Review

I am a long-standing science fiction fan and grew up on a diet of Arthur C. Clarke, Patrick Moore, Robert Heinlein and Isaac Asimov, to name a few. I had not come across Stefan Vučak until *Fulfillment* caught my eye and I am delighted to have made the discovery. Stefan is an accomplished author, technically adept, and a consummate storyteller. His tales transport you to the farthest reaches of the universe or the darkest corners of the mind in a direct, uncomplicated style. I will certainly be reading more from this author, and if you are a fan of the science fiction genre, I would recommend *Fulfillment*, a first-class collection of tales for the most discerning of aficionados.

Readers' Favorite

Books by Stefan Vučak

General Fiction:
Cry of Eagles
All the Evils
Towers of Darkness
Strike for Honor
Proportional Response
Legitimate Power
Autumn Leaves
F/X-26
28th Amendment
Night Sirens
Broken Rose

Shadow Gods Saga:
In the Shadow of Death
Against the Gods of Shadow
A Whisper from Shadow
Shadow Masters
Immortal in Shadow
Walking in Shadow
With Shadow and Thunder
Through the Valley of Shadow
Guardians of Shadow

Science Fiction:
Fulfillment
Lifeliners
All My Sunsets

Non-Fiction:
Writing Tips for Authors

Contact at:
www.stefanvucak.com

FULFILLMENT

By

Stefan Vučak

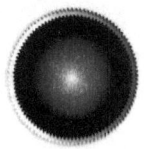

Note:

This is a work of fiction. All names, characters, places, and events are the work of the author's imagination. Any resemblance to real persons, places, or events is coincidental.

Updated edition: October 2025

‹

Dedication

To Julian ... when wearing two faces

Acknowledgments

Cover art by Laura Shinn.
www.laurashinn.yolasite.com

Foreword

The collection of stories in *Fulfillment* took many years to compile, because most of them were written a very long time ago when I decided writing is something I wanted to do, not realizing that once stepping on that road, I could not turn back. But we write because we must. We are driven, we are cursed, and it brings us joy. Let's leave it at that. In many respects, the first nine stories reflect my evolution as a writer, my training wheels, and I wanted to share them. I trust some will bring a measure of satisfaction.

These stories are also available on my website:
www.stefanvucak.com/short-stories/

Stefan Vučak
October, 2018

Table of Contents

Fulfillment

A sheet of blood covered the eastern sky. Overhead, the moon glowed, full and pale in dawn's light. Shadows lay heavy in the valley, and the mist lay like a gray blanket that hugged the steep slopes. A bull elk strode out of the forest, his sides wet from morning dew. His front hooves minced delicately and he snorted impatiently, his breath sharp and steamy. He tossed back his spread of antlers and bellowed. The valley echoed his call. Satisfied, he turned and stomped back into the forest, the snapping of broken branches marked his path.

On the small plain below, a gentle wind sent sheets of tall, spiky grass swaying on the sloping meadow. The breeze reached out in tentative fingers through the whispering grass, keening across the field. The wide blades of grass exposed their silver bellies and bowed after it.

Tall trees that bordered the grassland rustled their yellowing leaves. Wisps of gold, red and orange drifted down among the branches to lay a thick carpet around the gnarled trunks. Deep in the gloomy, cool forest, the silence broken by an occasional creak of a branch or the sound of soft footfalls as something scampered hurriedly deeper into the darkness. The wind did not intrude here.

Nearby, bubbling water swirled around moss and algae-covered rocks, gurgled its greeting, then raced down the brook. A tiny green frog raised enormous black eyes above the surface of a small pool and blinked solemnly. Then it leaped. Crickets chattered, secure in their covering of lush grass. A bird, all gold and fire, perched on a twig and voiced its joy.

A shadow drifted slowly across the field. The wind soared, playing with the sunning clouds. It pushed and chased, drawing wispy streamers from the slumbering white masses.

He lay on the grass, hands behind his head, the sky mirroring itself in the blue depths of his clear eyes. The muted buzz of insects filled his ears with pleasant music. Chewing a blade of grass, he smiled at the antics of a butterfly. He peered around a branch as the sun caressed his body with fingers of warmth and pleasure. He chuckled, content with himself and the world.

With a smooth flow of rippling muscles, he rose and spread his arms, twisting his body as he stretched. Tall, he stood with confidence as he gazed around the meadow. He walked toward the brook, sensitive to the grass beneath his feet. The frog sunning itself on a moss-covered rock croaked and jumped into the water as he knelt. He pushed his face into the stream and drank in big gulps. He paused, shook the water off his face with a snort and drank again. Satisfied, he stood beside the brook and looked once again down the sloping meadow.

It was a time of falling leaves and all the herds were moving toward the land of the setting sun. The forests and the plains far behind them were already bare, waiting for the sleep that would come as snow started to fall. The older members of the herd like himself were becoming increasingly tense and restless. He would wake in the middle of the night, unaccountably afraid. Images of oddly dressed figures and strange flat shapes in the sky filled his mind with terror. This unease happened only during the time of falling leaves.

The herd slowly made its way through the meadows, picking edible tidbits along the way. A youngster ran from the group and two more followed. They all ended up rolling through the tall grass, flattening it into irregular clearings. Sounds of laughter and gleeful shrieks drifted toward him. He grunted with contentment, his fear forgotten. On the far side of the meadow a youngster ran screaming between trees in his play.

A shadow drifted over him and a chill crept through his body. He shivered and looked about quickly, getting increasingly nervous as the memories returned. Shouts were coming from the herd as they ran toward the forest, fear contorting their faces. He started breathing rapidly and looked up at the sky. He watched the flat shapes fly toward him and felt the hair on his neck stiffen.

In the hills beyond, a flicker of lightning slashed at the ground. Thunder rumbled in the distance, rolling across the hills. With a last glance at the descending flat shapes, he turned and sprinted toward the forest, his heart suddenly loud in his ears.

He did not know where he ran or why. He only knew that he must get away. His legs, arms and chest were covered with raw lines, scratched by bushes and low branches. He stumbled and fell, sobbing as fatigued leg muscles throbbed with pain. He landed on rotting leaves and inhaled the strong, pleasant smell of decaying vegetation.

He rolled on his back and breathed deeply, shivering as fear rose and receded. The trees were around him, close and comforting, and he felt united with them. Behind the branches and the leaves, fire colored the sky. Thunder rolled over the forest and its deep voice made the ground tremble. Darkness settled quickly, drawing the shadows after it. The first drops of rain began to fall.

He lifted his face and licked the wetness off his lips, at last feeling safe.

* * *

He awakened, turned his head and listened. The hushed wind whispered among the branches above him. Leaves crackled as some small creature scampered about. Frogs conducted a concert nearby. A mosquito buzzed around his head and fled as he moved. He smelled water and dampness. A drop fell and touched his cheek with cold. He allowed his head to sink back into the leaves and closed his eyes.

A breath of wind stirred the leaf. Clear tears of dawn trembled and merged into one pure jewel. The teardrop slid down the leaf and hung at its tip. A fleeting ray of light, jumping from leaf to leaf, splashed itself against the drop. A rainbow flared in its depths as the drop fell toward the shadowy under-growth.

He felt the drop hit his face and he opened his eyes. He smiled at the deep blue of a clear sky, the silent trees and the noises of life around him. The air sharp and alive after the rain, he breathed deeply. Then he felt the pain of memory and hurriedly stood up.

Between the trees, he could see the meadow and the hills beyond. The herd would be there and he longed for the company of familiar faces.

He emerged out of the forest and ran through the dew-sprinkled grass. A white mist hung low over the field. Loose tendrils slowly reached toward the sky. He jogged to the top of a small hill and looked down, but he could see no sign of the herd. Puzzled, but not overly concerned, he knew where they were headed. Strange noises were coming from the other side of the rise and he tilted his head, listening, undecided. It might be the herd, but he could not recognize the sounds. Uncertain, he walked across the meadow and scrambled up the small rise.

Four oval shapes rested on the plain below and strange creatures walked among them. They looked like the herd and had pleasing faces, but from the neck down, all had red skin. One of the creatures looked up and stopped. About to turn away, he saw its eyes. His whole body tingled and he felt himself growing numb. His legs trembled as he stumbled and fell. He whimpered with fear and struggled to his feet, feeling the staring eyes on his back. He screamed as the image of those eyes consumed him and ran over the crest toward the welcoming forest.

Some time later, he fell in gasping exhaustion beside a rotting tree trunk that lay sprawled on the forest floor. He could run no farther. His lungs felt filled with tiny thorns. It was agony to breathe and he ached everywhere. The scratches on his arms and legs stung painfully.

He lay there moaning, realizing he had trapped himself. After an aimless flight through the length of the forest, he discovered nothing but meadows and valleys all around. With no way out, he dared not venture into the open. The thought of those strangely clad creatures waiting for him out there made fear cloud his mind. Those eyes! Unbearably thirsty, he remembered the brook at the edge of the forest. He could not wait for darkness while his whole body demanding water.

The forest was something he thought he understood. As he walked toward the brook, he kept glancing at the shadows around him. The trees were shifting strangely and shapes formed in the gloom. On the verge of panic barely controlled, he pushed through the undergrowth. There was no safety anywhere. Dry leaves suddenly rustled behind him and he yelled in alarm and ran. After a while, he stopped and looked back. Nothing pursued him.

The trees thinned and he could see the swaying grass beyond. Slowly, he moved closer to the forest edge. He could not see anything threatening out there. Haltingly, he emerged into the open, soaking in the warmth of the sun. He knelt beside the brook and glanced around before plunging his face into the water. It was icy and tasted delicious. After washing himself, he drank again. Then he laughed, his skin tingling with the radiant feeling of life.

The breeze played with his hair as he listened to the whispering grass and the nodding, rustling branches. A dry twig snapped and he whirled, looking into the forest. A slim red figure stepped away from behind a tree. Still in shadow, its eyes burned with inner fire. They seemed to grow and pulled at him.

* * *

He tried to look away, but his body refused to obey. He felt something snap and tear in his head and long forgotten memories struggled to rise, and it hurt. He screamed inside his mind, trying to hide from those compelling eyes.

Musical sounds came from the creature as it slowly walked toward him. The sounds were soft and soothing, and gradually calmed him. Confused, puzzled, he could not pull away from those compelling eyes. The creature looked like one of the herd, yet smaller and thinner. Seeing it close up, he realized it wore some sort of covering that ended at the neck and wrists. The creature stopped before him at arm's length. He watched with interest as the wind played with its streaming yellow hair, never seeing anything like it before. The pleasant face that looked at him smiled.

Slowly, it lifted a slender hand to the top of its red covering. The hand moved down the center of the body and he could see white skin beneath as the covering parted. The creature stepped out of its false skin and more soothing noises came from its mouth. Fascinated by the false skin lying crumpled on the grass, burning eyes pulled at him and he could not look away from the compelling curves of the creature's body that stirred some ancient memory.

Its skin light and delicate, the body rounded with no rippling muscles. Two upraised mounds of flesh shifted on its chest as it breathed and he stared at them in fascination. Then the creature stopped smiling, reached out with its hand, and touched his cheek. A pleasant, warm tingle ran down his spine and he shuddered. Strange sensations raced through his body. He felt hot and cold as images of sunlight, sky and trees burst in his mind, then faded.

He felt his body slowly sink into the grass. The creature looked down at him and smiled. Its eyes flared, boring into his. A gurgle rose in his throat as another memory surfaced. A memory of silver towers, the sky filled with flying disks. Creatures dressed in many colors walked along the broad boulevards. Little ones scampered among them. He knew that place from a memory of a past long ago, but did not understand it at all.

The creature knelt beside him and stroked his arm, chest,

and gently moved over his body. He felt himself respond in a way he never felt before and reached out with a trembling hand to touch the rosy tip on one of the fleshy mounds. The creature smiled broadly, murmured something, moved to straddle his body, and touched him.

After a time, with the climax of pleasure, he felt a sharp rip in his head and the eyes staring at him flared. He sobbed and reached for the woman above him, for he now knew what she was and why she sought him out. His mind screamed as he struggled to form the strange words that came into his mind as darkness covered his eyes.

* * *

The flat shapes flew low over the forest, glinting as light skidded over polished metal. A young male child ran from behind a tree where he hid and watched the shapes grow smaller and vanish into afternoon haze. He shrugged and scampered toward the others. He briefly wondered why some of the older ones were not there, but in the warm air, the sounds of laughter made him forget.

Beside the brook, the figure of a prone man lying in the grass began to change and became translucent. A leaf detached itself from an overhanging branch, fluttered toward the brook, hovered above the semi-transparent form before it settled on the ghostly outline of a face. The outline blurred like a patch of mist, and slowly, the form faded.

The leaf hesitated, then settled gently where the figure had lain. The flattened grass slowly straightened around it.

An earlier version of this story appeared in The Altered I, *Norstrilia Press, 1976.*

Reprinted by Berkley Windhover Books, 1978.

Even the Gods Cry

In a burst of scintillation the ship emerged from subspace high above the planetary plane, beyond the gravity well of the small yellow star.

The ship's secondary shield grid flared in violet discharge, then stabilized. It paused, oriented itself and moved deliberately down into the inner system toward the bright points of a double world. It slowed as the twin horns began to resolve out of blackness: one gray and the other brilliant blue-white. The ship made one terminator orbit around the moon before moving toward the dark side to hang above a narrow valley of the north pole where it waited. Below, twisted masts reached up amid the radial pattern of the base. Shrouded in shadow, the base lay dark and silent, cold like the cliffs that surrounded it. After a time the ship rose and slowly moved away.

It climbed above the horizon to be greeted by a blue crescent of a sleeping world. The northern ice cap shrouded under untidy clouds stretching their twisted whorls into night. In a burst of speed, the ship vanished into the black shadow of the waiting world. It moved into a polar orbit as the planet shifted ponderously beneath it. It made a single circuit, looking for the sentinel cruiser, noting the scanning sensor probes coming up from the ground. It found the cruiser hanging above the equator. The ship maneuvered until both flew silently side by side in a locked orbit.

* * *

"Status?" Kukll-nn demanded with an impatient growl.

Oryana lifted her head gracefully and looked where he stood before the high window, hands clasped tightly behind his back.

"They're sending down a landing boat," she said, her voice

soft and musical, now slightly breathless. Her black eyebrows were arched and traced a thin line above large brown eyes. She pulled at her small pointed chin with a slim delicate hand and turned back to the main display plate positioned above the sloping consoles. The tactical grid dissolved and the image re-formed into a wide-angle pattern. She glanced absently at the small repeater plates and sighed dreamily.

"A ship from home! I wonder how much things have changed," she mused, eyes misty, lost in memory. Absently, she fondled the long, white tresses that spilled across her shoulders. Long hair cascaded down the middle of her head, streaked with twin bands of dark gray of a mature Deklan female.

Kukll-nn stood silent beside the window, his eyes far in another reality. The observatory gave him an excellent view of the city below. The lake, its black waters lapping softly against the massive stone walls, stretched north and west as far as the eye could see. Shrouded in blue haze the mountains arched toward a violet sky. Ice and snow capped the peaks, shouldering the lower slopes. How fragile, he thought, almost brittle in their stark and serene beauty. So much like his native Kaplan. He shook his head, surprised at the nostalgia that overcame him.

"Recall acknowledged?"

"All continental stations reported in two minutes ago," he heard Oryana say behind him. "The intruder has matched with our ship and is maintaining neutral status."

The Center quiet, waiting, the stillness interrupted by the whisper of computer reports and an occasional shuffling of feet from the watchstanders.

"Sachmm-nn?"

For a few seconds, more silence. Oryana stared at Kukll's back, then climbed out of her seat and walked slowly to the window to stand beside him. Following his gaze, she watched the natives busy at their work. Lord of this world, it would all now end. They expected this, and some probably even welcomed it. As the years marched, the waiting had not grown easier.

She looked at his reflection in the window and the face she saw hard. A rough face full of slabs, chiseled with deep lines of power and determination. A face used to command. His hair rusty, shot through with patches of white. It had lost some of the gloss that used to make her breath catch. The years had been kind to all of them, she thought as she gazed at him with deep affection. And there have been so many years. Too many perhaps to face what they left behind.

"Do you really think that's necessary?" she asked gently and reached up with her hand, hesitating before touching his shoulder.

He tensed at her touch and turned to look at her, faintly amused. "Don't you? Yes…I can see it in your face. All the years we've spent here have not removed the longing. You still yearn for the worlds of Deklan. And me…" The fire in his black eyes waned and his jaw lifted with resolve. "Those worlds are no longer ours," he grated, each word a blow and she flinched. Slowly, he raised his hand and pointed a stubby finger at the ceiling. "The ship up there hasn't come to help us, remember that. You ask if Sachmm-nn is necessary. We shall see. Now, order it to power up and stand by."

Hurt, she turned to the operator behind one of the consoles. When he nodded to her, she looked at Kukll-nn.

"They have acknowledged," she said stiffly, torn with warring emotions.

They watched the city in silence. After a while, he turned to stare into the deep pools of her eyes and gently brushed her cheek.

"I am sorry, Oryana. I shouldn't have spoken to you like that. It's only—"

"Don't." She clasped his hand and held it. "I understand. But…" She left it unsaid. Nothing left to say when the yesterdays suddenly came crowding.

"We better go and meet them," he said at length and managed a faint smile that didn't touch his eyes.

* * *

The voice from the temple boomed and the people stopped their work and stood silent in the streets, markets, homes and farms. The gods were speaking. Leoichan, High Priest of Tiahunn-cc, heard the voice and listened. As he listened, his excitement grew. When the voice stopped, he ordered the priests to send a message to the king and gather the people to direct them to the star nest. The gods were coming!

Slowly, then with hurried fervor, chanting, the people moved down the broad avenues toward the star nest where the gods would come. The King, the High Priest, the Oracle and the multitude of peasantry waited at the gates of Tiahunn-cc. Black marble doors rumbled as they slid open. Clad in tight red coveralls, Kukll-nn emerged with Oryana at his side dressed in blue. The people held their arms high and sang the names of the two gods. With slow dignity the gods mounted an air chariot and it began to move. The populace shouted and danced and walked with them toward the star nest.

The valley walls fell away and the baked plain opened before them. Leoichan started the sixth chant of observance as he stared in awe at the two metal birds perched on their stone pads, surrounded by spidery towers. The minions of the gods moved about on flat air chariots and Leoichan watched it all and chanted.

Assembled, they murmured and waited, eyes fixed on the heavens from where the gods would come. A deep rumble shook the air and the ground trembled. The heavenly bird glittered in white light high above them. Leoichan began the eleventh chant and the priests around him held their arms high.

Clad with fire and light, it looked like a descending star. With thunder that shook the heavens, white smoke billowing, the heavenly bird fell quickly. It slowed and hovered for an instant, roaring in tortured anger, and then it touched the pad. The fires stopped and thunder echoed through the hills. Smoke drifted slowly down the valley. In the sudden silence, only the chanting could be heard.

The bird sat there breathing hot air, shimmering in the haze and everyone waited for the gods to emerge. Leoichan turned shyly and smiled at Kukll-nn and Oryana, proud to be near them. They smiled back and he felt warmed in his soul.

A hush fell over the crowd when one of the towers began to slowly move toward the bird. Kukll and Oryana mounted their air chariot and sped quickly down onto the baked plain.

Leoichan watched the chariot stop at the base of the tower. The gods climbed down and stood before the bird, waiting. A box descended within the tower. When it stopped, doors opened and he stood there, tall, his hair bright red and clothing silver. When Kukll-nn saluted, Leoichan gaped, his surprise complete. The other stared back a long time before returning the salute.

* * *

Kukll allowed his hand to fall to his side as his eyes raked over the thin form of his visitor. The man's long hands swayed and his fingers twitched in characteristic agitation. His small yellow eyes darted restlessly as they moved over everything. Hidden behind bushy orange eyebrows, they glinted with cold fire. The face pale white and pinched, fixed with a thin nose. Arrogance and hidden cruelty marked the face. The twin bands of thick red hair were rich and prominent. Kukll decided they weren't going to get along.

"Master Scout Kukll-nn, and my executive officer, First Scout Oryana," Kukll said evenly, trying to keep the distaste out of his voice. The man was a political busybody and the quicker he dealt with him the better. "I see Prima Scout, that the Serrll Combine has not forgotten us after all."

"No, they have not forgotten, Master Scout," the other

grated heavily and looked about him pointedly. "I am Virrchaa, on a special Executive Council Mission to look you over."

"Look me over or take me over? I suppose I should be flattered, but after nineteen years, taking into account four time dilation jumps, you'll have to forgive me if the excitement has kind of worn off."

"I should imagine." Virrchaa snorted and swept his hand before him. "Holy Master of Sin, man! What have you done to this world?"

Kukll glanced at the assembled multitude. "I have brought it life."

"I'm not in any mood for your worm shit!" Virr growled and lead the way to the sled-pad. "Let's talk."

* * *

"Is that all?" Virr said with icy politeness as his fingers drummed impatiently against the desk.

Kukll nodded and took a sip from a frosted tumbler. "I guess that's about the size of it, Prima Scout."

Virr glared at Oryana, but she became suddenly busy studying her nails. He pushed back his chair and started pacing. Kukll sat back and a faint smile creased his chiseled face. Whatever Virr expected, he certainly didn't like what he found.

With a growl of exasperation, Virr stopped before the wide window. The city below lay spread before him in neat patterns. It looked simple, belying the sophistication of its design.

"You were sent here on a follow-up survey mission," he hissed impatiently and turned to glare at Kukll. "Nothing else!"

"That sounded okay nineteen years ago," Kukll pointed out.

Virr pursed his lips. "Look at it from my point of view. I break out of subspace and I think maybe I'm in the wrong system. There is no SC&C, no patrols, nothing. And the moon base? Abandoned. You were sent here to watch them, not mold them!"

Kukll shrugged and reached for the decanter. He filled the tumbler, stared at it for a moment, then looked up, his mouth hard.

"We set up bases here for one reason and one reason only: genetic engineering experiments. Don't tell me you didn't know. So let's drop this indignant posturing nonsense, shall we? We don't need to pretend here."

Virr exhaled and bared his teeth. "I expect a measure of respect from you, Master Scout!"

Kukll laughed. "What are you going to do? Send me home?"

Virr glared, pursed his lips and turned to stare out the window. "They look happy down there. How much do they know?"

Kukll glanced at Oryana. "They know I teach and heal. When necessary, I punish. I leave it at that."

"How many other bases?"

"Two; one farther north and one on the western landmass across the ocean. We had a base on the southern island continent, but we had a reactor accident and were forced to abandon it."

"The natives?"

"They're developing. Not as fast as predicted, though. It's being looked into. The western continent is dry and getting worse. Here, we have a chance and the polar ice is receding."

Virr turned and looked directly at Kukll. "You will shut down all bases and terminate the experiments."

"Does that include the natives as well?" Kukll asked calmly.

"This doesn't come from me."

"Tell me one thing. If the Executive Council intended to close us down, why the regular resupply ships? In all my years here, there has never been even a hint of abandoning the project."

"I don't know—"

"Don't give me that! Not after coming all this way. What happened to make everyone suddenly want to salve their conscience? Look at them!" Kukll swept a hand at the window and stood up. "That's an indigenous population and this planet is a protectorate. You're sworn to defend what's here."

Virr smiled grimly. "You're right. The natives will be left alone. They can struggle on as best they can. But this," he said and looked about him, "this has to go and you'll return to Captal for a well deserved promotion and rest."

Kukll glanced at Oryana and chuckled. A mirthless laugh full of irony.

"What do you think of that, my dear?" He looked at Virr and shook his head. "No, Prima Scout. It won't be so easy. Our work here isn't finished yet. Too many things still need to be done to ensure the natives' survival."

"You like playing a god, Kukll?" Virr studied the other man, past the mask of a Serrll officer at the mantle of power radiating from him.

"A god?" Kukll lifted his head in genuine surprise. "You're a fool to think so, Virr. This, for what we left back home? I am prepared to return. We all are. Holy Master of Sin, who wouldn't be? Only if the Mission Plan is maintained and we're replaced. Only if the Mission Plan is maintained," he repeated, his voice flat and uncompromising.

Virr shook his head. "I cannot do that, and you know it. My orders are clear."

"And you don't have the guts to do the right thing."

"Even if I sent a message to the Executive Council pleading your case, my orders will not be rescinded. They don't have any reason to."

"Who the hell cares? By the time you get back, how many months will have gone?"

"Seventy-three days. We can do two hundred times the

speed of light now."

"At max boost perhaps, but you cannot push max for that long. Not all the way to Salina. Anyway, it's long enough for the Council to change its mind. Think, man! This goes beyond mere political expediency, or this experiment would never been allowed to continue."

"There is nothing I can do," Virr said flatly. "Begin preparation for immediate evacuation, Master Scout."

"I have a ship up there and this place is defended," Kukll said softly.

Virr stared. "You mean it?"

Kukll's eyes were cold with resolve.

* * *

Leoichan watched the air chariot leave the gates of Tiahunn-cc and speed toward the star nest just as the summons arrived from Kukll-nn. Torn, wanting to watch the air chariot, the summons could not be ignored. Chewing his lip in frustration, he motioned to his retainers and the little group moved quickly toward the black marble gates.

When he reached the gates they opened with a low groan. With a feeling of religious awe and dread, he walked in. One of the minions greeted him and he indicated to his retainers to wait on him before following. He stood before Kukll-nn and the goddess Oryana many times, but each time he stood in their presence, he felt vulnerable and his soul naked before their gaze. His sins were many and it was never certain how the gods would judge him. He gave an involuntary shudder and hurried after the minion.

The door slid aside and his footsteps were loud in the quiet of the Great Hall. Light streamed in yellow shafts through tall windows and made warm pools through which he walked daintily. The god stood before one of the windows. Oryana, all in blue, sat on the reception dais and smiled at him. He sank to his knees and bowed.

"Your humble servant awaits your word, Lords," he whispered, not daring to breathe.

"Stand, our faithful Leoichan." Oryana's voice soft and clear and sent a tingle of excitement down his spine.

Slowly, he straightened and stood and waited.

Without turning, Kukll said, "Tell the King that all his people must leave Tiahunn-cc immediately. Tell him they must not stop until they've reached Tiukk-ll. Start now," he growled and waved his hand in dismissal.

Leoichan stood stunned as he heard the words, not believing. Leave the city? Uproot their lives?

"Lord, have we offended thee that you should send us away?" he whispered, greatly daring.

Kukll didn't say anything. He merely stood there, his hands clasped tightly behind his back. Oryana got up and walked slowly toward Leoichan to stop before him.

"The gods are angry, my servant. Fire may fall from the sky, consuming all."

"The gods are angry with the people?"

"No, Leoichan," she said softly and placed a slim hand on his shoulder. "I am well pleased and so is Kukll-nn. My friend, a messenger from the stars brought us news of troubles. We must stay here and defend Tiahunn-cc, but you have to leave so that your people may be safe."

Leoichan did not understand. However, the gods have spoken and therefore it must be so.

"I shall stay here with you. All of us will stay and help you in your need," he said with sudden resolve and straightened. "Have you not cared for us?"

As Oryana looked at him, he was awed to see a tear glisten in her eye and slide down her cheek. "Thank you, faithful servant," she whispered. "The fire of the gods cannot be stopped. You must flee."

"To pack...there is so much..." He faltered and looked helplessly at her.

"Don't pack, just go!" Kukll snapped and Leoichan

blanched, feeling himself tremble.

"Lord," he whispered and bowed low.

Relenting, Kukll walked up to him. "Don't be afraid, Leoichan. I didn't mean to be harsh, but time is limited. I shall not abandon you. Wait for me at Tiukk-ll. Don't forget the writings and the laws, my servant," he added, then abruptly turned and strode out of the Hall.

"Go quickly," Oryana whispered and followed.

Leoichan knew something terrible was about to happen if the gods were so troubled, but leave Tiahunn-cc?

* * *

The display plate cleared and Virrchaa glared at her.

"I want to speak to Kukll, First Scout," he said impatiently, his head held high and haughty.

"I speak for Kukll, Prima Scout," she said unflinchingly.

"Very well, then." He glanced at the chronometer readout. "Tell him he must evacuate all stations in fourteen hours. If he doesn't, I shall close them by force."

"I shall tell him, sir." Oryana nodded and his image faded. She turned to look at Kukll standing nearby and bit her lip.

"You heard?"

He barely nodded.

The black waters of the lake lapped below the walls of the fortress. Whitecaps curled and sent spray flying before the wind. About him, the city stood silent and empty. The last patrol reported all the natives evacuated. Something positive at last, he mused wryly. After all the time and effort, it'll now vanish in fire. What a waste. If the natives survived, it would still be worth it.

Beneath him the floor shook slightly and he turned toward the command consoles.

"The last of the boats has taken off, sir," the technician said, his eyes wondering, asking the same questions Kukll asked. "Low orbit in four-point-seven minutes."

Kukll placed an arm over Oryana's shoulder. "Virr could be right," she said after a moment.

"Yes, I know." A cold smile tugged at the corner of his mouth. "If we leave, then *they* would have lost it all." He waved at the window. "He'll wipe it all clean to remove a political embarrassment. He might not like it, but he'll follow orders. Who knows, in three or four thousand years the remnants might climb back to where they're now. The species will survive."

"And us?"

"We do what we must." He shrugged, turned and looked questioningly at the technician.

"Sachmm-nn is fully powered up and all stations have acknowledged. The local population has dispersed. All boats are in position. Target is in low three-hour equatorial orbit. Our ship will shift to a geosynchronous position in twelve minutes from now."

Kukll nodded. "Open channel to Virr's ship."

When the plate cleared, the two men stared at each other, both resolved, determined to carry it to the end. Virr pursed his lips.

"Damn it, Kukll! This is madness."

"I agree, Prima Scout, but I cannot permit these people to be wiped out. Orders or not, it's murder."

"I cannot permit Sachmm-nn and Tiahunn-cc to remain operational, Master Scout. You've made the population dependent on your technological and social infrastructure. You cannot be with them always."

"No, but without it, they'll revert to savagery, or worse."

Virr looked hard at Kukll and seemed to reach a decision. "I give you my word as an officer of the Serrll that I shall take no action against the natives. Provided all the bases are neutralized, with the exception of the moon base, of course."

"I might go as far as to believe you, Virr, but that doesn't bind the Executive Council."

"I meant the Council, damn it! I'll file a report with the

General Assembly and the Council won't force the issue. As you said yourself, it's not worth it. You'll be free to return. I don't want to shed our blood for a cause I don't believe in and reasons that are expedient. Don't force my hand."

"On one condition."

"And that is?"

"The Serrll must send follow-up missions, to check up."

"It might not be so easy."

"Make it easy. Virr…you cannot afford to have your ship damaged. It's a hell of a long way to Captal."

"So it is."

When the screen faded, Kukll looked at Oryana. "What do you think?"

She tilted her head and frowned. "He appears sincere, but I don't trust him. He gave in too easily."

"Just so." He nodded and turned to the watch operator. "Maintain alert status and give me position of the primary target."

"They're maintaining neutral status, and their shield grid is up."

"Then we wait."

* * *

The comms alert beeped and Kukll turned as the image cleared.

"Sir, it's three hours plus," the operator said.

"Status?"

"All landing boats maintaining low orbit. The target has assumed a geosynchronous position above Sachmm-nn. All other bases—"

"I know," Kukll snapped and slammed his fist against the desk. "Is Virr's ship in line-of-sight?"

"Affirmative."

Kukll looked disgusted. "Get him for me, now!"

When the image cleared, Kukll stood straight, hands

clasped tightly behind his back.

"You shifted orbit when I wasn't in a position to see. Why?"

"I don't make explanations, Kukll," Virr snarled, his eyes almost hidden by flared eyebrows. "I simply want your compliance."

"You're not in any position to make demands, Prima Scout."

"A missile might change your mind, Master Scout!" Virr bellowed as he finally lost his temper. "I want your answer and I want it now. I'm tired of this whole mess. And I'm especially tired of you! Copy that, Mister?"

"Sachmm-nn has weapons capability, in case you have not been informed."

Virr turned abruptly, nodded and the image faded.

"Sir! Sachmm-nn reports they're under missile attack. Our defense screen has responded."

Oryana drew in her breath. Her eyes glistened as she looked at Kukll. "After all we have done…"

"He won't risk total confrontation," Kukll said flatly, thinking furiously. "He hasn't launched any scouts…yet. He wants to pull our teeth first. I cannot risk my ship and neither can he." He walked to the tactical plot and studied the plate. "Order Sachmm-nn to fire a burst at his ship. Rattle his shields a bit."

"Kukll!" Oryana cried. "This can only end in destruction for all of us. Then everything we've done will be a waste."

"It's already a waste. He'll either destroy us now or someone else will do it tomorrow. Unless the Executive Council intervenes, the politicians will erase everything we've done here."

She walked to him and looked gravely into his eyes. Her hands reached for him.

"You know, I have even forgotten what a Deklan sky looks like. Isn't that terrible?" she said tragically and her voice trembled. "I remember black sands washed by a warm ocean and the smell of flying spray, but it's only a memory now. Our reality is here. Understand me?"

He stared at her for a long time before squeezing her hands. "Are you sure this is what you want?" he whispered and she nodded. "Once committed, there is no going back. Not for a long time."

"I am sure, my love."

"Sir? Sachmm-nn received a near miss and our defense grid is holding. Prima Scout Virrchaa has shifted orbit."

"Open channel," Kukll commanded.

"The next attack will be on you, Master Scout," Virr spoke softly, but his eyes were hard and uncompromising.

"That will not be necessary, Prima Scout. I wouldn't want any stray missiles heading toward the natives."

"You don't trust me, do you?"

"What do you think?"

Virr's mouth twitched. "No, I guess you don't. Instead of wasting away in this backwater, your talents can be better employed elsewhere. When we get back—"

"We're not going back."

"What do you mean? If you are—"

"Don't worry. I'm not planning to throw away my life in some grand gesture. I have reconsidered our position. Particularly the follow-up missions."

"And?"

"We've been here a long time, Prima Scout. All of us have. Long enough to develop a certain affection for the natives and this planet. For me, Kaplan is a faded dream, albeit a fond one. I intend taking volunteers and make a time dilation jump of fifteen years. It will buy the Council more than enough time to sort things out. Many of the people I know here will still be alive when I return. Enough for me to pick up the pieces, anyway."

After a moment of silence, Virr shook his head. "Damnedest idea I ever heard of."

"But it'll work. Besides, who do you have willing enough

to exile themselves here?" Kukll asked, his voice full of irony. "About the Mission Plan. The General Assembly may pretend that this place doesn't exist, but they'd still love to have it followed through. At least through Stage Two."

"I agree," Virr said.

"On one condition, Prima Scout."

"And that is?"

"Tiukk-ll and the other population centers must remain intact. This is not negotiable."

Virr sighed, then nodded. "Very well."

"And, Virr? My ship will remain in orbit and ready until you transit into subspace."

Virr didn't say anything as he cut contact.

* * *

Leoichan found it hard to breathe the hot, sticky air.

Overhead, the sun a white furnace, too painful to look at. Few people were about and the temple grounds shimmered in the heat. Somewhere, a child wailed and there came a startled cackle from the poultry. A fly buzzed, then the sound faded.

He hobbled slowly along the avenue, his stick tapping on polished stones. Bent, the skinny legs showed blue veins and tight, stringy muscles. Yet he enjoyed good health, even if he had trouble chewing with the few teeth he had left. Life had been harsh, but he did not complain. He had his sons and his family were powerful. He frowned as he recalled some of the practices at the temple and the loose interpretation of the laws. The king strong and the people have prospered. Surely not as in the days of his youth, but obedient to the laws nonetheless.

He sat in the shade of the temple wall, lost in memory when shouting and the pounding of feet caused him to open his eyes. Squinting, he watched with amusement the running figures. In dismay, he realized they were coming toward him.

A messenger from the High Priest, and Leoichan frowned.

That man would have to go if things did not change, he re-flected darkly. One of the boys, still panting, sank to his knees and bowed before him.

"Venerable One," the boy gasped and looked up with fear and wonder.

"Speak!"

"The Observatory!"

Leoichan's ears roared and his heart began to pound. No, it cannot be.

"What about it?" he whispered, hardly daring to believe.

"The dome opened and a shiny dish-like shape rose from within and started turning. Then it stopped and I was ordered to tell it to you."

Leoichan nodded and closed his eyes in quiet happiness. The gods were coming at last. He should have believed, he should have. Did not Kukll-nn promise he would come?

"Tell the High Priest and the King to assemble the people at the star nest," he ordered and smiled at the gaping faces. "The gods are coming."

He sat back and relaxed, content. He feared to die before setting eyes on Kukll and the goddess Oryana again, but he knew himself to be an old fool to hold such a foolish dream.

He remembered that fateful, terrible day fifteen years ago. Seven of his priests and he were hidden in the mountains, far above Tiahunn-cc and the black lake. They could hardly see the massive walls of the fortress in the hazy distance. The star nest on the plain far below clearly visible. They waited, want-ing to see the anger of the gods, realizing that death may be their only reward for such presumption.

He watched as the last heavenly bird roared in anger, fire billowing from its base. He trembled in fear as it climbed into the sky. Fire and thunder followed it to the heavens and the ground shook beneath him. When the thunder stopped, only a column of writhing smoke remained. He remembered talk-ing to one of his priests, arguing whether they should stay longer, when a flash of blinding radiance seared the hills around them. One of the priests screamed and tore at his eyes.

Leoichan turned to see a strangely shaped cloud hang over where Tiahunn-cc once stood. Then the wind roared and clutched at them, threatening to sweep them from the mountain. Terrified, they fled. That night, huddled together against the cold, he remembered Oryana's tears and he wept unashamedly for things lost.

The memory of that writhing cloud had stayed with him always.

Four of his priests died of a mysterious, wasting illness. Although he took sick, he recovered, the illness leaving him old before his time.

* * *

Arms raised, the priests toned through the seventh chant of observance. The multitude buzzed with excitement. The King sat adorned in feathers and gold, hands folded as he stared at the emptiness of the star nest. Slowly, he turned his head, looked at Leoichan and nodded. Someone shouted and pointed and heads turned toward the heavens.

Brighter than a star and Leoichan squinted to look at it. It had been a long time, a long time since he witnessed the coming of a heavenly bird. He did not mind dying now. He watched the light sink swiftly and heard the first rumble of thunder.

Flame and smoke filled the small plain. The very air trembled as the pillar of fire hung briefly and touched the earth. In the sudden silence the echoes boomed in the distance and faded. The priests finished chanting and they waited. The smoke cleared quickly and a hole appeared in the side of the bird. Leoichan clenched his fists with gleeful excitement as an air chariot glided out, sank slowly and started toward them. He turned and nodded. The retainers moved his palanquin forward, away from the waiting priests and royalty.

The chariot drifted to a stop and sank toward the ground,

but did not touch it. Its glittering bubble opened and Kukll-nn, all in red, stepped out and looked curiously about him. Oryana moved close beside him, her blue coverall shimmering in the heat. Leoichan stared at them with hunger, drinking in every detail. They were just as he remembered them, unchanged. They were gods, no?

Kukll turned and smiled as Leoichan stood and bowed low. "Lord, I have waited as you commanded."

"My faithful servant." Kukll placed his hand on Leoichan's shoulder. "I have come, as I promised."

Behind them, the chanting rose in waves.

* * *

A cool breeze ruffled his long faded hair and Leoichan grasped the fine red llama blanket closer to his thin body. His gnarled hand trembled and his breathing labored. Gold thread woven into the blanket glinted in the afternoon's dying light. Dying like him. The prospect of death did not trouble him. He had lived a long and full life, and in the nine years since the gods returned, his people prospered again and spread into new lands in the west where Qatzeltal, the new god protector, held law. He carried out the will of the gods and was content. One last thing to be done.

They placed Leoichan's palanquin on the knoll so he could see the star nest below. The retainers stood back respectfully. His sons waited in silence. The King had sent the Oracle to attend him, the shrew not pleased at the honor done to her. The woman too interested in the trappings of her position than the exercise of her duties to the gods and the people, thankful he wouldn't have to deal with that problem. The High Priest and his attendants softly chanted the litanies of observance.

A coppery glow smeared the setting sun and painted the thin streamers of high cloud red. He knew this would be his last sunset. Unperturbed, Leoichan waited. The gods had promised, but would Kukll and Oryana come? It was always dangerous to presume on the will of the gods. Not that Kukll had been harsh, and the laws were just, even if the people did not always obey. He so desperately wanted to see the god again before Kukll and Oryana returned from wherever the gods came. A glint of light high in the sky brightened and he squinted. His eyes were not as they used to be, but he felt a prickle of anticipation race through him. Kukll had returned his faith.

Shrouded in a shimmering yellow cocoon the thick gray disk descended silently toward the stone landing pad of the star nest. The Oracle reluctantly began her chant. The heavenly bird grew in size, paused above the pad and extended its landing skids. The yellow light faded around the ship and steps dropped down from its side. An air chariot raced toward the waiting ship from the maintenance hangar at the edge of the landing pad. Two figures emerged from the ship and Leoichan's breath caught in his throat. He could not mistake Kukll's red uniform and Oryana's blue coverall. The two gods climbed into the waiting air chariot and the machine sped toward the gathered crowd on the hill.

A respectful hush fell as the air chariot slowed and stopped beside Leoichan's palanquin. Kukll stepped down, cast his eyes over the assembly, then smiled as he strode to the palanquin. Everyone bowed low. Leoichan struggled to rise, but Kukll gently pushed him back.

"My lord," Leoichan husked, "it is not seemly that I lie in your presence."

"My faithful servant," Kukll said warmly. "We're past such foolishness, you and I."

Oryana stopped beside Kukll and her tender smile lit Leoichan's soul.

"My Lady…"

"Leoichan, this day you shall sleep with the gods," she said in a trembling voice.

"Then my life will have been fulfilled, goddess," he

breathed. The gods were powerful, but even they could not stay the hand of Death.

What happened next shocked him. Kukll bent over him and gathered him into his arms.

"Lord!"

"Rest easy, my friend," Kukll whispered.

The Oracle and the High Priest gaped as the god carried Leoichan to the air chariot and sat down. Oryana took the controls and the chariot turned and sped toward the star nest.

Kukll hardly felt any weight in his arms. Leoichan a frail sack of wrinkled skin and bone with little life left in him. Kukll climbed the steps into the scoutship and placed his servant on the reclined formchair. Oryana came up behind him and sat in the command couch. The nav bubble cleared and Leoichan marveled at this wondrous vehicle. Once before, long ago, he had the privilege to sit inside a heavenly bird, but what he saw now overwhelmed him. The hatch cycled shut and he felt a change in pressure.

"Won't be long now," Kukll said beside him.

The ship hovered, then surged into the sky. Leoichan gasped when the sky lost its softness and he could see the stars.

"Lord…"

"Wait."

The stars spun and Leoichan saw the sharp curve of a blue world laid below him like a distant shore. And the world was like an island in a black lake, and the clouds were mists that painted the waters. He could almost embrace it. Did his people really live on this seemingly small orb? His labored breathing eased and he felt a quiet warmth steel through his body. He envied the gods their heaven. Were they here to take him there?

"Lord, I have tried to be a faithful servant."

Oryana knelt beside him and brushed his forehead. "You were more than that," she whispered and smiled, her eyes glistening bright. "You were a friend."

"I don't mind dying then," he tried to say, but the words

would not come. He stared at the blue world even as life left him.

The fires of death burned high in the temple that night.

Hunger

I favored Blink's Bar after a movie or a do-it-yourself dinner in my apartment. Inside, they played thin, reedy music, the kind of stuff that used to be popular in the eighties—preferred by the oldies and the sentimental at heart; like me perhaps. Half the time I couldn't hear anything anyway above the blanket of noise and anonymous chatter of guests. A little open square among the tables had room where I could dance if I wanted to, or simply cling to someone warm and feminine. The drinks weren't watered and the bartender would talk to me if not busy. Cheaper than a session with my shrink and delivered about the same kind of service.

Maybe it was the slow pace or the square atmosphere, but there were always a lot of young people hanging around. Some came to enjoy the novelty, liked the mood and the dated sounds, and many of them became regulars, proud to have discovered a real cool place.

That's how I met Dan.

We were both checking out the female scenery after ordering. Mine a bourbon and dry ginger ale, no ice. When the drinks arrived, he appeared to scrutinize the amber fluid in his glass, gave me a sidelong glance and shrugged.

"If I wanted a decent drink, I wouldn't be here," he decided and raised the tumbler in a salute.

He wore a gray corduroy blazer and black trousers. Clear blue eyes regarded me with amused cynicism. He wore his light brown hair, streaked with white, in a thick mop. He had the kind of rugged exterior that made women fall at his feet and men take orders from; lucky bastard.

I tried to suppress my jealousy and returned the salute, wondering what he did in his day job.

"Check," I said with a grin and glanced briefly at the crowd. "Being here is a diversion from what's waiting for us outside."

"You got that right," he muttered, leaned against the bar and scanned the room.

The bar was a very good place to get picked up—by either sex.

"All the good ones are already taken, my boy," I said.

"You must have been out of circulation, man!" His deep, rich laugh lit his eyes. No pretense there and I began to warm to him. The eyes told me a lot about him. "The name is Dan," he said and stuck out a meaty a hand.

"Frank," I said and nodded.

His hand cool and dry, we both maneuvered for a knuckle crusher. Childish, but what the hell. He had height and reach on me, but I only smiled as his expression changed from a confident smirk into a surprised grimace of pain. I let him go before he was reduced to squirming. Considering what I was, he had a strong grip.

"Damn!" he grunted, massaging his hand. "It's been a while since I came off second best."

"I'll be around whenever you want a reminder." We had a hearty chuckle and clicked glasses again.

Looking around, he suddenly jerked his head. "Frank! Take a look at that chassis, man."

I followed his glance and almost missed her.

Not tall, something about the way she stood radiated a power held in check that made me stare. Her black hair spilled across her shoulders and hung above a slim waist. Her oval face framed ebony eyes, a delicate nose and generous lips. I couldn't see any makeup. She wore a brown knee-length dress that clung without being tight. Attractive enough, but I had seen better. I could swear that for a second every male eye in the room turned on her. Must have been my imagination, but I decided not. Something about her made me take a second look and I recognized her. A hunter, and I wondered what prey she'd catch tonight. It wouldn't be me, but I wasn't hunting just then.

"Not bad," I said offhandedly.

Dan shook his head and gave me a pitying grin. "You happen to leave your eyeballs at home or something? Step aside. This is man's work, sonny." Without taking his eyes off the woman, he placed the tumbler on the bar top and stood up.

Amused, I watched as he walked up to her and said something. She gave him a quizzical look, nodded and smiled. I took a sip and when I looked up, they were gone. Dan didn't know it, but he was in for an interesting night, lucky stiff.

I forgot about them, figuring it was none of my business. A grown man, Dan knew what he was doing, and the woman wouldn't take too much from him. The ordinary people around us provided what she and I needed to survive, and we had to be careful not to abuse our gift. I did remember the scowl hanging on the bartender's face when he gave me a refill.

"You figure I should have warned him?" I demanded.

He merely grunted and walked off. To hell with him. I didn't need a conscience. Dan might get some scar tissue of the heart, but what she'll give him in return would even things out.

* * *

A few weeks later, I bumped into Dan again—and didn't recognize him.

I stood leaning against the bar for emotional support when this old geezer quietly slipped on a stool beside me. He had peppery hair worn kind of long and skin hanging off his jowls. Powerful once, he was now only another old timer trying to recapture something he happened to leave behind in his youth.

"Pops," I said pleasantly and nodded.

His blue eyes sparkled as he grinned. "How you doing, Frank?"

The voice sounded kind of familiar and I frowned. Then my jaw fell as I took in the gray corduroy blazer and dark trousers.

"Dan?" I asked, not believing my eyes, alarm bells clanging in my head.

"I always knew you were a pretty sharp boy, Frank," he wheezed, nodding.

"What the hell happened to you? You look…" I trailed off, but deep down I knew, and the knowledge made me angry. Why did she do it? This wasn't the kind of advertising any of us needed. Once ordinary people started noticing, we would become the hunted.

"Yeah, I know. I look like hell and I feel like I'm pushing eighty." He raised a finger and ordered a drink. He didn't say anything, just stared into space as he waited for that drink. I let him have his moment.

The bartender shook his head as he slid the tumbler across the top.

"On the house," he growled and stomped away, but not before giving me an accusing glare. I pursed my lips. How could I know she would do this to Dan? Secretly, I burned with guilt, remembering her. She had that wild look in her eyes I should have recognized.

"Don't mind him," I told Dan. "He's only sore at the world."

"Can't blame him. Let's find a quiet place," Dan grunted and we carried our drinks to an empty table tucked into a dark corner. The music followed us, but I didn't mind. Looking at him, I still couldn't believe it. It had been a while since I'd hunted, but even when I did, I never took too much. We were supposed to leave something behind, or the victim would never recover.

"Dan?"

"I know, I know," he said tiredly. "I'm dying."

"Dying? From what?" I demanded, but I knew. The signs were all there. She shouldn't have done it.

He smiled and his eyes lit up. "Would you believe love?"

"Come on, Dan. I'm serious."

"So am I."

When he looked at me, there was no pretense, no regrets. "It was her."

He didn't have to explain. "How?" But I already knew. He shook his head and shrugged.

"I don't know. Something about her made her different from any other woman I have ever known. She made herself like that for me. She wanted me bad. I could tell, and she didn't hold back. Neither did I."

"What are you talking about?"

A wistful smile creased his face and some of the years seemed to fall away. I could see a face before he became old. Then he looked at me, an old and weary man.

"When I picked her up, or maybe she did the picking. It doesn't matter. Anyway, we both knew where it would lead to. She had me captivated, or bewitched. I don't know."

"Yeah, you were taken in by her, all right. I saw."

He snorted and took a quick gulp. "It's not that. Pretty enough, but nothing spectacular. What I mean is, when she looked at me, I knew I was the only man in the world for her. That's a powerful weapon, my boy. I was hers, and something in the back of my mind told me to get the hell out of there in a hurry, but I left it too late. My hormones were doing my thinking for me."

"So you were swept off your feet. A one-night stand."

"Sure, except it lasted three weeks. Then one morning, I looked in the mirror and saw a stranger. No sign of her and her things were gone. I tell you, in those three weeks, I lived a lifetime."

He looked at me, eyes glistening and a shiver ran down my spine. Obviously, she has gone rogue. Not good. Not good at all.

"And you know something? I didn't care. I didn't! Who knows, maybe she left that with me as some kind of compensation."

I twirled my tumbler, brooding. "You still haven't told me what happened, Dan."

"I don't *know* what happened! All I know, as I grew weaker, she grew stronger, more radiant, more compelling. When we made love, I could feel my strength draining from me. Frank, making love to that woman, I lost myself."

"You did," I said dryly, knowing exactly what happened. "Dan, you know what you're saying? How do you know she made you old? You could have caught something…" I trailed off. I was making lame conversation and knew it. It shouldn't happen like this!

"You know she did it. I can see it in your eyes, Frank," he said gently and I looked away, surprised at the pain I felt, seeing him reduced to this. "All women take something from you when you love. This one just took a bit more than most."

Yeah, his life.

* * *

A week later, he was dead.

And I started to have doubts. Sure, he was suddenly old and then he faded away, but there were a lot of other plausible explanations for that. Weren't there? I wasn't fooling myself and sighed in disgust. Something would have to be done, and it looked like I would be the one to do it. I hoped I could hack it, or I'd wind up like Dan, which wasn't part of the plan.

On one cool evening, the wind keened softly through the alleys. A thin fog began to drift in, shrouding the city lights in a soft blanket. I never meant to drop in for a drink that night, but I'd had a long day and the thought of making my own dinner didn't hold much appeal.

I finished my drink when silence settled around me as she slid onto the bar stool next to me. She ordered something in a low contralto voice. Our eyes met and I could feel my face tense.

She wore the same brown gown and her eyes seemed to widen as I looked into them. They were completely opaque and I couldn't see any reflection in them. Her hair tied in a knot above her head accentuated her narrow features. She touched the corner of her mouth with the tip of a small tongue and smiled slowly.

"Hi," she murmured huskily, revealing even teeth, not recognizing me for what I was. I would need that to protect me. "You look like I remind you of someone."

"You do remind me of someone," I said after a moment, drinking in her face. Her power radiated from her and I fought not to sink under her spell, remembering what I had to do.

"It must have been a painful reminder. Perhaps I should leave?"

"No," I said firmly, wanting her to think of me as merely another victim. "A memory of a thing long ago."

She smiled, the charm exuding from her making me wary. We were the same, but that didn't mean she couldn't take me if I wasn't careful. For a moment, I wanted to ask her about Dan. Luckily, I had enough sense to keep my mouth shut. For what I intended, I had to keep my wits about me, or I could end up like Dan. That simply wouldn't do.

With another smile that didn't touch her eyes, she placed a small hand on my arm.

"I'll make you forget her," she whispered. "There will only be us—forever."

I believed her. I slipped some notes on the bar and stood up. We made our way between the tables and walked out.

I had a fairly large apartment not far from downtown a ten-minute drive away. While the car hummed to itself, she didn't say anything. She sat there, the silence broken by the whisper of tires and the traffic around us. I felt strangely content and at peace, warm in her presence. I didn't want to spoil it with hollow words or too much introspection. Besides, no one said I couldn't have a little fun while I dealt with her.

She touched my arm and I glanced at her outline, her face in shadow. On impulse, I pulled over, and for a while, we listened to the throb of the engine as we kissed deeply.

"I don't even know your name," I said softly, trying to make out her features.

She seemed to hesitate, then turned her head. "Kaneel."

The air seemed to tremble as I savored the sound. "Mine's—"

"Frank, I know."

I was pleased that she remembered. I leaned toward her and brushed her soft lips with mine.

When I reached home, I pulled into the curb and helped her out. We walked up the steps into a gloomy foyer. The elevator sighed to a stop and the doors slid away. Our footsteps were soundless in the thick pile as we walked slowly down the corridor. I gave her a brief smile as I fitted the key into the lock of my door.

I hung my jacket and found her in the lounge, eying the rows of books lining dark shelves, and little trinkets that cluttered the rest of the furniture. I kept the place neat. That always went down well with the ladies.

"You have a very nice place, Frank." She flashed me a grin and opened one of the two bedroom panels. She didn't turn on the lights.

I walked slowly toward her. She had her back to me, outlined in black against the backdrop of outside lights. Gently, I placed my hands on her shoulders and felt her stiffen as my arms slid down her body. Then she turned and melted against me.

Her lips were soft and cool against mine. Fire ran down my back as our tongues touched. I looked into the black pools of her eyes, cold and unblinking.

The zipper hardly made a sound as I moved it down her back. I pulled at her shoulder straps and the dress caught at the swell of her breasts. Breathing rapidly, her chest strained against me as fingers worked on the buttons of my shirt.

My head whirled and I couldn't do anything to stop it even if I wanted to, which I didn't. Then her cool flesh pressed against me, hair spilling across her shoulders, arms around my neck.

"You're mine," she whispered against my ear as I picked her up, desire welling within me even as part of me thought black thoughts. She had it coming to her.

* * *

I figured I had about four days.

At least I had none of the crap that goes with old age: rheumatism, stiff joints and constant pain. I was just old and a little senile maybe. Not an affliction of only the old. I'd get over it. I had done this twice before and it always passed, but there is a risk. I knew of somebody who did this and didn't make it. It could easily have happened to me had I given into temptation.

She stayed for five days, then left suddenly. One morning, I woke in a lonely bed filled with pleasant memories. I knew what Dan must have gone through, suspecting the truth, but still willing to pay the price. For what she had to give, any man would. I did, a bit of it anyway.

I took some time off work and waited. She came back on the eight day.

Her hair white, streaked with gray, her face had gone all wrinkly and dry. The eyes were still compelling, but some inner fire had gone out of them.

I knew how she felt.

"You bastard!" she croaked as I opened the door.

"Come in, Kaneel," I said easily, enjoying how she looked.

"You knew what I was and you still did it! Why?"

The smile slipped off my face and I stared at her, my eyes cold. "You took too much."

"I gave them a lifetime of love!"

"You took too much! We need the life force ordinary people give us to survive, but you turned that need into a sport. You took everything they had, not giving them a chance to recover. You risked having us exposed, and that's something I couldn't let you do."

"And who are you to set yourself up as my judge? You're a hunter like me, preying on them like I did."

"Yes, I preyed on them, but I never took more than they could give. You took Dan, knowing what you were doing broke our code, but you did it anyway. You used him and discarded him like a broken toy. For that's what he was to you, simply to make yourself more powerful. No, Kaneel, you brought this on yourself."

She broke then, sobs racking her body as she buried her face in her hands. The power still in her touched me. For a moment, I felt sorry for her, but only for a moment. Those tears would have worked on anyone else, but I wasn't just anyone.

Finally, she lifted her head, her face wet. "I really cared for you, Frank. You weren't like the others. Maybe because I sensed something, I couldn't go through with it."

"Is that why you left me after only five days?"

She nodded, her eyes swimming, pleading.

I shook my head and smiled. "I wish I could believe you, Kaneel, but I felt your unease and doubts. You were beginning to suspect what I was. You left to save yourself."

"I don't want to die!"

I knew she meant it, but I couldn't undo death. It had been too late the minute Dan died.

I felt better the next day. My hair had some of its color back and my skin tone felt firmer. It would take some time before I became my old, mean self again, but that was all right. I could wait. Waiting came easy when I had all the time in the world.

Three days later, they found her body behind Blink's Bar, a wistful smile on her face.

This story appeared in an anthology Monster Attack, *released in November 2014, edited by Samie Sands.*

Ice Maidens

With a clash of grinding transmission and a snarl from the diesel, the coach swayed as it entered the parking ramp. I squinted through the window, the glass smeared with frost, sparkling from the fluorescent strips that hung from power poles outside. The brakes sighed and we squealed to a stop, the whir of air-conditioning suddenly loud.

Across the aisle a figure stirred beneath a blanket and a head slowly reared up. Someone coughed. A ripple of suppressed muttering and shifting of cramped bodies ran the length of the coach. The lights came on, suddenly bright and intrusive, and I saw myself reflected in the window.

"Appelton!" the driver growled into the intercom and pried himself out of the seat. "Stopping for twenty minutes only!"

The door hissed as it opened and powder snow swirled into the coach. The driver muttered something as he strode toward the luggage compartment doors. I stood up and groped for my jump bag in the overhead rack.

Pulling up the zipper of my ski jacket, I joined the queue inching its way down the aisle toward the door. I paused on the first step and breathed deeply. The sharp air smelled of snow. Looking at the old diner, I tried to sort out my feelings. How long had it been? Certainly longer than I cared to remember.

Outside, it snowed gently. The large flakes clung like feathers where they touched. Someone bumped into me and muttered an apology as I stepped off. The figure brushed past me, hurrying toward the diner entrance. The sidewalks were almost deserted. Bent figures moved through thin fog, only to vanish as silently as they appeared.

I turned and looked around, drinking in the sights. It hadn't changed at all. Pete's old BP station still stood on the corner, a blurred pool of white light that cut through the snow. A car whispered by, trailing a cloud of white exhaust, its parking lights glittering as it vanished down the street. The Walmart store stood dark and shadows lay thick around it. A lonely huddled figure hurried on the other side of the street and disappeared into the bright interior of the Kentucky Fried Chicken eatery.

With a stiff hand, I pushed open the diner door and walked in. The air felt hot and heavy, a mixture of body odors, smoke and the acid reek of thin beer. As I stood there, a small black cat rubbed itself against my leg, looked at me and purred. I grimaced and pushed it away. I have always been wary of cats. Suddenly, I felt alone and lost, wondering where the years had taken me. As I tried to find a familiar face, a finger jabbed my shoulder.

"You getting in or admiring the scenery?" a strong rasping voice demanded behind me.

I turned slowly, stepped aside and grinned at him. "Sorry, bud. Wool gathering."

He looked at me in disgust and shook his head. "Well, gather it someplace else, okay?" He pushed his way through the crowd and vanished in the gloom of coiling cigarette smoke.

I dropped my jump bag beside the door and rubbed my hands. Maybe coming to Appelton wasn't such a great idea after all. I walked to the bar, leaned against it and reached for a bowl of mixed nuts. As I chewed, snatches of conversation washed over me; laughter and shouting drowned in a sea of noise.

"What'll ya have?" a brusque voice jerked me back to reality. The barman looked at me with pale washed-out eyes as he wiped the counter with an impatient sweep of a crumpled rag.

"Bourbon," I said. "A double."

As I sipped, I sighed. I was wrong. The place and the people here hadn't changed. I had changed.

The empty tumbler clicked as I placed it gently on the bar. I pushed it away with a flick of my forefinger and walked out, feeling the liquor burn in my belly, tempted to climb back into the coach.

* * *

It had stopped snowing. Through breaking cloud, stars shivered in frosty silence. I pulled up the collar of my ski jacket, and with a grunt, heaved the jump bag over my shoulder. Late in the evening the street stood deserted. A church bell tolled mournfully and the hair on the back of my neck twitched.

With an impatient jerk, I pulled out my gloves and a postcard fluttered into slush on the sidewalk. I stared at it for a moment before picking it up. I unfolded the stiff cardboard and read the single line. All it said, 'Come to me now. I need you'. Signed with his usual scratchy scrawl, I pursed my lips as I unzipped the jacket and slid the card into the breast pocket of my woolen shirt.

Why now, Dad?

I've been asking that question all day, but there were no answers. We had a curious relationship, my father and I. I sent him a card at Christmas and sometimes I remembered his birthday. Since Mother died, he lived alone on The Hill, and from what people said, he rarely came down into town. They said a lot more things besides, few of them flattering; just idle village talk. There had always been something of a mystery regarding The Hill and our place. Folks loved to frighten kids with tales of witches and devils. Remembering the kind of people that lived up there, I often wondered if some of those tales might be true.

I shifted my jump bag to a more comfortable position and started down the street. The snow crunched and squeaked beneath my feet and my face tingled from the cold. I had a two-hour slog along a steep, winding road to The Hill, but I knew a shortcut. I couldn't see any point paying a motel good money to hang around till morning. Besides, the walk would do me good.

The icy sidewalk gave way to a narrow frozen road and the houses gradually thinned out – black outlines in the night. An occasional yellow circle of light from a power pole scattered the shadows. Overhead, a half moon glowed hard white, streaking patchy clouds with silver, making the frozen fields glitter. The silence lay thick around me, broken only by the regular crunch of my footfalls and my uneven breathing.

After a while, I felt that someone followed me. I even stopped to look back along the road, but couldn't see anyone. Away from the noise and bustle of a big city, I was letting my imagination run wild.

As I walked, I thought I could hear the sound of mincing steps. The more I tried to ignore it the louder they became. I stopped suddenly and whirled, but there was nothing there. I shook my head and chided myself for a fool.

Bare birch and oak began to reach toward the road from the blackness of the forest. I started looking for the trail, but couldn't see it, probably lost somewhere beneath the snow. Hands on hips, I stared at the road as it wound its way up, clinging to the edge of the hill.

I checked my bearings, certain the trail should be here. Somewhat puzzled, I felt annoyed that I couldn't find it. I must have walked through here hundreds of times. Snow or not, everybody always used it – at least they did when I was a kid. Listening to my breathing, I felt unaccountably cold, a chill that came from within. Shadows moved around me, but when I looked, everything lay shrouded in silence and night.

With a sigh, I jumped over a narrow ditch along the road and plowed through the powdery snow that covered the un-marked field. Twenty minutes tops and I would be home. Well, what used to be my home.

* * *

It was bright beneath the moon and the air crisp. The snowline curved gently upward and disappeared among the pines. My legs were beginning to ache, but at least I walked on familiar ground. Transformed in summer, filled with clean smells and the buzz of insects, this meadow used to be my playground. Those were happy days, but my heart felt lighter then.

Tall pines lined the hill and I walked closer toward them. A branch creaked and a flurry of snow cascaded among the branches. I looked around, sensing shadows moving between the trees. I felt a cold touch on my cheek and jerked back. It was only the fur of my ski jacket.

I hurried then, unexpectedly anxious to get to Dad's cottage. The Hill lay just beyond the forest ahead of me. I had gotten used to city living and its cloying intimacy. This cold wilderness was suddenly alien and I did not belong anymore.

A soft patter of small footfalls broke the silence behind me and I stopped and turned. The brittle surface of the snow lay unbroken and I couldn't see anything. I don't know what I expected, but I waited until my heart slowed before moving on. Foxes and raccoons would be prowling the forest, I told myself. That was it. Nothing unusual about that, and the animals were light enough not to break the snow's crust.

I didn't believe any of it.

Ice crackled and snapped and the snow squeaked beneath my boots as I pushed my way up the slope. Perhaps I should have spent the night at a motel after all. The coach journey had been long and I felt more tired than I realized.

When the footfalls sounded behind me again, I whirled around, my breath a white fog in front of me. A large cat, coal black, its glowing orange eyes stared at me fixedly. It sat on its hunches and licked its right paw, tail swishing back and forth. It lifted its head, the eyes never leaving mine. It yawned with deliberate dignity and I could hear its rasped purring. I had a moment of fear as I looked into eyes that glowed with open malevolence. Hell, it's only a cat! With a snort, I turned and began to walk.

With each step the pines drew closer, but I couldn't get that cat out of my mind. Every time I paused to listen, nothing but silence and my labored breathing. I had a dreaded suspicion it followed me. I wanted to stop and see, but I couldn't bring myself to do it. Ridiculous, but there was something about that cat that set my teeth on edge.

Stupid!

Then I did stop and stared hard at the wall of the forest ahead. I clenched my teeth, willing myself to turn. When I did turn it sat there, staring at me, its tail working in agitation. I crouched and waved, hissing at it. It didn't move. Almost as though it laughed at me. I picked up a handful of powdery snow, crunched it into a ball, and threw it. I missed, but as the ball shattered, fragments of snow fell around the cat. It jumped, back arched and spitting, its orange eyes glaring.

Burning malice lay in those eyes and I felt a ripple of apprehension. Then I went pale. Another cat slowly emerged out of the pines. Silent like a black ghost, its red eyes stared at me. The unease I felt quickly turned into a sense of danger and I hurried away from the damned things. When one of them yowled, I shivered with dread.

Pushing my way through the snow, I imagined one of them leaping on me, tearing at me. Absurd, of course, wasn't it? Whoever heard of a cat attacking a man? Even though it seemed unreasonable, I knew they were behind me, waiting.

A narrow wagon trail wound its way through the forest, cut long ago before my father's time, and I breathed a sigh of relief as I stumbled across one of its furrows. I stopped, turned and froze. There were dozens of them, all sitting on the snow, their glowing eyes staring and I stood rooted, unable to move. The apprehension I felt before grew into real panic as I pictured them swarming over me, clawing and biting.

But they simply sat there, staring, tails working.

"Man, most mortal," a harsh female voice grated close to me and I yelped in terror.

Beside me were only trees: pine, oak and birch. Then I noticed a slim black form perched on one of the low oak branches.

"Who are you?" I demanded and harsh laughter echoed around me. The cats began to yowl.

* * *

I have always considered myself religious, but I had long ago ceased believing in the reward of heaven or the pain of hell. As with sin, these were inventions of priests to keep the believers in check. Now, all the childhood horrors instilled into me reared their dark heads as I stood staring at the sinuous shape sitting on the branch. I could just make out the slow lashing of a long tail. There may not be a hell, but there were certainly devils around. Unless this was some horrible nightmare and I would wake, still on the bus. Somehow, I knew this to be altogether too real.

"Why have you sought me now?" I whispered hoarsely, trembling uncontrollably.

"So, you recognize me," the evil creature snorted with derision. "Not at all what you expected, is it?" Its nasty laugh mocked me and my skin chilled. The cats, her minions, were all around me, waiting.

I fought to push back the tide of imagined horrors that waited for me when the demon dragged me into hell.

"Answer me!" the creature shrieked and I gasped.

"But I don't seek you!" I managed to stammer.

Her laughter was the sound of ripping steel as her tail swished. "Yet you're here. You fear me, mortal. That's good, for you have much to fear," she grated, the sound setting my teeth on edge. "You were told never to walk here at night, for your soul would be in peril. As with other things, you chose to forget or ignore the warning. I demand your answer!" she screamed and the red glow of her eyes held me horrified as I tried to understand what she had said.

I couldn't recall anyone telling me ever that I couldn't walk here at night. Then, like a window opening, I saw myself sitting beside my father one dreamy afternoon as we gazed together at the forest below us. He clutched the bowl of his pipe, the aromatic smoke pleasant. Then he spoke to me. Only a boy, too restless and not much interested in his tales.

I did remember his words, though.

"Our family has held that patch of forest as far back as any of us can remember," he growled, nodding to himself. "It's ours to do as we wish, but only during the day. Only during the day," he had said, nodding solemnly.

I remembered how he turned to look down at me, his eyes intense.

"Never go there at night, boy. Never!" His words were cold and I was afraid. I had played there often, at night too – well, late into the evening anyway.

"Why, father?" I had managed to ask.

"Later, boy. Just remember what I told you."

I had forgotten the warning, and perhaps I would now pay the ultimate price for my foolishness. How could I answer this thing when I didn't understand the question?

A small part of me reared itself in admonition and the burden of my guilt for neglecting my Dad lay heavy.

"You were following me," I said accusingly, greatly daring. If I was going to lose my soul, I could afford to dare.

"Ah, silly creature," she sneered and the tail coiled. "I was always there when you sampled the pleasure of my flesh, but when you came tonight, you opened the door to me willingly."

I looked around and the cats were there, licking their paws, staring at me in anticipation. Their turn might come too. Was that to be my punishment, to be torn forever into pieces by snarling cats?

My soul appeared to lay in judgment and my omissions were many. True, I had opened the door for her, if only a little.

and I had done that a long time ago. Although I had never strayed along the dark side that lies within all of us, I knew its shadows. The craving for material possessions and the lusts of the flesh had claimed me, and I measured success with their coin, ignoring the needs of the spirit. That part of me had withered somewhat, but it was still there – waiting to be nurtured.

When his postcard came, I *could* have stayed away...

"I may have strayed, but you have no claim on me," I said defiantly, the empty achievements of my life tasting bitter in my mouth.

"By answering your father's call, you mean to redeem yourself?" the devil chided.

"I have not finished my work yet," I said lamely.

"Your work?" she mimicked and laughed, the tail whipping. "You crave mercy, then?" she roared and one of the cats sprang on my shoulder. I stood rooted, terrified as it bared its fangs and hissed. The smell of death lay on it and its eyes burned into mine.

"All I have to do is reach with my hand and you'll be mine," the devil hissed, and the cold menace of her voice came from the depths of hell.

I may have been half crazed with fright, but I wasn't about to give myself to that thing.

"You can't –"

The cat on my shoulder snarled and sank its teeth into my neck. I screamed and clawed at the thing, but it sprang away. Blood flowed warm between my fingers and tears stung my eyes.

"I can't what?" the devil demanded softly.

"You can't touch me," I grated in defiance. "I may be in terror of you and your minions, but I have never walked in your shadow. You and yours be damned!"

She chuckled and her eyes blazed. "Oh, very good, mortal. Lame, but good. You may not have walked in my shadow, but you have touched me nonetheless."

"You tempted me, yes, but I have never given into you!"

"One day you will, and then you shall be mine for real. You chose to walk the dark path, as you chose to come to me tonight. You didn't have to, but you did."

"I will never walk your path!"

She let out a shrill laugh. "I can feel your terror, and the lust you harbor for my shape. One day, you'll embrace me willingly."

"Never!"

"We shall see. You are warned. Next time our paths cross, the fear you now feel will be justified."

One by one the cats slowly padded into darkness. A warmth seemed to descend on the forest, and with it, a pervasive friendliness. The branch where the terrible thing had perched now stood empty. It took a while before I stopped shaking. With tentative steps, I walked to where the cats had sat, but the snow lay unbroken, except for my footprints.

I saw a dark stain on the snow and bent down. It was a fluff of cat hair. A drop of dark blood fell beside it from the bite on my neck. It was then that I sank into the snow and silently sobbed.

* * *

The coach lurched as it entered the parking ramp and I opened my eyes with a start. Across the aisle a figure stirred beneath a blanket and a head slowly reared up. The lights came on, suddenly bright and intrusive and I saw myself reflected in the glass of the window.

"Appelton!" the driver growled into the intercom and pried himself out of his seat "Stopping for twenty minutes only!"

The door hissed as it opened and he winced as powder snow swirled around him. I could see his hunched figure fumbling with the luggage compartment doors.

I blinked in total confused. Had it all been only a dream?

I hurriedly touched my neck, but there was no wound. I opened my hand. In it lay a fluff of cat hair. I went cold and started to shake. I swallowed, but it went down hard.

Pulling up the zipper of my ski jacket, I moved down the aisle toward the door. I paused on the first step, breathing deeply of the biting air, trying to sort out my feelings. With heavy feet that carried the whole world, I descended the steps. When I looked up, he was there, waiting for me.

"Dad?" I managed to mumble with relief, my throat suddenly tight.

He walked toward me and smiled warmly. When he saw my eyes, he frowned, then nodded slowly.

"Dad, I…"

"It's all right, son. You're here, that's all that matters," he said gruffly and we embraced. He smelled of wood smoke and tobacco. He let me go and patted my back. I followed him to the car, flooded with relief at seeing him. I should have done this much sooner.

He opened the door for me and smiled ruefully. "Don't worry. I didn't heed my father's warning either, boy. Get in. We have much to talk about."

A slightly different version of this story appeared in an anthology Swallowed by the Beast, *released in January 2015, edited by Samie Sands.*

July 2015 Fictuary contest winner.
http://fictuary.com/feed-me-fiction-volume-3/

Memories of Tomorrow

I mean, he couldn't really tell anyone. How could he? Who would believe the poor guy? So, Sam Appleby told me. I didn't believe it, and Sally Withers didn't either. Who was she? Well, ...never mind. I'll tell it later.

You see, something about the whole thing simply didn't make any sense.

It was an ordinary suburb, you know. The kind where you've seen one, you've seen them all: tree-lined streets, brick veneer houses with no front fences, and neatly mowed lawns. Kids kicked footballs around parked cars and dogs chased the mailman. You could even see the Dandenong Ranges beyond the broken city skyline – when the smog wasn't around.

Anyway, Sam lived in a modern house of his own design in a quiet road lined with white gums and wattles. The neighbors didn't have bothersome kids underfoot and they mostly left him alone. He didn't mind it at all. A place where you would expect to find a rocking chair, not a civil engineer in his early thirties.

You see, Sam was kind of shy and withdrawn, and saw no practical use for women – much to the exasperation of one particular woman. The quiet life he led made for looks of respect from his neighbors, but Sam did not enjoy the comforts of his work. His gray eyes often held a glazed, vacant look as they roamed far horizons. He had the true spirit of a hopeless romantic. He yearned for adventure, daring, and feats of physical courage. That explained civil engineering – physical activity. A hobby in electronics and computers satisfied his more natural inclinations.

Sam dreamed, a lot. Perhaps that's what started it all. Well, the only way to achieve his desires, if he couldn't have the real thing, he'd have it in his dreams. Right?

* * *

Sam wheeled his restored Mazda RX-7 into the driveway. With a squeal of tires, he rocked to a stop before the garage. He removed his black leather gloves, stepped out of the car, greeted the old geezer next door, and waved to the woman across the road; something he did on most days. Once inside the house, he got the percolator going and changed into more casual gear. Despite his apparent good humor, Sam wasn't happy.

The new downtown building site he worked on had fallen behind schedule. The chief architect had nothing pleasant to say about it. For the most part, Sam agreed with him. It was partly Sam's own fault anyway. Easygoing by nature, he couldn't handle tough, one-track-minded construction gangs. They walked all over him. He *tried* to be stern. It was laughable. They knew him for a fake and that made him angry. Sam didn't have the backbone God gave a cockroach.

Drinking his coffee – black – he puzzled over sheets of circuit diagrams. The basement was quiet, the silence disturbed by the soft sigh of computer cooling fans. He frowned, reached for the keyboard, called up the program he'd been working on, and began coding the changes. Almost ready, he rubbed his hands in anticipation. The computer hummed and the cursor blinked at him.

Next to the server cabinet stood a used bunk. Where a pillow usually stood lay what looked like a large crash helmet. Cables of thin multi-colored wires trailed from the helmet and disappeared behind the server.

At that moment, unknown to Sam, a certain pretty brunette chemist chose to visit her reluctant victim. She had it in mind to put some backbone into Sam through physical experience, with *her* if she had anything to say about it.

The doorbell rang and the repeater in the lab clanged. Sam frowned and passed a hand through his hair, then walked up the stairs into the house. He opened the door and groaned as

Sally Withers gave him a sunny smile and brushed past him. It was *that* girl again! Without pausing for breath, she maneuvered him onto the couch. They sat down, Sam uncomfortable, Sally predatory.

The next hour passed in agony. They talked about his/her job, the weather, smog, but nothing about their relationship. Sometimes she wondered why she bothered. She stood up, placed her hands on shapely hips and glared.

"Look, Sam. We're friends, right?"

"Sure, Sally." He grinned and nodded, wishing she'd go away so he could finish his program updates.

"We've been friends long enough. It's time for the next step."

"What step is that, Sally?"

She left, disgusted.

Sam let out a sigh of relief and happily went back to his lab.

Next morning, his neighbors saw him cheerful and chipper – whistling, a thing Sam never did in public. They wondered if Sally and he…and Sally wondered if he and some other floozy…

Sam didn't bother with explanations. He had his dreams and he was happy. The machine worked better than he expected! All it needed were a few minor adjustments to the cognitive sensor booster to make it perfect.

So it went on for two weeks and Sam began to change. He became more outspoken, more sure of himself, and less embarrassed, a new man. On Friday, he didn't appear for work. In fact, no one saw him until late Saturday when Sally paid her call to check what was going on and have it out with him.

* * *

Sam opened his eyes and looked about him in terror. He sat up and swung his legs to the warm floor, holding the edge of the bunk with both hands to stop his trembling. He breathed deeply, willing himself calm down. A glance at his right arm convinced him of the appalling truth.

With a savage jerk, he tore the helmet off his head and straightened. Without a backward glance, he climbed the stairs, locked the lab, and staggered into the kitchen. A stiff jolt of bourbon brought some color to his face. In the living room, he sank onto the couch and sighed. He glanced at the wall clock. It's been thirty-two hours.

Sally rang the bell, no answer. She opened the door and walked in. Sam faced her without recognition. A cold chill ran down her spine at the sight of his dishevel form, and stifled a biting remark.

"Sam, is anything wrong? You look terrible!"

He stared at her, blinked, ran a hand through his hair and strode toward the couch.

"Sally…I…"

"What happened? Are you ill?"

Absently, he rubbed his arm. He tossed back the last of the bourbon and waited for her to sit down. He sat on the edge of the couch and looked at her.

"I suppose you know about my tinkering in the lab?"

"Must be something important that you never let me see it," she confirmed darkly.

"Well, I've developed a Synaptic Response Synthesizer. Or more simply, a dream machine."

"A what?"

"A dream machine," Sam explained patiently. "A machine that excites the brain synapses and induces dreams; dreams indistinguishable from reality. You must have noticed the change in my behavior lately."

"Yes, and I don't know whether I approve," she said primly.

"It was the SRS. I programmed it to make me dream about things I wanted to experience in real life, but never could. The machine built a synthetic personality for me and it worked, but it worked too well. By tinkering with it, I went beyond a mere dream," he declared, staring at her.

"What do you mean, beyond?"

Sam took her hand in his. "Instead of a dream, I created reality."

* * *

It felt very much like metal and his head pulsed with pain. Then came a shudder. Something tore at the cloth of his right sleeve and he fell. He blinked at the cork-like floor a centimeter from his nose just as the pain began to burn in his arm. He heard noises and shouting and smelled shorting of high-powered machinery.

He couldn't get up. When the floor stopped heaving, there were hurried footsteps and gentle hands moved over his body. He winced and groaned at the pain in his arm. A voice talked urgently and it seemed important, but Sam didn't understand any of it.

Hands moved under him and turned him on his back. Unrecognizable faces hovered above him. He looked at them with alarm.

"Shock. There is a bump on his head the size of a fist," someone said. "And he has a cut on his arm."

"That's great!" another voice snarled. "Get him to Sickbay and see what you can do, Doc. I have to get that raider before it reaches the shuttle."

* * *

Sam didn't know how much time had passed, but he felt snug and lazy. He looked around, intensely curious at the strange gadgetry, and what looked like computer screens. He could also smell a faint odor of antiseptic. He pulled out his right arm from under the sheet and looked curiously at the orange material of the sleeve. It looked metallic, yet felt soft and warm.

He remembered the corridors, the uniformed figures hurrying, and the intercom sounding orders, everything so military. A ship under way – a warship? Judging by the sophisticated technology, it did not look like any warship he had ever seen. Strange, he felt no movement of the deck.

A figure dressed in light green appeared in the doorway and walked toward him. The man glanced at the display beside the bunk and smiled with satisfaction.

"How do you feel, Captain?"

Captain? Oh, God!

"Don't worry about a thing. It's only mild concussion and a lacerated arm. You'll be up and about in a few hours. Tankard isn't very happy, though."

What the hell was the man blabbering about?

"Tankard?"

"It seems that our first officer is findings things rather difficult at the moment."

"How is that, Doc?"

"It looks like the Dee raider will catch the shuttle after all. The ambush they pulled on us, which knocked you out, by the way, gave them just enough time to do it."

Sam sighed and sat up. "Doc, I –"

"Wait a minute." The other put out his hand. "You're not fit for duty yet. I –"

Sam ignored him and pushed back the covers. "Stow it. I have to find out what's going on. Get the first officer for me."

The medic looked like he was about to say something, then shrugged. "Have it your own way, but don't blame me if you fall flat on your face on the bridge."

Sam grinned as he pulled on the orange uniform lying beside him. The doctor snorted, gave him a passing glance and walked out. He sat on the bunk, staring at a blinking console when a young man wearing a deep frown walked in.

"You wanted to see me, Sam?"

Sam felt torn between opposing forces. One wanted to deny what his senses told him, screaming at him to snap out of the SRS-induced nightmare. The other told him to reveal himself as an impostor, face the truth and its consequences.

But this was only a dream, right?

"What's been happening while I took my nap?" he demanded crisply, allowing himself to play out the charade.

Rolan Tankard relaxed, and with a tired smile, sat on the edge of the bunk.

"I'm glad to see you back in action, Sam. Have you been told?"

"Told what?"

"That ambush cost us Leerod's ship. It's a gutted wreck now. Nothing left. We were damn lucky to get away with only a shaking up."

Sam stared at Tankard and felt his skin crawl. What was he supposed to say? And who the hell was Leerod?

"No, I didn't know," he muttered, straightened his uniform. "What's our status?"

"Some twenty minutes behind the Dee raider. The bad news is the shuttle will be in its range long before we can get there. You know what that means."

Sam didn't, but couldn't very well ask. "What do you suggest?"

"We have to catch the raider and take it out before it can get within comms range of Dee patrols."

"How far are we from him?"

"Bit over two light-years." Tankard shrugged.

Two light-years? Sam could feel color drain from his face. This wasn't a ship, but a *starship*!

Tankard reached out with his arm when he saw Sam's face. "Hey, you don't look so hot. The doctor told me you're not fit for duty."

"I'll be all right. Just dizziness. Let's get on with it."

Sam had his hands clasped behind his back when the elevator doors closed before him. The polished metal revealed a stranger. He expected it, but the shock of looking at a hard chiseled face almost broke him down. Why carry on? What was he proving?

The control room was something he didn't even attempt to understand. Faces looked up briefly, then bent over their consoles. To his horror, he automatically walked down the small ramp and sat down in the lone command seat. On the curved bulkhead before him, a huge screen showed stars, naked space and a tactical window overlay. A blue and a red blip were slowly drawing closer. Beneath them, columns of figures flashed.

"Tankard, what's our present speed?"

"We're pushing maximum boost now, Captain," Tankard replied evenly.

"Go to overload."

Tankard looked at him briefly then nodded. "Helm, go to 110 percent boost."

"Aye, sir. 110 percent."

No protesting whine came from the engines and the deck did not shudder. Everything seemed normal and Sam felt disappointed.

In silence, they watched the Dee raider close with the shuttle, the enemy shields enveloping it to prevent it jumping into normal space. Five minutes later, the raider pulled away, leaving the shuttle an expanding sphere of cooling gas.

"ETA on intercept, Tankard?"

"Four minutes. That'll leave us eight minutes before they reach comms range."

"What do you suggest?" Sam looked at his first officer with interest.

Tankard hesitated and raised an eyebrow. "There isn't much we *can* do. The raider has its prisoners and the information they were looking for."

"We can destroy them," Sam said simply.

Tankard opened his mouth in astonishment. "You cannot do that, Sam! You know the stink it would cause with the Admiral if we wiped out those VIPs?"

"They're as good as dead now anyway. When we get into range, you will open fire and maintain it until the enemy has been destroyed. Regardless of cost, copy that?"

"I don't like this, Captain." Tankard shook his head.

"You don't have to like it," Sam snapped. "Just do it!"

It didn't take long. When they overhauled the Dee raider, Tankard glanced at Sam and nodded. "Commence when ready," he said quietly and waited.

Sam watched the screen trace two yellow tracks of energy toward the pulsing blip. As they merged, a halo flared around the blip. The Dee raider fired back and the ship shuddered around him. The deck heaved under Sam's feet and he went flying. He crashed against something hard and lay sprawled on the deck. He could not feel his body and his mind went mushy. He welcomed the darkness as it settled over him.

* * *

Sally watched him in silence with concerned eyes. For once, words did not come easily to her, he mused. Finally, she laughed uncertainly.

"Sam! What you told me is pretty fantastic. In fact, it's so fantastic, the simplest explanation is the one most likely to be true. It *was* all a dream. A bit weird, I must admit, but still a dream."

"That's what I thought when I woke up." Sam looked at her soberly. "But for one thing."

"What's that?"

Sam smiled faintly, then slowly rolled up the sleeve of his right arm. From elbow to wrist, a pink scar marked tender flesh.

Sally stared at his arm and her jaw sagged as she tried to comprehend the impossibility of it all. He knew how she felt.

"What are you going to do?" she whispered at length.

"Well…"

He looked at her, smiled, and gathered her into his arms.

* * *

His laughter echoed in the empty Sickbay.

"You sure can spin a wild one, Sam," I grinned.

"It was absolutely incredible, Doc! It seemed so real. Anyway, I better get back to the bridge. Tankard just called. We have a faint echo on our starboard side and I told him to send Leerod to investigate. That Dee raider won't get away this time."

"Right, I'll see you later, then," I said, watching him disappear into the elevator, and shook my head.

Two minutes later the alert sounded.

Nightwalk

I pulled back the sliding door and stepped out onto the back veranda. Quiet and still, the wind barely stirred the branches of the tall spruce that lined the fence boundary. I dragged the door shut and paused as it clicked and locked. I stood there listening to the buzz of insects. From the paddock next door came the sudden squawk of a magpie. A hurried beat of startled wings, then silence.

Dad had mowed the grass in the morning, the drying rows looking like plowed furrows. The smell sharp and pleasant, far removed from the metallic smells of the city with which I was more familiar.

At that moment, a dark band of cloud appeared above the hills and I shivered as something cold went through me. Annoyed at being disturbed by dark clouds, I walked quickly to the tool shed. The old tin door groaned on worn hinges as it opened and I peered inside. I squinted and looked around, spotting the large axe propped in one corner. It felt unusually heavy when I tried to pick it up. Either it had grown some since the last time I used it, or I had gone soft.

I decided to take only two steel wedges. The things were bulky and I had enough to carry already. One of Dad's neighbors shuffled along the road, paused and waved in greeting. I nodded and waved back. A shadow fell across me and I looked up.

The band of black clouds had grown and were drifting overhead. Something strange about those clouds I could not pin down, and I paused to watch them. On the lawn, a magpie looked up from his pecking. With a startled flutter of wings, it headed for the giant spruce in the neighbor's yard.

I noticed the silence then. Not a whisper from anything. Branches hung limp as though the wind itself had fled. Somewhere down the road, a car backfired and I jumped. Two sparrows flew quickly toward the gums that lined the road.

* * *

My boots crunched on loose gravel. The trail ahead twisted as it vanished among the towering gums of the forest. The smell of eucalyptus overpowered everything and the branches high above me hung unmoving. My steps were light. The water bottle thumped against my rump.

There is magic in a forest that drew on the strings of my soul. My cares dropped away as I craned my head, staring at the thick canopy above me. Pushing my way through the forest, I stopped beside a broad white gum, reached with my hand and touched the smooth bark. It felt warm and I imagined I could feel it breathe.

I shifted the axe to my left shoulder and repositioned the saw hanging at my waist. The path before me was narrow and worn, a path I had taken often over the last few days. On my left the ground fell away into a steep cutting where a small stream gurgled as it wound its way through the undergrowth. I stepped over a fallen trunk and followed the path deeper into the forest. By the time Dad returned, I would have cut the logs and his grudging smile sufficient reward for my labors. He doled out his praise in meager amounts and I was content for any crumbs he cared to throw my way. We didn't have a close relationship, but managed to get along, albeit warily.

It took longer to reach the logs than I had thought. At one point, I stopped and stared at the silent trees around me, wondering if I had taken a wrong turn somewhere. They had a strange, lost look that made me pause. Dad and I used only one trail, and I had not taken a wrong turn. I knew this part of the forest like the back of my hand. Now, some strange difference about it made me pause, something alien. A cold gust ruffled my shirt and I shivered, annoyed at allowing myself to get spooked like some city tenderfoot.

I finally reached the logs, dropped the tools and stripped off my shirt, letting the soft air wash over me. Walking around the logs, I frowned, debating which one to tackle first. I pulled on leather gloves and rubbed my hands in anticipation.

* * *

The heavy axe swung high above me. With a whispering sigh, it arced through the air and came down. The steel wedge clanged and sank deeper, the clap flat and muffled. I exhaled loudly, propped myself against the axe handle and wiped sweat off my brow. It was hot work, but I enjoyed the exertion.

Gradually, I noticed the overpowering silence, thick and oppressive like a blanket. As I leaned back, something touched me and I froze. I turned my head slowly and snorted. Only a branch. Hell!

Overhead the clouds were gathering. I looked around and the shadows were all about, growing black in the forest depths. Somewhere a branch crashed through the canopy and I waited for it to strike. Nothing. It must have caught on the lower limbs.

The log groaned, and with a crackling like frying bacon, a thin line ran quickly down its length. I took another swing and the axe slammed against the burred top of the wedge. The echo rang hollow. With a crack the log split to reveal its dark, almost red core. Sinewy strands bound the two halves. With quick swings of the axe, I cut through, grunting with satisfaction as the halves rolled apart.

I sat on one of the logs, tilted back my head, and drank deeply from the water bottle. The water tasted warm and flat. I looked up and saw the band of darkness had covered the sky, and the air had turned gray. I slowly stood up and stared at the clouds.

There was something strange about that blackness normal storm clouds should not have had. I've been caught in storms before, but even during its fury, it had a sense of familiarity, knowing it would pass. This thing was ominous and unaccountably, I felt it courted death for company.

I screwed back the top of the water bottle. Annoyed at being spooked, I spat on the ground and grabbed the axe. Next, I would start to imagine voices! Just storm clouds, that's all. I grunted and rolled the split log so that it lay flat, then paused to catch my breath. Polishing a chair in an office hadn't done anything for flabby muscles. Maybe I should have waited for Dad. I could have used some company right then.

Holding the steel wedge, I tapped it tentatively until it caught in a crack. Something stirred the undergrowth and I looked up. A low dark shape bounded in the gloom and vanished without a trace. Only a wallaby, I mused. A branch creaked above me and I stopped. I held the axe tight against my chest and felt my face drain.

When the touch came, I jumped and swiveled, but saw nothing, not even a branch. I could still feel something on my back, crawling. With a frantic swipe of my hand, I brushed my back and felt something rustle. With a suppressed yelp, I stepped back and watched as a gum leaf fluttered to the ground.

I stared at the leaf and my hands shook. I knew I was on the verge of screaming with rage. With an effort, I willed myself to calm down. Afraid of a falling leaf! If I told anyone, I would never live it down.

* * *

The axe fell in slow motion and I didn't hear it fall. A strong gust made the branches groan and my bush hat was whipped away. Muttering a curse, I bent to pick it up. Suddenly, I found myself bathed in light. Startled, I looked up and knew I had gone nuts. Where a thick forest had stood before, I looked at a gently rolling meadow. Tall grass swayed beneath a black sky, pushed by a stiff wind. Where I stood, everything was silent and still. The forest hissed behind me.

The edge of that dark sky touched what looked like low hills. Beneath the blackness, a stubby black funnel reached toward the ground and I imagined raging winds sucking everything in its path. I heard no roaring, saw no debris flying, nothing. The funnel seemed to pause as if waiting for something, then it slowly moved toward me.

I had no time to rationalize what I was seeing. I clamped my teeth to prevent myself from whimpering. Behind me, what sounded like stifled laughter stirred me into movement. When I turned, I saw only the gloom of shifting shadows. The forest should have been familiar, but there was only darkness within which strange shapes moved. The laughter came again, this time closer.

When I looked at the meadow, the funnel was almost above me and the wind keened thinly – the wailing of trapped souls. Like a window opening, the funnel moved over me and I could see into it. I could not discern any depth or distance and I felt if I reached up, I could touch it. Shapes moved inside it and I stared in helpless fascination as a gray, elongated, planar face formed. The eyes, black pits with no irises, stared back at me. The mouth split into a jagged gash and moved, but I couldn't hear anything.

I didn't know what was happening, but I knew I had to get away from that funnel. Laughter followed my footfalls as I broke into a run toward the trees.

* * *

My foot caught on a root and I sprawled, scraping skin off my palms. Rain started to fall, cold and invisible. Something touched my legs. With a muffled scream, I scrambled up and ran down the trail. Shadows shifted around me. The trail

wound its way down the side of a cutting and I did not remember taking a turn.

When I reached the stream, it had turned into a raging
creek, boiling and hissing, its water oily and black. Beyond it
lay a dirt road and I jumped, landing waist high in the foamy
water. I struggled toward the bank, my hands clawing at the
mud.

In panic, I scrambled up and sagged weakly against the
bank. Almost dark now, the road before me became indistinct,
but still recognizable. The forest around me groaned in pain,
branches whipped in agitation, but there was no wind, only
the cold rain falling softly.

"Run, Man," something whispered close and I whirled, but
I was alone. Distorted shapes twisted and melted just outside
my reach and I moaned.

Something cracked above me like a gunshot and I could
hear the ripping of timber. I jumped and rolled as a heavy
branch crashed onto the spot where I had stood. Gasping, I
ran down the road.

The road looked unfamiliar, but I knew that I could not go
back into the forest, or cross that creek again. Alive, the forest
had now filled with something sinister, and it wanted me. I
remembered the stories my father used to tell me, of witches
and devils and strange happenings. They were good for a
laugh, but I wasn't laughing now.

I always imagined a devil with horns and a pitchfork, a long
tail lashing back and forth as it prodded its hapless victim. I
almost wished to see one now. At least, I would know what
was after me. This invisible presence, though, the shifting
scenery and horrible laughter, was harder to take. I kept running, knowing if I stopped, it would win.

* * *

The road seemed to end in a thicker patch of blackness and
I paused, exhausted. I turned and a shadowy hand reached for

me. Muffled laughter followed my strangled scream as I ran into the black wall.

I burst into daylight and skidded to a stop.

My heart hammered and my chest heaved. I stood frozen in a crouch as hot sunlight washed over me. I slowly looked around. Behind me lay the overgrown tracks of the Daylesford railway. On my right ran the main Trentham road. A low slung Ford Falcon topped the gentle rise and whispered past. I glimpsed a startled face of its driver, then it was gone.

I sank to the ground and sobbed. Shaking, I wiped my face with the back of my sleeve and patted my matted hair. It was streaming wet. I looked at myself and terror welled within me. I patted my muddy, wet shirt, as were my jeans. No wonder that driver looked startled. I managed a weak cackle of relief.

The sky was clear, deep blue and without a cloud. Insects buzzed soothingly and I breathed deeply of the scented air. I didn't know what had happened, but there would be time to sort it out later, happy to be back in the real world – and sane.

I pulled off my shirt and tied it loosely around my waist. My Dad's place was about a kilometer away and I started to walk. My first few steps were tentative and unsteady, but being in familiar surroundings reassured me and I picked up my pace.

The terror still lurked inside me, vivid in my mind, but I could face it now. I paused in front of a store and stared at my reflection in the display glass. The face looked thin and drawn and the eyes were wild. A hot shower and it would all vanish into the bad dream I felt it was.

I almost laughed when I reached the spruce-lined fence. The gate stood open, so Dad must have returned. I paused at the gate and looked fondly at the house. A magpie pecked at the grass. It turned and looked at me. With a squawk, it flew away. I grinned and walked to the front door.

As I reached for the handle, the door opened with a heavy groan and a blast of cold air washed over me. The face staring at me was gray and long, with sharp, planer features. The eyes were black pools and I saw my horror reflected in them.

"You have come to me." The voice was cold and deep, drawn from the depths of my nightmares and I heard myself scream.

Empire Builder

-1-

I could see the locus points form around the Free Planets cruiser's shields and knew what was coming. Twin tracks of pale blue ionization lanced toward my ship and the deck shuddered beneath my feet. Our return fire made the enemy's screens flare and metal boiled from the outer frames where the primary shield had collapsed.

"Keep firing, Opturkarh," I said urgently. "We've got to get closer."

"He'll roast our ass if we keep this up, Karhide." Taris pointed at the holoview enveloping most of the operations platform below. I glared at him and snorted with impatience.

"We've hit him hard! This isn't the time to back off," I snapped, watching the tactical mainframe plot overlay.

The enemy cruiser fired and I counted the seconds before the beam would hit, cursing silently. The deck shuddered and I clutched the armrest.

"Caution. Levels three, four, and six are penetrated. Areas are isolated," the housekeeping computer declared. "Caution. Secondary shield overload. Primary shield active."

Taris looked up from the command seat on the operations platform below. "Its Engineering, Da."

"And?"

"We're down on our secondary shields."

"I'll go and hold Makkee's hand some other day. For now, all I want to know is when that ship out there is giving up. What's the report? Tactical plot says we made direct hits."

"So did they," Taris growled.

"That last pattern must have hurt him."

Taris glanced at the mainframe plot. "Target is stationary and locked into our fire control. Approaching optimal acquisition point. Ready to engage."

"Cent Comp copy?" I demanded.

"Ready."

"Clear auxiliary tactical plot."

The repeater screen lit up showing the enemy ship apparently immobilized by the running fight. No indication of surrender came from the battered hull.

Skies!

We closed in. Their shields flared in overload under the impact of our projectors. I grinned savagely at the thought of roasting a few of my enemies. Their screens pulsed, flickered and vanished. Metal boiled, surrounding the ship in a dispersing cloud. Wreckage drifted around gaping holes. I wasn't surprised to see survival NS-5 needles emerge from the stricken starship.

I nodded to Taris. "You may cease firing, Opturkarh. And well done."

"I'd like to board her, Lee," Taris looked at me and grinned. "Souvenirs."

"I'll handle the souvenirs. You stay here and clean up this mess. Get ten men to Boat Bay Two. And Taris…"

"Da?"

"Right now, he's playing dead, but he might change his mind. If he attempts to maneuver, you do what's necessary. Copy that?"

"With pleasure!"

"Yeah." I chuckled and headed for the lift-well. Taris wouldn't mind blasting away if he thought it would get me as well.

* * *

Docking the shuttle, the security detail followed me to Primary Flight Control. Standing there, I surveyed the wreckage of the enemy command deck. My own PFC didn't look much better. The crew lay prone against torn equipment, moaning, clutching bleeding limbs.

It wasn't nice.

The command chair swiveled, revealing a haggard young man. His clothes were rumpled and he looked the way I felt. He stood at attention and brought the tips of his fingers to his forehead in a salute.

"Opturkarh Salon of the Free Planets. I surrender my ship, Da." He exhaled heavily, trembling.

"Karhide Zor-Lee of the Orieli Space Arm, at your service." I didn't return the salute. Not to a rebel. "Okay, Opturkarh. Care to give me your version of it?"

"Go to the pit," he hissed.

"All in good time," I grated, my lips bared into a snarl. "You've been a pain in the neck ever since I spotted your stolen ship. I haven't spent all day chasing you just so we could have a quiet drink somewhere."

He glared at me, defiant and proud. "I'll see you rot first, you bastard." He turned and touched a prism on his armrest.

"Caution. Self-destruct in final sequence. Commencing final count. Five…four…Caution. Self-destruct malfunction. Sequence terminated."

Salon stood there as the realization of his failure slowly became clear, then he lunged at me. I stepped aside and whipped the edge of my hand against his neck. He blocked, twisted, and his right hand shot out and slammed into my face. Stars popped all around and I felt myself falling.

-2-

I made the switch from sleep to wakefulness in two steps. The first was becoming aware of the bunk and crisp sheets. That felt pleasant. Second, a stab of pain on my jaw shattered the brief moment of peace.

Why did I feel so alone and miserable? When was the last time I felt truly happy? What did I fight for anyway? The greed and rot that was so much part of the Concordiat? Or it could be nothing more than a drive to show all those ass lickers in the Orieli Space Arm how it should be done.

I didn't know. Perhaps it was a bit of everything. One thing I knew with certainty. I was hated by my so-called brother – bastards most of them – officers even more than by the enemy. They hated me because I was an eye gouger and a ball kicker, and because I got results.

Where are you now, my son?

I opened my eyes and looked around. I began wondering how long I'd been here and climbed off the bunk. Pulling on a shirt, I reached for the Command Console Screen.

"PFC!" I yelled, cursing my daydreaming.

Taris appeared in the screen looking worse for wear. "Da?"

"What's our status?"

"We're heading back to our initial contact point with the FP cruiser, Lee. Rendezvous in three hours."

I stared at him, then grinned. "Well done. How long have I been out?"

"About four hours. I had Dr. Malfe give you something. You needed it."

"You take a damned lot on yourself, Mister," I grumbled, looking at him closely.

"Well, the last time I checked, you were in no shape to give orders to anybody," he replied cheerfully. "Then there is damage to –"

"Never mind. That was a smart piece of thinking, about heading back, I mean. You'll make Karhide rank yet."

"Hell, there's no need to get nasty, Lee."

I switched off and chuckled. I meant it, though. A fine exec, Taris was more than ready for his own command.

The Personal Transport system took me down to Sickbay. Dr. Daran stood up and hurried toward me.

"Some, ah, bad news, I'm afraid." He dabbed nervously at his sagging jowls.

"Tell me about it, doc."

"Well, it all boils down to, ah, their conditioning, Da. The fact of the matter is, I cannot break their conditioning in three hours."

I grunted and paced around. Daran hovered near me, dabbing nervously at his face. "Doc, I need that information now. I cannot hang around while you tinker with their damned brains." I saw him studying me and grinned. "What's the matter?" I pointed at one of the empty medicrib bunks. "I'll bet you'd love to get me onto one of those, eh?" He turned white and I laughed. The man was a fool. The time for clowning over, I had serious business to do. I stared at Daran shuffling nervously, avoiding my eyes. I didn't care if the fool hated me as long as he did his job.

"Okay, doc. Get Malfe up here. Then you can go and play with your instruments."

"You mean that, ah, I'm relieved of this case…Da?"

"That's right."

He stared at me, mouth hanging. Then he dropped his eyes and his shoulders sagged. I watched him go and shook my head. After this, I promised myself there were going to be some changes around here. I wasn't running a cruise ship!

Humming a nameless tune, I sat down behind the CCS and pressed a button. "Security? Bring Opturkarh Salon to Sickbay Two." I switched off and waited.

* * *

"You can't mean it, Lee." Malfe grabbed my arm, staring at me in horror.

"Why shouldn't I mean it?" I said harshly. "What do you think this is anyway? Some afternoon picnic?" Peeved, I expected him to understand, not have his wounded sensibilities paraded before me.

Skies!

"But not like this!"

"There isn't any other way." I slammed my fist against the desk beside the CCS console. "And there isn't time to do it your way either. I can't afford to screw around."

We walked into the examination room and Salon looked up as we entered. I nodded to the two security types and they faded. I paced around for a while, hands behind my back. It might get Salon nervous, but I doubted it. He didn't fit the part. I stopped in front of him and looked into his eyes.

"This is it, Opturkarh. No more leisurely tinkering with Dr. Daran's probes. From now on it gets rough and nasty." I paused and gave him a disarming smile. "But, should you choose to be cooperative and tell me what I want to know, I can be generous. Well, what's it going to be?"

"Screw you," he said.

I sighed and shook my head. "A hero type." I pointed my thumb over my shoulder at one of the manned medicribs. "See that?" Salon glanced behind me and his lips tightened.

"One of your crewmen, Opturkarh. As you can see, I've got him all wired up there. You know what that means." I studied his face and grinned. "Tell him, Malfe."

"I'm sure that —"

"Tell him!"

"The medicrib —"

"I know what the thing does," Salon grated.

"I'm sure you do," I said and pointed at the man lying on the crib. "I'm not asking any more. I'm telling. He's only the first."

He looked at me and shook his head.

I walked to the crib and looked down at the strapped body. He looked awfully young to be playing grownup games.

"Now, son. You heard what I said. Don't make the mistake thinking I'm joking. A demonstration." My hand moved toward the control panel and hovered. I watched the anxiety build on his face and closed a contact. His face twisted into a grimace as the medicrib began to tear down his internal tissue. He gurgled through clenched teeth, then screamed as he convulsed against the straps.

I switched off the machine and glanced at Salon. "You want to talk?" I asked and he shook his head, taking in quick breaths. I closed the contact and turned, shutting out the screams. My conscience didn't even twinge.

A disciplined officer, Salon knew the rules. He stood there, face drawn as he listened to the screams of his crewman. The play of emotions clear on his hard face.

I switched off the machine. "Ready to talk?"

"No more...no more," the boy sobbed, his body shivering, muscles twitching. Blood oozed from his earns and nose.

"What was your post?"

"Nav control."

"Your course before we made contact?"

He mumbled coordinates figures. I frowned and closed the contact. He leaped against the harness in shock and howled. Malfe hurried over and glanced at the console. He gripped my arm.

"Lee, you're killing him!"

"If that's what it takes," I said calmly and shook him off. I leaned against the bunk.

"Those figures, son. They don't seem right to me. Maybe you were trying to pull a fast one?"

"It's the truth! I swear it," he whimpered, then blanched when my hand moved toward the console. "No more," he kept repeating, shaking his head from side to side.

Was he telling the truth? Nothing out there but an interference barrier – a singularity event horizon.

"What ship were you supposed to meet?"

"I don't know!"

"Your base?"

"The Syke..." he trailed away and I grinned at him.

"It couldn't be the Syke system, boy. Ceti is a peaceful world of the Concordiat."

"It's Syke," he whispered.

"How many ships in your group?"

"I don't know."

"Name some of your other bases."

"I can't! I don't know where they are. I don't know, I don't know."

"You did just fine," I said and pressed a red pad on the console. I looked away from the body as Malfe stepped in front of me.

"Lee!"

I cut him off with a wave of my hand. "Don't say it, Malfe."

"Not like this!"

"He was a rebel," I snapped. "He deserved to die." I took two quick steps and stood before Salon.

"I want to know everything, Opturkarh. As traitors against the Zaron Concordiat, you'll die. How you die is up to you. I only warmed up with that boy. I'll go through every one of your crew if I have to, and you'll be the last."

"You're lower than a canal slime," he hissed. "An animal."

"Negative, Opturkarh. This is war! There is no place for sanctimonious tirades in this game. What would you have done? Exactly the same thing. You'd justify it as a deplorable necessity, a sacrifice for the noble cause of the Free Planets, anything to overthrow the Concordiat yoke."

"We'll not fail, Karhide. History is against you. Everyone is against you," Salon snarled.

"Nice sentiments, Opturkarh. I'm all chocked up. Let's look at a few facts." I ticked off the points on my fingers. "One. You were in some damn hurry when I spotted you. Two. Instead of picking a fight, you ran. Three. You must have carried something vital and couldn't take the risk of having it fall into my hands. Four, and this is the clincher. You attempted to destroy your ship to prove it. Tell me, Opturkarh. How can I regain your civilized esteem when you persist in being uncooperative?"

"What you did there," he snarled and pointed at the body in the crib, "was nothing but sadistic brutality."

"Brutality? You cowardly son of a bitch! And you're righteous and holy, right? I would like to know how you explained to your conscience all the men you killed when you defected with one of our ships. Ejected them into space! Brutality, eh? All in the name of freedom, a convenient hook on which to hang your morals while you pursue your so-called freedom.

"Your precious Alkarh Aron, hero of the Free Planets. He had my son for three days. I got him back eventually, but he didn't last long. The poor bastard didn't even know anything of note. Not even in the military, a plain civilian. That didn't matter. Aron was acting for the Free Planets and everything was forgiven. Nothing but revenge for a grudge against me. Not man enough to get me himself, he got someone who could not defend himself." I stared at Salon and wiped my mouth. "Brutality, Opturkarh? You haven't seen anything yet. Malfe! Bring in the next one."

I breathed deeply and swallowed. I shouldn't have gotten so emotional about it. The bastard wasn't worth it.

Skies!

"I'll tell you what you want to know," Salon said heavily. "Just leave my men alone."

"No, Opturkarh. I have to be sure. You might tell me a fib and I wouldn't like it. No. You've had your chance."

"On my honor!"

I snorted. "Honor is cheap these days. Still, talk."

"We…we were out to meet some brass from Zaron. I don't know the names. I was to hand over a new set of operational grids to a Space Arm Alkarh who's on our side. When you disabled me, I had them destroyed. That's all." He glared at me, then hung his head.

More traitors. I wasn't surprised. "Coordinates?"

Salon gave me a string of numbers. "The interference barrier?" I stared at him. "This changes nothing, Opturkarh."

"Better an honorable death than that," he said, glancing at the medicrib.

I walked to the CCS and punched a glowing prism. "PFC?"

"PFC, aye."

I gave them the numbers and grinned at Salon. "We might not be too late after all. If I had not made the intercept, you'd reach that singularity in some two days from now. We might still make it."

"You're mad!" Salon hissed.

"Yeah," I nodded and waved at the security detail. "Take him away and don't let him wander around."

-3-

"Approaching the interference barrier, Lee," Taris announced quietly.

I nodded. "Anything from the targets?"

"Nothing." Taris barely glanced up from his screens. "They're only sitting there."

"Caution. Interference barrier, strength: point two. Advise course deviation," Cent Comp noted.

"Slow approach," I said. They were waiting for me, a scout and a heavy battlecruiser. I didn't feel particularly happy about the last item. Tangling with one of those wasn't my idea of bravery, regardless of my mission priority.

"They're requesting the recognition pattern."

"Comms?"

The operator pressed a glowing blue pad and looked up. "Code sent and accepted, Da. They request you maintain neutral status."

"Figures. All stop, Opturkarh." My attention was on the tactical mainframe plot where the enemy ships were skirting the singularity event horizon.

Columns of data flickered in the holoview overlay. A pulsing green blip that identified the enemy battlecruiser broke away from the scout and slowly crawled toward me. I glanced at the main chronometer repeater line and pulled at my chin.

"The cruiser is requesting a visual, Da," the comms officer said and looked at me.

"Time to make our move," I said quietly and nodded at Taris.

I didn't feel any vibration beneath my feet as the ship hurled itself toward the enemy. We fired twice before the blip veered a fraction – into the first ring of the interference barrier. I grinned, rubbing my hands with happiness.

"Scout breaking away," Taris said, pointing at the holoview plot.

I glanced at the comms officer. "Notify all units in the area to be on alert for a PP-6 interceptor dart. Suspected Free Planets VIPs. Seek and destroy, and keep them informed of any course changes. Give them time and position."

"Copy."

The nifty little thing would have to have a cast-iron alibi to escape the hell I planned for it. If I could keep the battlecruiser off my back for a couple of hours, I might conceivably catch the thing myself. I doubted it, though. The interceptor was all legs.

"The cruiser is still locked within the event horizon boundary, Da," Taris announced.

I nodded, hoping the rebel had his engines burned out. Humming a tune, I watched the tactical mainframe plot. After a while, I glanced at the chronometer line. Only six minutes since breakaway and the PP-6 was fast drawing away.

"Interceptor changing course, sir. Coordinates..." The tactical officer rattled off a string of numbers. I followed the projection on the screen and frowned. Nothing out there but hard vacuum. Could it have detected a patrol ship so soon?

"Enemy cruiser has broken out of the interference ring and is on intercept course. ETA, thirty-one minutes at present speed."

Skies!

"PP-6 changing course again. Coordinates…" More numbers.

I scratched my head. What the hell was going on? Things were going according to plan, but it wasn't my plan. I stared intently at the screen trying to read information not there. I had a hunch so strong I could taste it, but was I right?

Had the rebel jettisoned an NS-5 survival pod with the VIPs, then scooted away hoping I wouldn't chase it? A neat trick – if that is what happened. With the enemy cruiser hot on my tail hoping to pick me off before help arrived, I had run out of options. I glanced at the chronometer again and swore. Should I follow my hunch?

"Drop normal," I ordered.

"I think it's a trick, Lee," Taris cautioned.

"Don't give me a hard time now. Just do it, okay?" I stared at him. He turned and gave the order.

The screen blinked as the ship dropped out of subspace. Energy patterns flickered in hazy lines across the tactical mainframe plot. Data flashed in continuous streams in the overlay, but without the telltale neutrino flow from an NS-5 power plant. The pod was empty. I ground my teeth in frustration. A blind bait and I had fallen for it. Precious minutes lost and possibly my ship as well.

"You may transit, Taris," I growled testily. "Status?"

"The PP-6 is now sixty-seven minutes away. Loss of tracking in eleven minutes at present speed. Enemy cruiser ETA, eighteen minutes."

Time for evasive maneuvers. I touched a prism on the armrest.

"Engineering, aye," a grumpy voice answered from the bowels of the engine deck.

"Say, Tanner," I said affably. "Can we get any more go out of this tub? I need it, bad."

"Well, maybe. How much did you have in mind, Lee?"

"How much can you deliver?"

"I could override to one hundred and ten percent, but, Lee –"

"Yeah?"

"It's not gonna last long."

"It won't have to. Override."

"It's your bucket," the engineer said and switched off.

My ass as well. I looked up and Taris stared at me. "You want to say something?"

He shook his head and bent over his station.

The extra speed might not be enough, but it was all I had. The PP-6 swiftly drew beyond the range of my sensors. As far as I was concerned, it might as well have vanished into perdition. I hoped those fools out there had tracked it. And me? Left to the tender mercies of the rebel battlecruiser.

Skies!

I heartily approved of the enemy commander's tactics, but wished the devil pursued somebody else.

"Da, message from Sector Command. They have the PP-6 on positive track. They have two light cruisers dispatched for your assistance. ETA in eighty-three minutes."

"Great!" By then the only thing those ships would find would be a cloud of iron filings. "Opturkarh!" I snapped.

Taris stood beside me.

"Damn your eyes!" I bellowed. "Stand straight when I'm talking to you, you gutless fool. Where is your blasted pride?"

He stiffened with anger and his eyes locked with mine.

"Better. Practice it. That's an order." I placed a fatherly hand on his shoulder. "What would you do if you had the con? Speak up."

"Reinforcements can be disregarded, seeing they're too far away to matter," Taris replied immediately.

"Good, good."

"The enemy can outrun and outgun us, and we're still carrying damage from our previous engagement. However, we can just about match him and he might sustain damage before destroying or disabling us. Seeing how the Free Planets are short of capital ships and trained men, this might induce their commander into caution."

"Excellent!"

"I cannot see any alternative but to keep dodging him until help arrives. Sorry, Lee."

"You're no good to me," I growled and shook my head. "Didn't you say that reinforcements can be disregarded? Think, man! By increasing our speed, we showed him that we have more than showed in his manual of tricks. We might have other things. That will keep him guessing, and doubt is a sure way to hell. Besides, if we go, we take him with us, no?" I saw the confusion in his eyes and laughed. "Resume your post, Opturkarh." I clapped him on the back. "Cent Comp? Set condition two." I climbed into my seat and looked around me. I had to endure an hour of hell. So be it.

The ceiling changed to throbbing orange and banks of dormant displays flickered into life. "Status. Primary unit active. Fire control ready. Condition two active."

I waited, listening to the whisper between the decks and the muted sounds of machines. The ship primed to unleash its stock in trade. The men were tired and the ship was tired. We needed a few months on some soothing, warm world that had never heard of the Zaron Concordiat or war.

"Target at extreme firing range," Cent Comp announced. "Recommend going to condition three."

I glanced at the tactical mainframe plot and the blip of the enemy cruiser. "Secure from condition two. Execute condition three."

The ceiling immediately changed from its glowing orange to pulsing red. There was movement around me as men and machines settled in for battle.

"Condition three commencing. All decks secured. Primary fire control active. Primary and secondary screens on lock. Primary unit active. Status. Escape sequence active. Status. Condition three active."

The enemy fired. On the screen, two tracks of blue death streaked toward me. The ship made an automatic shift in course and the energy pattern swept harmlessly by. In the next pattern, my luck ran out. The deck shuddered under a direct hit and the crew grabbed for holds.

"Opturkarh? You may return fire."

I carefully studied the effect my fire had on the enemy. He didn't even bother avoiding the bombardment, intent on drawing closer where his more powerful projectors would make short work of my ship.

"Caution. Target at optimum range. Lead impact time, zero."

Next time they fired, it would be a direct hit every time. I needed to roll out another plan if I were to get out of this.

"Mr Taris, drop normal."

"Breaking out of subspace now."

I watched the chronometer repeater line and the tactical mainframe, noting how long it would take the battlecruiser to emerge. After fourteen seconds, a faint shimmer of energy registered far ahead. I told Taris to transit back into subspace. For what I had in mind, I would need those seconds.

I looked around the command platform. Faces stared intently at displays. The quiet whisper between decks broken by an occasional command.

"Mr Taris?"

The exec looked up from the fire control console. "Escape sequence fully operational?" I asked softly, studying his face.

"Set," he said simply.

"Good. Cent Comp?"

"Ready."

The enemy ship also transited and drew closer. This had to work first time, because there wasn't going to be a second. I needed to get away and leave the devil to himself. I sat back and quietly issued my instructions. The pending maneuver would be executed too quickly for human direction; machine against machine.

Cent Comp waited for the enemy ship to come into range and start firing. We took a few hits before dropping normal relational. I stared at the chronometer, my fingers tapping against the armrest. The indicator line crawled with maddening slowness. I clamped my mouth and waited. It either worked or that cloud of iron filings would be my ship.

Cent Comp fired and twin lances of energy lanced toward a point in space where the enemy ship was calculated to emerge. A second later, another pulse, then another. I stared at the tactical mainframe. The first pulse decayed and my fingers drummed against the armrest.

A shimmer on the screen indicated the emergence of the enemy cruiser. Twin tracks of death reached the point and the image in the screen wavered and flared. The ship dropped normal as the third pulse crossed its position. The enemy screens fluctuated as they tried to stabilize after emerging into normal space, but the sudden surge of energy from my projector overloaded them.

The sphere of incandescent gas still expanding when we approached. I scanned the twisting patterns of plasma for possible survivor pods. There were none.

* * *

I lay on my bunk staring at the ceiling, my thoughts wandering aimlessly. The ship at last headed back to base – rest, repair, and then? Back to war, hate and killing? And Salon? I couldn't get him out of my mind.

I remembered how he stood facing the open hatch. Salon and what was left of his crew had seconds to live before being dumped alive into space. Not nice, but simple.

"Do you want to say anything, Opturkarh," I asked him.

"I hope to see you damned real soon, Karhide," he snarled, eyes filled with loathing.

I shook my head and nodded to the operator. The hatch closed and the outer Boat Bay doors opened. With a rush of expelled air, Salon and his men were gone.

I reached with my hand and touched a glowing prism. The ceiling dimmed to a restful green. What did they feel? A few seconds of excruciating pain, followed by oblivion. At least they were at peace now, which is more than I could say for myself.

I felt drained and weary. Like the ship, I also needed rest and repair. The crew were strangely cold and distant. Did they resent how I escaped from the enemy battlecruiser, or how I dealt with the rebels? I saved their stinking hides! It was either the cruiser or me, a simple equation of survival.

The image of my son drifted before me.

When Stars Die

I stormed through Kliff's buffer zones without collecting more than my usual quota of hostile stares. His prim-faced secretary squawked as I brushed past her.

"Don't bother announcing me," I said smoothly. "I'll just let myself in."

I strode into Kliff's luxurious office slung with low couches and deep rugs from Katalan, his native world. I made myself comfortable without waiting for an invitation. He was used to this routine. That did not mean he liked it. He positively scowled.

"Feeling quite comfortable, Lee?" His voice was hard and gravelly, the characteristic wheeze hardly audible. A short sawn-off runt, he had a dour suffering expression and an undertaker's smile. Maybe it was the eyes: tiny black points, cold and remote; or the dry, leathery yellow skin, crinkling around the eyes and mouth. Whatever, there wasn't any love lost between us and we both knew it.

"You bet," I said and gave him a smile designed for maximum irritation value. His jaw muscles were jumping, mouth a thin line.

"You should have come here sooner," he suggested, his fingers drumming softly against the desktop.

"I landed at Skaro Field an hour ago, Kliff, pursuant to your orders. If this was so damned important, you could have met me or commed."

He ignored that one. "Your squadron still in orbit?" he demanded, lips white as he glared at me, knowing very well they were.

"That's another thing. We could use a few days leave on Zaron. The crews need rest and my ships need overhaul and resupply. I want to bring them down."

"Permission denied!"

I sighed. "That's what I figured. Let's cut the crap, Kliff. What do you want?"

He went through the usual routine when giving me a particularly nasty piece of work: a pass through the white hair, the placing of fingertips together on top of the fake stone desk, and the throat clearing bit. This time it took him a while – guilty conscience perhaps. I guess I didn't go out of my way to make things easier.

Skies!

"All right, Lee. The bare bones," he wheezed and cleared his throat. "You must know that you have a lot of enemies in the Space Arm."

"Screw them," I said.

"That's what I mean. You rub people the wrong way. However, your unorthodox methods do get results…sometimes. As far as the Concordiat is concerned, that's all that counts. As you know, I don't totally subscribe to that policy. I'll be candid with you, Lee."

"Okay."

"You got this assignment over the heads of vastly more senior people. Alkarhs," he added ponderously, his black eyes studying me.

"I'm really touched, Kliff." I chuckled nastily, knowing his voice probably figured prominently trying to block me from getting whatever the Orieli Space Arm had in mind.

He gave me a hard look. "As you please, then. Your job is to destroy Ceti."

I stared at him, feeling the weariness heavy on my shoulders. "Ceti? There must be some mistake."

He shook his head, relishing my confusion. "Hard copy of your orders are waiting for you aboard your ship. You'll open them at 1700 hours today. By that time, you should be on your way. Your squadron is being resupplied even as we speak. Accrued leave will be granted on mission completion. After all, how long does it take to blow up a planet?" he said and smiled with genuine satisfaction at my bewilderment.

I sat there looking at his cold black eyes, hating him. "Differences aside, okay?"

"All right, Lee." He nodded, enjoying himself.

"You're talking about billions of people, Kliff! This will not solve the rebel problem. It will only stiffen resistance against the Concordiat. Even the moderate systems will join the rebel cause if we go through with this madness."

"I know all that."

"Then why?"

"I only carry out orders, I don't make policy." He leaned back, his hands forming a neat bridge above the polished desk.

"Whoever dreamed this up must be insane."

"Careful, Lee. Those are dangerous words. Some would say even treasonous."

"Skies!" I spat out. "Tactically, you think Ceti will be sitting on its hands while we move in a squadron and interdict their system?"

"Probably not. But then, they're not expecting anything, are they? As far as they're concerned, this will be another Space Arm maneuver off the Syke system. For once, a secret plan has remained secret."

"What about the population?"

"That's all been taken care of. Your orders are clear. Carry them out and don't try to formulate policy for the Concordiat." The warning in his voice unmistakable.

"Hiding behind orders! Is that supposed to make me proud, Alkarh?"

"It's supposed to make you obedient, Karhide!" he thundered, jumping to his feet.

"You're talking about a whole world, Kliff!"

"A world that's one of the organizational centers for subversion and rebellion against the Concordiat! You have your orders, and I'm tired of debating this with you. Now, get out!"

I stood up, looking at him in disgust. "You're a phony, Kliff, and I'm beginning to understand why you handed this mess to me." Prepared to add a lot more to that, he simply wasn't worth it. "Orders of the Space Arm will be carried out, Alkarh, and damn you for it." I turned and stormed out.

Skies!

* * *

Gray clouds lay heavy among the glowing spires of Skaro. The eastern sky, muddy and sullen, reflected my mood. I slowed my walk as the tower appeared out of thin fog. I stood at the main entrance to the building and shook the dew off my cape. The doors slid away and I strode through, folding the cape over my left arm.

I stepped into one of the empty transport booths and mumbled the combination. The aftereffect tingle of the personal transport transceiver left me and I walked into a brightly lit room.

"Eryne?" I tossed the cape in the general direction of the chair.

A happy squeal came from the lounge and she ran into me. She flung herself at me and locked my neck with her arms. We laughed and I swung her around. Then she pulled away, her large eyes searching mine.

"Lee, how I've missed you," she murmured huskily, eager and excited.

I reached out and touched her pale cheek. It was soft and warm, like her smile, no pretense. Small and delicate and I needed her very much. We held hands, her eyes laughing at me. It was only then that I noticed her long silver-green gown rimmed with blue fur. She wore matching slippers. She caught my glance and smiled.

"You like?"

"I've seen better," I said and shrugged, pretending indifference. She was so much like an innocent child in her small pleasures.

"Beast!" she pouted. "You're a crude man and I hate you."

"You'll get over it."

"Beast!"

I held her, suddenly feeling cold with pending dread. "Eryne?"

"Mmm?" She nestled her head against my chest.

"I won't be able to make it tonight."

"Are you in trouble?" She pulled back, all concern.

"I have a most ultra-top secret mission and I haven't read my orders yet. I'll get shot for it. Dawn. Tomorrow."

"So? What are you doing here, Karhide?"

"They granted a dying man's last wish to see an angel."

She fisted me in the ribs and I gasped.

"Lee?"

"Mmm?"

"How long this time?"

I shook my head. "I don't know, sweetie."

"What's going to happen to us?" she whispered, searching my face. A slim hand reached up and gently touched my cheek.

What could I say? What was there to say?

She pulled at my arm. "Let's go somewhere where there is still some peace and sanity. The Orieli Cluster is full of wars and killing. Please, Lee!"

"And where could we go to find peace and sanity?" I asked softly and stroked her cheek.

"Leave the Cluster. We could go to the frontier worlds in the White Cloud. The galaxy is a big place."

"I can't do that, Eryne. You know I can't."

"Why not? All you have now is horror and grief."

She had a point there. I pulled away from her and paced around the room for a while.

"I have a job to do, my duty." It sounded lame even as I said it.

"Killing and destroying?" I could sense the hurt and anger in her voice.

She stood there, regal and defiant.

"If that's what it takes," I said.

Her eyes were large and round and it wouldn't take much to fill them with tears. I didn't want that. I walked to her, stood in front of her and opened my arms.

"Love me?" I whispered.

She hesitated, then laid her head on my chest.

"Oh, Lee," she mumbled into my shirt. "Loving you is so hard sometimes."

That was Eryne.

* * *

Darkness lay around me and I could hear the gentle whisper of inter-deck comms and the muted computer status reports. Hands clasped behind my head, I stared moodily at the holoview surrounding me.

The Syke's sun only a yellow point and Ceti hung there like a red horn on a black tapestry, majestic and beautiful. Its two gray moons were like pearls adorning a jewel. The stars of the Orieli Cluster were thick here. Above me, the galaxy core blazed with harsh light, its arms a lazy swirl. After twelve days in subspace, Zaron now only a distant memory. I didn't relish the cup from which I was about to drink.

The CCS blinked and I stared at it for a while. I reached with a weary hand and touched a glowing prism. Taris stared at me, looking grim, his face shiny with sweat. He had reason to be grim.

"Yes, Karhide?"

"It's 1800, Lee," he said, his eyes full of accusation.

"So?"

"You wanted a status report."

"Then give it to me, damn you!"

He winced, jaw muscles working. "All ships have completed their orbital grids as instructed, Da," he declared formally, and I knew what bothered him. "We're in position and ready to initiate firing sequence."

"Any hostile signatures?"

"Outer patrol ring is showing normal commercial traffic, but that's being rerouted. There are two scout ships, SL-3s, maintaining a holding pattern outside the active area. We could pull them in if you want."

Sublight patrol darts from Tioni hanging around to see the Space Arm in action. "No. If they're Free Planets scouts, there's nothing they can do now. Anything from Ceti?"

"An interrogative from the Primate Council and two calls from our resident Commissioner. We've intercepted military band scans, but show no combat assets in the area."

"Naturally," I said sarcastically. "Ceti is a peaceful planet of the Concordiat. You may initiate active jamming of all sub-space comms, Taris."

"Aye, Da."

"Have you got the inner-system scans in yet?"

There was a perceptible pause before he spoke. "I think you should come up to Primary Flight Control, Lee." His voice sounded strained and haggard, and I looked at him sharply. He better the hell not let me down now. This wasn't the time to get squeamish.

"I'll be right up," I said and shut off the Command Console Screen. Feeling a thousand years old, I stood up and reached for my cape. I swung it around my shoulders and fumbled with the clip.

In PFC, men and women were quietly going about their duties, tense and unsmiling. There wasn't a hell of a lot to smile about. I climbed into my command seat, took a glance at the operations platform below and grunted. Taris stood beside me, not looking at anything in particular.

"Okay. Let's have it," I grated.

"I saw the scans, Lee," he whispered fiercely. "The planet's still full of people! There wasn't any evacuation at all. They never intended to have one, did they? As far as I can see, the only thing Ceti is aware of at this moment is a squadron of heavy line cruisers of the Orieli Space Arm holding grid pattern above the planetary plane and jamming all comms. There are four and a half billion people down there, Lee!"

"Your analysis of the situation is quite accurate, Karhide, as usual," I growled, irritated at having to explain it all. "There never was a possibility of an evacuation. How could there be? If this little maneuver had become known, why, every bleeding son of a bitch would have fronted up here in some rusty bucket either to watch the show or fight us." I could see some of the watchstanders casting nervous glances in our direction. "And besides. Who would take them all off, anyway? And where would we put them?"

"You're a cold blooded bastard, Lee."

"They invented the word *mean* just for me. What the hell's the matter with you, anyway? Let's take a look at those damned scans."

"This is murder, Lee, and I don't have to like it."

"That's right, Karhide," I hissed, thinking of Kliff and his oily smiles, of Eryne, her gentleness and trust. "Nobody gives a shit whether you like it or not. Carry out your orders, is all."

"Under protest, Karhide." His eyes locked with mine.

I swung myself out of the seat, my cape swirling about me as I stood over him.

"You sanctimonious heel! Eager enough when things are smooth, but when the crap starts flying, quick to see that none sticks."

"You can say what you like, Da, but this is wrong!" He shook his head and pointed at the repeater screen.

"Wrong or not, Mister, those are our orders."

"You could have refused those orders."

"Refused my orders? It's not your hand carrying death and fire. What the hell do you think we're playing at, eh? Some elaborate game? Honor and glory? There is no honor in this and damned little glory. So your fine sense of morality is a little rattled, eh? You should have stayed where it would have been safe, or resigned! While you remain in this ship and wear that uniform, you take whatever is being dished out. Copy that, Mister?"

"Lee, I —"

"Shove it!" I said wearily and slumped into my seat. "One more word, Karhide, and you're relieved." I fumed and glared around me, then slammed the top of the armrest. "We have a job to do!" I bellowed. "Let's get on with it!"

The watchstanders hurriedly turned to their screens. The silence thick and uncomfortable. I could sense Taris standing beside me, but I had no time for him.

"Karhide?" I said without looking at him.

"Da?"

"Signify all ships. Arm all antimatter pods and stand by for firing on my order."

"All ships report ready to comply, Da."

"Status?"

"Outer patrol ring is sealed. The two SL-3 scouts are still maintaining a holding pattern."

"Okay. You may arm the pods." I climbed out of the seat and headed for the personal transport alcove. "When they're all ready, contact our commissioner and the Ceti Primate, in that order. Is all."

"Da, there is nothing in our orders about communication with Ceti."

"So what?" I demanded and waited.

He colored and nodded. "As you say."

I grunted and stepped into the alcove. When the aftereffect tingle passed, I paused before entering the lounge of my quarters. The door sighed as it closed behind me and I leaned heavily against it. I threw the cape over a chair and buried my face between my hands. I slumped on the couch and closed my eyes.

Forgive me Eryne.

* * *

The CCS went off just as I was ready to forget, for a little while anyway. Taris looked haggard and shrunken as I scowled at him.

"We have a channel open to the Commissioner, Da."

I nodded and touched a series of glowing prisms. The screen cleared and I stared at another fat political appointee of the Concordiat. Probably given Ceti for licking an appropriate ass, no doubt. Who cares.

"Commissioner, this is Karhide Zor-Lee."

"Karhide." He nodded, looking bemused, his jowls sagging. Soft living does that. "Ah, forgive me for asking, but –"

"Quite all right, Commissioner. Did you receive any messages from Orieli Space Arm Command within the last sixteen hours?"

"Why, no. Should I have?"

I muttered something vile under my breath. "No, I guess not. Still..." It would have been nice to be surprised. "No doubt, you may be wondering what we're doing out here."

"Well, our Ceti friends were a little frantic since you showed up in the system, Karhide." A faint smile touched his smooth face.

"To be sure. To business, Commissioner. My orders are to neutralize Ceti." His face turned green and his mouth worked. "I suggest you notify your staff and leave immediately. Do not bother packing. Just leave. Do you understand me?"

"But...But...That's murder! This is insanity! The Concordiat cannot –"

"Save the speeches and recriminations for the Council. Goodbye, Da." I cut contact and stared at the blank screen.

Skies!

"Comms? Got the Ceti Primate?"

"Affirmative, Da."

"Good." I wondered where they picked up all that *affirmative* crap from? Couldn't he have simply said *yes*? Not that I was a hard commander or anything...

The screen lit up again. The face looked old and wizened,

like it had seen everything. Well, almost everything.

"Karhide Zor-Lee, Orieli Space Arm, Da."

"Councilor Catlankt." He gave a stiff bow.

Well, the head man. It would make things easier – maybe. "Councilor, you must have noticed the maneuvering of my ships off Ceti. My orders are to –"

"Destroy this planet, Karhide?" he finished for me, showing no expression on his lined face.

Something heavy rolled across my shoulders and I sagged. I held his eye and nodded. "To destroy Ceti."

"When?"

"You have twenty hours. Ships leaving Ceti will not be interdicted, military or civilian. And Councilor, no heroics, please. This is difficult enough as it is."

"There doesn't seem to be much heroics about any of this, Karhide," he said gravely.

"I can't argue with you about that one, Da."

He nodded and managed a tragic smile. "Why the warning, Karhide?"

"Call it a token of mercy," I said savagely and cut contact.

* * *

"It's twenty-nine hours now, Lee," Taris said tightly, avoiding my eyes.

I stared at the red glow of Ceti filling most of the holoview of the operations platform below. Like fireflies, bright blue points flickered on the tactical overlay in a pattern that surrounded the planet: lights of death – antimatter pods armed and waiting to unleash their fury at the helpless planet. The cruisers had already formed a holding position at the edge of the system in case Free Planets warships decided to call, but the area was empty. It would have been a futile gesture, as was mine about to destroy a world. All so futile...

I kept my word. We did not molest ships leaving Ceti. Call it a salve for my conscience. Nevertheless, only an insignificant fraction of the population had managed to get away. Somehow, I knew that Catlankt would not be among them. Still, if they took to underground shelters, a lot could still live through what was about to come; long enough for further evacuation later.

"Status?" I demanded.

"Pods armed, in position and ready for firing, Da."

"Very well, Karhide. Cent Comp copy?"

"Ready, Karhide," the computer replied gravely.

"Initiate firing sequence on my mark...mark!"

Like a star in mortal agony, Ceti flared bright as the pods ignited. The atmosphere burned with consuming intensity. I watched with horrified fascination as the world died. Long after the flash that ignited it, living flame stormed over the planet from which unheard voices screamed their defiance to hell.

I stared at the boiling, swirling eddies of smoke and steam without blinking. Without a word, I stood up and walked to the transport alcove.

I sat alone in the Observation Deck bubble. All cruisers of my squadron were leaving. I looked at Ceti's gray crescent and the dull glow of its night side. The atmosphere still burned halfheartedly, choked with superheated steam. Scanners and tracking devices circled the cinder, noting everything for the amusement of bright-eyed thinkers on Zaron.

When the ship moved and the stars began to shift about me, I kept staring at the spot where Ceti smoldered, listening to its cries. It would take a few days to get back to Zaron and I had some thinking to do. I didn't look forward to it.

* * *

Clouds raced low over dirty, battered shingles; black fortresses tumbling over the heavens. Ribbons of jagged light danced in their bellies. A rolling low rumble shook the ground. Slanting walls of rain moved quickly to surround the cowering towers.

A black giant winked and a sheet of white light licked the earth. With a hideous crash, thunder bellowed in defiance. The sound rolled ponderously over the heavens. Low on the horizon, the advancing wall of broken cloud lay bathed in blood. White swords flickered in its gray depths. Where they touched, gold and fire danced. The rain came in cold, heavy streams over Skaro. It softened and blurred where it touched.

I clutched my cape around me, walking quickly. A slimy torrent of water gurgled as it sluiced down the center of the alleyway. The patched muddy walls gave me claustrophobia. I cursed slowly and steadily. An icy trickle tickled the back of my neck and ran down my spine. I pulled my collar tight, but it made no difference. Eryne had to pick a nightclub in the rundown historic quarter to work!

Skies!

I gave a deep sigh of relief when I saw the glowing sign above the club's entrance. Here was comfort and warmth. I stopped, shook myself and walked quickly inside. Some gloomy creature dressed in a green uniform wished me good evening as he bowed.

"Damn your eyes!" I snarled, struggling with the clip on my cape. I finally got it undone and dropped the sodden mess into the outstretched hand. The porter smiled, but his eyes were frigid. I turned and walked away, not giving a crap.

I paused before the entrance to the main floor. I hate doormen, especially doormen with phony brass smiles. Better a man who showed his hate openly. I screwed my face into a grimace of disgust as I looked in.

The place was lousy with people, all types and sizes, all chatting gaily to annoy and antagonize me. I hated them all. The air moist and heavy and clung to my skin with cloying intimacy. I squirmed, thinking of the crisp air outside.

Smoke curled thick around suspended light strips, and the ceiling pulsed with shifting colors. It flared bright yellow as a party around one of the tables began a shouting match.

"You have a reservation…Da?" I could see the headwaiter, dressed in immaculate pale green one-piece outfit, measuring my drab gray mufti with suspicion, probably thinking of his bouncers.

"Yeah," I said.

"Uh, the name…Da," he looked apologetic, but still measuring.

"Zor-Lee."

"Ah, yes, of course, Da!" More phony smiles. He raised his right hand and snapped his fingers. A servant walked quickly around tables, expertly avoiding flailing hands, swaying drinks and strings of curses. The headwaiter tapped his foot impatiently.

"Take, ah…" he glanced at me expectantly.

"Try…Mister." I glared at him.

"Take, ah, Mister Zor-Lee to table eleven. Chop!"

The servant bowed and preceded me through the jungle of tables. He snatched the reserved sign off the cloth and nodded at a small table neatly tucked against the wall. I sat down and relaxed. A ribbon of soft yellow light sprang around the table edge.

"Refreshments, kind Da?" The servant stood unmoving.

"Sabrion on crushed ice with a slice of bandrine peel. Chilled!" I growled, looking at the empty stage.

The ceiling flared bright blue and the strips turned into bars of crimson. The stage lights shimmered. Heavy green curtains moved oily as they slowly drew aside, swaying gently when they stopped. The chatter died like a whisper of receding surf and the ceiling throbbed. Heads twisted for a better angle and chairs scraped.

She sat on a high carved stool, her long legs crossed, revealing a generous length of smooth thigh. Her hands were folded in her lap. Waves of thick violet hair spilled over her shoulders. Her skin light blue, darkening around glowing black eyes and mouth. She did not smile as she turned her head to stare at me.

My face softened beneath her gaze. I could feel the warmth of her gaze spreading like fire. It was very pleasant. I grinned, staring at her with longing hunger.

Slow beats of pulsing music wove between the tables as everyone waited. Hands in her lap, Eryne began to sing. The accompanying band wasn't too loud. A hush blanketed the floor. I had not heard her sing that song before. The melody was moody, tragic and tender, a ballad of youth, beauty and lost love. Of war and terror, of death and pain.

Needles crawled down my back. She sang slowly, softly, her words gossamer that drifted gently over the audience, but her eyes were sad. A window to a broken heart and fleeting glimpses of what might have been. When she finished, her eyes were glistening with tears. The curtains closed with a rush and the audience sat there stunned. Then they were on their feet; cheering, demanding more. The ceiling rippled in response.

I nursed my drink. I knew the song, of course. It was about us and I could feel my heart flutter with anxiety. I looked up and she stood there.

"Can I sit down, Lee?" She looked shy and apprehensive and my heart went out to her. I glanced around. People stared at us, smiling knowingly. How I wished to wipe those smirks off their faces!

"Please," I said, my eyes never leaving hers as she bowed and sat down. I raised my right hand and snapped my fingers. A servant came beside her in an instant.

"What would you like, Eryne?" I asked as she put a slender finger into her mouth.

"Ah, a small Alatri special, Manargee." She smiled at the servant.

"Your wishes, gentle lady." The servant bowed low and left. I found myself frowning after him.

"You shouldn't waste your kindness on dirt like that."

She placed a small hand over mine and shook her head. "Poor, Lee. Still bitter. The world in your eyes so different from mine. Let your heart be glad tonight." She smiled and I couldn't resist her warmth. I turned her hand until it rested in mine.

"Your song, Eryne. I know it."

"You wrote the words."

"I'm not a disillusioned youth drowning his sorrows in abandonment of war," I reproached her gently.

"No. You know exactly what you're doing all the time. Your every move is perfectly calculated." She stared at the table, fiddling with her drink. Slowly, she raised her head and looked at me. Pain and sorrow clouded those eyes and I felt myself tense.

"Lee...I...I won't be seeing you anymore," she said with a rush.

I stared at her in disbelief. My world crumbled around me and I felt unbearably weary. I clutched my tumbler and gulped the last of my drink. When I laughed, it was a hollow, empty thing.

"Why, Eryne? Why?"

"Because I love you so much," she whispered brokenly and kissed my hand.

"That doesn't make any damn sense!"

"Remember the night we met?"

I stared at her. "I remember," I said at length.

"You were alone, drinking. Lonely and lost, and I was a brand new attraction at the Slee Club. Remember?" Her eyes moved over my face, her hand in mine.

"Because I destroyed Ceti?" I didn't mean it to sound cold and accusing. It just came out that way.

She flinched and shook her head. "No, of course not. It –"

"World, fleet, ship. What does it matter? They were nothing but rebels."

"Don't!" she begged, but I ignored her.

"My publicity isn't good for the Club, is that it?" I regretted the words even as I said them. I sighed and touched her lips with the tip of my finger. "I'm sorry, Eryne. That was stupid of me. I'm just not thinking straight. Forgive?"

I stared hard into her eyes. After a while, a ghost of a smile touched her mouth. "Forgive."

"I still want to know why, Eryne."

She laughed and shook her head. "Still the Karhide. Standing on his deck waiting for acknowledgement. Da!" She made a face.

I didn't smile. "I take my duty very seriously. I will not attempt to deny for a moment the hell and injustice that is the Concordiat. Nor will I point out the other side of the coin. I simply do my job as best I can, and my best is a damned sight too good for a lot of my brother officers. Bastards, most of them. They would love nothing better than to see me stretched out on some bloody deck."

"That's why I cannot see you anymore."

"Love me, Eryne," I pleaded in desperation. "I'll resign my commission. There is nothing more I can do," I begged and it came hard.

"My love. Every time you saw a starship, a little bit of your heart would go with it. After a while, there would be nothing left. Nothing for me, nothing for you. Where would that leave us, Lee?" Her voice trembled and her eyes filled. A drop sparkled and slid quickly down her cheek. I moved my finger and wiped it away.

"What about the moments of love we shared? The dreams we made? All the sorrows we conquered? Are all those things lost? Write them off to experience?"

"That can never be lost, Lee. I sit here and I can feel the pain tearing at your heart. Don't you see?" She gripped my hands fiercely. "I die a little every time you go out, wondering what's happening to you. Lying somewhere, mutilated, tortured or dead. Oh, Lee!" She sobbed, eyes streaming. "I love you because you're strong, unshakeable, full of purpose and duty. But your path takes you through the worst that life has to offer, and I'm not strong enough to follow."

"I can't give you up, Eryne." I gripped her head, my heart hammering.

She sat up, wiped her eyes and sniffed. "I have another song. The patrons are getting restless. Goodbye, Lee."

"Love me, Eryne! Love me!" I cried out, searching her eyes in vain. She gave a strangled sob, tore her arm free and ran into the crowd. Faces stared at me, but I didn't see them.

I searched the bottom of my tumbler. Empty, like my heart. My throat tight, I blinked rapidly and swallowed. The world had slammed its door in my face and I hated it for it.

I don't know how long I sat there. After a while, I stood up, threw money on the table and walked away. The porter hastily rose to his feet and held out my cape. I put it on and drew the collar tight. I paused as the crowd fell silent and the lights dimmed. I turned and looked at the main floor.

She stood straight before the gently swaying curtains. Her orange gown glowed as it clung to her figure. Like an ornament, she was delicate and frail, meant to be cherished, not used. She was right. She wasn't strong enough to follow where I walked. She would only be in my way, be my conscience. The last thing I needed in my job is a conscience.

As she started to sing, I hastily turned and walked out. It still rained, soft and caressing. Lightning ripped the sky, followed by rolling thunder.

I waited for a moment, then hunched my shoulders and stepped into the rain.

Interim

-1-

"…And then Man created STOR, and STOR was given dominion over the whole Earth. Then Man went to the stars in search of glory and beauty while STOR kept Earth safe from her enemies. STOR waited patiently. Centuries passed and STOR still waited for Man to return from the stars. STOR worked hard and waited. He built cities that shone like the stars and rivaled the mountains with their towering spires. Earth flourished and creatures from all over the galaxy come to admire her beauty.

"One day, THAR came and challenged STOR for the dominion of Earth, and STOR bade him depart. Then there was a battle such as the galaxy had never seen. Whole stars grew dark as their energies were drained for the mighty battle. STOR fought for Earth, but in the end, THAR defeated him. Thus began the Dark Age," she spoke softly, lost in a far dream as she stroked the boy's hair. "THAR hated Man because they had banished him from Earth long, long ago. For revenge, THAR destroyed everything of Man left on Earth and swore to destroy Him when he returned from the stars.

"THAR needed slaves to work for him while he made ready for the coming of Man. Thus he created us. The battle with STOR had damaged him and he created us imperfect in his eyes. He imposed his will on us and punished with death for the slightest disobedience. THAR waited for centuries for the return of Man, but he did not come. Now, we all must work hard for THAR and wait patiently for Man to come and free us."

Although late, the evening remained warm and still. On the edge of the meadow, the forest already lay deep in shadow. Overhead the brighter stars winked shyly, scarcely visible.

"Always remember, Doby," she told him. "Man will come one day and sweep THAR from the sky, and Earth will be the jewel of the galaxy again."

The little boy clung to his mother and stared at her golden face, his eyes round with wonder. He never tired of listening to his mother tell him the Tale of Man. Every time he heard it, it brought the same wonder and excitement that sent him squirming with anticipation. He wriggled in her lap as she looked down at him and smiled.

"Mother?" he ventured tentatively.

An insect buzzed nearby. "Yes, Doby?" she whispered.

"What does Man look like?"

His mother clutched him to her breast, tussled his burning mop of hair and laughed, a sound of sweetness echoing through the woods.

"They were tall and proud, with dark eyes and skin of gold. The stars were their domain."

"Skin as smooth and golden as yours, Mother?" Doby suggested shyly. "With long brown hair like yours?"

His mother chuckled, sending ripples of joy through his body. "I suppose so. No one has seen a Man. We only know what the Tale tells us."

That night, Doby dreamed of blazing starships and Man coming to Earth in fire and glory, sweeping THAR away forever. And he would be there when Man descended from the skies.

Doby woke, screwed his eyes, felt something tickle his nose and sneezed. Stretching under the coarse blanket, he yawned mightily. A tiny gray bird fluttered on the window sill and twittered excitedly.

He climbed out of the straw bunk and tiptoed across the dirt floor toward the window. Slowly, he extended a small finger toward the bird. With a squawk and a flutter of wings, it rose and flew low toward the forest.

He clapped his hands with glee and gingerly climbed over the sill, feeling for the upturned old water barrel with his toes.

The frame creaked in protest, but held as he scrambled off it. With a wary look at the closed bedroom doorway, he ran toward the forest. The grass, sprinkled with dew, glittering like strewn jewels, felt cold to touch, but he hardly noticed. Still in shadow the lower slopes of the rolling meadow were clothed in streaming sheets of white mist.

He paused at the edge of the forest, staring into its dark interior as images of unknown dangers lurking within burned in his imagination.

"Doby! Oh, Doooby!"

Far away the hills heard the call and threw back the echoes. With a last look at the forest, he ran back toward the house. He would explore later. His mother stood outside the door holding a wooden basin. On hearing the crash of his passage, she lifted her head and heaved the water at the ground.

"Doby, did you have your breakfast?"

"No, Mother."

"You had better hurry up. The Keeper will be here in a minute. Skat!"

"Mother?"

"Yes, Doby?"

"Where is father?"

She stopped wiping the basin and looked at him. "He…he had to return to the City."

"Why?"

"Enough of that. Go and eat," she swung her hand at him, but he scampered away.

He ate in subdued silence, remembering what the Keeper did to his mother when it had to wait for them until she had fed him. It pointed something at her and she screamed and fell. He remembered rushing to her where she quietly sobbed.

He was never late after that.

He swallowed a last piece of black grain bread and dry fruit and heard the familiar warble outside. He rushed to the doorway and waited. His mother walked toward the hovering black platform. Attached to the control console, the glowing sphere of the Keeper pulsed yellow. She knelt on her left knee and bowed deeply.

"I am ready, Master," she whispered.

He walked to the platform in defiance, knelt and bowed quickly. A harsh grating sound came from the sphere.

"Unit Doby will be taken for duty testing today."

His mother drew her breath sharply, sprang to her feet and embraced him. "No! He's too young. You can't, you can't!"

Doby felt a dread of premonition and shivered.

"The Monitor is not to be questioned."

"No!" she clasped him to her.

"You defy me?" The sphere glowed brightly and a red nozzle slid out.

His mother backed away, her knuckles white against her mouth. "No, no, I didn't…"

"Come!" it commanded.

She kissed him hurriedly on the forehead and ran her fingers through his hair. "Go, Doby, and don't be afraid."

Hesitating, he slowly walked toward the platform, not wanting to leave his mother. He remembered Alos who taught him to swim, climb trees, and told him about the forest and the animals. One day a Keeper took him away and Doby never saw Alos again. As he stepped on board, a faint yellow film enveloped him and the platform slowly rose, heading in the direction of the shining city towers. As he watched the tall spires grow, he knew what the other boys in the crèche would think when he did not appear that morning. The same thoughts he'd been thinking when they took Alos away.

The platform descended and hovered above a flat metal roof protruding from a tower high above the ground. The Keeper slowly moved toward a blank wall. A doorway slid up and the sphere glided in. Doby followed the Keeper along two corridors whose walls slanted and merged above his head. The Keeper stopped before a panel of frosted crystal and he sighed in relief. His legs hurt and he was thirsty. Color rippled over the sphere in silent communication. It dimmed and the

Keeper drifted back down the corridor, leaving him alone before the door.

The door slid quietly up into the wall and he heard a hum of machinery and saw flickering lights on wall panels. Wiping his clammy hands against his leather shorts, he watched the lights as they flickered faster. He walked slowly toward the center of the room.

"Step into the green circle," a familiar harsh voice grated from somewhere.

Doby spun around searching for the Keeper that spoke to him, but he was alone. Only then did he realize he was in the presence of the Monitor, and he began to tremble.

"Obey!" The command made him jump.

His scalp crawled as he stepped within the area of the green circle. He whimpered and wished that his mother were here. She would comfort him and take away his fear. The green floor beneath his feet pulsed and the lights on the walls were racing.

"Doby?"

He gasped at the change of tone, soft and musical. He knelt on one knee and bowed.

"Yes, Master," he whispered in total humility.

"Do you know the Tale of Man?" The voice was compelling, but there was hidden malice in its smoothness.

"Yes."

"Do you believe?"

"I...yes!"

"Why do you believe?"

"I..." Doby faltered in confusion and fear.

"It is merely a tale, nothing more. No matter. You have grown into a satisfactory work unit and I am pleased."

The lights on the walls pulled at his eyes and he watched in fascination. He tried to draw away, but his body would not obey. He seemed to float and something pressed within his head. He felt tearing and ripping, and he whimpered, trying to scream. And then he did scream, endlessly.

When he woke, he found himself on a platform enclosed in its protective field. He sat behind the Keeper drone, his mind observing, taking in the landscape below. The platform slowed as it approached a cottage and hovered above the yard. Doby sat up when he saw the rough wooden door fly open and a young female run toward him. He stepped on the ground and looked at the tall grass nearby, noting with detachment that its photosynthesizing process functioned satisfactorily. The female stopped beside him and stared at him. He felt strong arms go around him and press him against her chest.

"Oh, Doby! My poor baby! What have they done to you?" she sobbed and a tear fell on his cheek.

Hesitating, he touched the tear with his finger and looked at the drop. He brought the finger to his tongue. Nothing but a basic saline solution.

"Oh, my baby! Don't you know me? Your mother?" she cried out.

Mother? He recognized the word associated with the rearing process of the young. He looked at her without emotion, savoring the sound. It was simply a word to him.

"You and unit Doby are to be transferred to Central Two for reclassification. Prepare yourself," the Keeper grated.

"No! He's too young!"

A blunt red nozzle slid out of the sphere and pointed at the female. Doby noted that a powerful electric discharge could seriously damage the female.

"You defy me?"

"Doby is mine! I will not—"

A blue flash and the smell of ozone. Charred clothing covered her fallen body and there was a stink of frying flesh. A red stain slowly spread around the burn wound.

"Disobedience is punished with death!"

Doby stared at her with detachment. The unit was obviously on the point of termination. She lifted her head and smiled at him. "Never forget the Tale of Man…my son." She coughed and her head slumped.

"Mother?" he ventured softly.

"Come!" the Keeper grated.

He stepped onto the platform. It rose and moved toward snowcapped mountains in the north, leaving the City far behind him.

-2-

Work unit d-37251 picked up a hollow shell of the mining tool from the conveyor belt and adjusted a silver clip to the glossy metal. He glanced at the display panel beside him. The screen traced orange circuit lines as it projected the tool in various geometric profiles. The trace stabilized and glowed green. He placed the tool on the small bench in front of him and picked up a circuit assembly. He mounted the assembly under the circuit tracer and slid it into the machined slot in the mining tool. He slid the completed tool onto the conveyor where it moved to the next bench. He looked up at worker units down the line with detachment, then picked up another mining tool.

Sudden pinging cut through machinery noises of the factory floor. Unit d-37251 placed the partially assembled tool on the bench and waited. He followed the other worker units as they slowly filed through the door where two Keeper drones hovered. From another doorway the next shift marched to occupy the vacated benches.

Down two levels, he waited in a queue before the Interrogation booths. Standing in his assigned place, he watched as blank-faced units entered the cubicles when their designation number was called. After a while, the units would emerge. Sometimes they came out looking different. He knew that some suffered impairment to their motor functions during Interrogation, which brought the attention of the Keepers on them. After another session in the Interrogator, they would be normal again.

"Unit d-37251!"

He hesitated before the cubicle entrance, then walked in. He sat down and waited. The checkerboard pattern of lights on the ceiling raced. A hiss of shorting circuitry disrupted the pattern and he felt pain in his head. The malfunction light flashed bright red. His vision blurred and he whimpered as pressure built in his head. He felt a tearing and ripping and heard himself scream.

Doby…Doby…Doby…

The chamber door slid aside and two worker units dragged him out.

"Report your status!" the Keeper grated.

"Unit d-37251…Unit…"

Someone pushed him into another booth. Blinking, he sat down. When the door opened again, he hesitated, then followed units from his shift heading for the refectory. After the meal, they were marched into the dormitory. Feeling unusually lethargic, he crawled into bed and fell into deep sleep.

The trail wound around ancient gnarled trunks and sheets of light slanted through the thick canopy. A doe with a spotted fawn drank, her ears twitching. A muted rumble of thunder rolled over the forest. Tall clouds, their snowy fronts hiding bulging black bellies, moved to cover the sky. Doby emerged from the forest and hurried toward a small stone cottage. He could feel the sweat rolling from his brow as he ran, panic burning within his chest.

"Mother?" he whispered.

A peal of thunder shook the earth beneath him.

He sat up with a start, breathing heavily. He recalled the dream and wondered, not understanding. The door slid up and a Keeper glided toward his bed.

"Unit d-37251, report your status."

"I am functioning within normal parameters, Master," he said coldly.

After the morning meal, he marched into the factory.

Several days later, a disturbing thought assailed him during his work shift. *What am I doing here?* This was a wasteful use of resources, he observed analytically. His hand stopped as he stared at the drive core of the induction motor. Surprised at his question, he quickly searched the faces round him. No one had noticed his lapse of concentration.

He was concerned at the changes taking place within him, and his reaction to them. He knew he should alert a Keeper and report for Interrogation, but something held him back. He had grown aware of the complex within which he and others lived and worked, and its evident age. He wondered what went on in the towers around him. Mostly, he sought to apply a straight line methodology to explain the changes in him, and the genuine danger he faced by not reporting his condition.

Holding the drive core, his chain of reasoning left him profoundly disturbed. Until recently, he had not questioned his purpose here, his work, or the presence of other units. Nobody talked as they fulfilled a menial function he did not understand. Disjointed memories that bubbled into his consciousness at night, memories of meadows, fields, forests and play, and a female unit he thought he knew, teased his waking moments. No matter how many times he performed the straight line analysis, it always produced the same inescapable answer.

At some point, the Monitor must have imprinted him, inhibiting memories and emotions, implanting knowledge to make him a productive unit. To detect and correct emerging anomalies, every unit underwent daily Interrogation to ensure that the memory pattern had not been degraded. So far, Interrogation had not detected his aberrant behavior, but cumulative changes he felt within him would not escape detection for long. Then what? Would he receive a new imprint, as he had seen others get when something went wrong with them?

When sharp pinging signaled the end of the work shift, he moved quietly with the others toward the Interrogation booths, wondering if he would emerge corrected.

That night, he lay on a bed of tall, sweet-smelling grass, staring at fluffy white clouds. They looked so solid and he wondered what it would feel like, lying on one of those clouds looking down. He plucked a blade of grass, stuck it into his mouth and chewed. He turned on his belly and grunted. Beside him, a stream of cold water gurgled over slimy rocks, making him thirsty all over again. It did not matter that he drank only a minute ago. He edged forward, gazed at the clear sandy bottom and plunged his face into the water. Satisfied, he sat up and sighed with contentment.

"Doby! Dooooby!"

The forest swallowed the echoes.

He scrambled to his feet and walked slowly down the winding trail, wondering where the echo went as it lost itself in the distance. Mother would know, he concluded confidently, and began to run. He rounded the corner of the cottage and saw her.

"Mother!"

Unit d-37251 sat up with a jerk, his body covered with cold sweat. The dormitory quiet, the silence broken by an occasional snore coming from one of the many bunks around him, lit by a dimly glowing blue ceiling strip. He wiped his forehead and slid out of the bunk. He padded over the cool floor toward the broad window and gazed at the glittering towers of the city, shielded by the soft orange glow of its protective field. For the first time, he really looked at them, wondering what they were and his role in it. How many years had he spent here? He did not know, but fleeting memories of his childhood told him it had been a while. He tried recalling his mother's face, but something terrible lurked there and he shut out the images. Mouth set in a tight line, he returned to his bunk. A long time later, he gratefully sank into a dreamless sleep.

The next day, he began forming his plan. He felt the changes crowding him as more memories surfaced, and he feared the next Interrogation session. As he worked on the assembly line, casting furtive glances at patrolling Keepers as they floated through the plant, he planned his escape from the city. The obvious thing to do was take a platform. He could not simply walk out with Keepers everywhere. The Monitor directed everything moving within and outside the city, but he had no way of knowing how far that influence extended, or whether it would permit a platform under manual control to depart. That information had been denied him.

At the end of his shift, sharp pinging cut through machinery noises of the factory floor and he followed the other worker unit to the Interrogation booths with mounting dread. Would the Monitor detect the difference in him? Would he ever know if it did? He would walk out of the booth corrected, forgetting everything.

"Unit d-37251!"

His feet heavy, he walked into the booth and sat down. The checkerboard pattern of lights on the ceiling raced. He felt nothing, but the session seemed to be taking longer than usual. The lights eventually faded and the door slid open. Relief washing through him, he stood up and made his way to the communal cafeteria.

Sometime during the night, he got up, dressed, retrieved his bag of food and headed for the elevator shafts. The brightly lit loading bay held neat rows of cargo haulers, flatbed carriers and commuter platforms. Worker units did not look at him as he strode quickly toward the nearest platform. A Keeper paused and he felt his mouth go dry, wondering if he would be questioned. After an agonizing moment the Keeper floated away. Heart hammering, he climbed onto the hovering platform and grasped the drive lever. The platform lifted and he steered it toward the faint glow of the city's force field. Watching the orange shimmer draw closer, he wondered if he would crash.

-3-

Behind him, blue haze obscured the hills and the valleys. Ahead, a jagged chain of snow-capped mountains clawed into a clear blue sky. Below him, a placid river wound through a broad meadow bordered by thick forest. An amber light winked on the control display indicating a low powered tracking beam sweeping over him, the source thirteen-point-two kilometers away on a heading of zero-two-zero. Over the last four days, he had traveled some 2,800 kilometers without spotting any sign of habitation. He had seen lots of wildlife, but no worker units. More importantly, he had not been pursued by Keepers from Central Two.

A tracking beam unlike that employed by the city Monitor, which meant a settlement not under THAR's control. It was only logical. If he had managed to escape, somewhere at some time, other units must also have escaped. He shifted the drive lever toward the new heading, not sure he was doing the right thing.

Last night, he slept fitfully. Snug in the protective cocoon of the platform's field, he dreamt of thunder, lightning and driving rain. He hung suspended in the air watching a small stone cottage, inexorably drawn toward it. Fear gripped his chest and he wanted to flee, but he could not stop his descent. He saw a Keeper clad in yellow light approach the cottage and a woman rush out. He wanted to shout out a warning, but the words failed him. Her golden face, framed by cascading brown hair, looked serene as she stood there, her arms reaching for him. A lance of light speared her and he screamed as she fell.

"Doby!"

He remembered waking with a jerk, terrible memories unleashing dark emotions.

"Mother?"

He was not unit d-37251. He was Doby, a person! The realization had not given him any peace. His mother's broken body haunted what remained of the night.

Looking up, the sun almost overhead, he decided to rest before proceeding to the settlement. He brought the platform down on a grassy meadow beside the river and climbed off. After drinking, resting against the hovering platform, he munched on a ration pack. He knew he should feel something, remembering how his mother died, but the images were remote, from a past that was no longer his. Too much time had passed for genuine emotion, and his objective outlook did not permit morbid introspection.

Sitting in the grass, savoring its clean smell, relishing the sun's warmth, he did feel something confusing. Right now, he should be at the factory working on mining tools, understanding what he was doing, but with detachment. He gazed at his surrounds, the buzz of insects, the sharp bird chirping, and analyzed his emotions. *I am content*, he decided in startled wonder, amazed that he could *feel*.

A warning beep from the control console made him frown. He heaved himself up and glanced at the display, wondering what had set off the proximity alarm. A roving animal? The blip in the screen moved and he turned toward the forest.

Bushes parted and a young male unit walked toward him. It appeared to be his age, nineteen or twenty, broad shouldered, wearing what looked like skin shorts and shirt, far removed from Doby's dark blue coverall. He held a long firearm in his left hand. The youth stopped and lifted his right palm.

"May I approach?"

Doby gaped at the youth's clean features and flowing black hair. Apart from the harsh grating from the Monitor and the Keepers, he had never heard a voice before. Swallowing hard, he nodded.

"Who are you?" he demanded awkwardly, uncertain what was the correct accepted behavior. The young unit smiled and Doby tucked away the datum.

"Klent." The youth planted the butt of his rifle into the grass and leaned against it. "It's been a while since I last saw someone from a city driving a platform. You lost or something?"

Trying to analyze the conflicting questions, Doby decided to play it safe. "I escaped from Central Two."

"Never heard of it, but then, I have never seen a city."

Doby goggled at him. "You have never—"

"I was born here."

"You…are free?"

Klent shrugged. "You could call it that, I suppose."

"How did you…ah, the tracking beam."

"Tracking…oh, you mean our radar. I was hunting game when I saw you come down," the youth said casually. "You were heading for our village?"

More confident, Doby nodded. "I wanted to rest first. Ah, you want to come with me, Klent?"

"Hey! Not on that thing! Besides, I have a deer carcass I need to clean up."

"It would take us some undetermined amount of time to reach your settlement on foot, and I don't want to abandon the platform."

Klent frowned, bit his lip and sighed. "Well…" He walked up and gingerly stepped onto the platform.

Doby powered up and the platform lifted, climbing quickly. It did not take long to reach the sprawling settlement. To Doby, it didn't look much from the air; a sprawl of mostly single-story dwellings, double and triple-story brick and stone buildings, and what looked like factories, dark smoke oozing from tall chimneys. If THAR controlled everything, he wondered how this ramshackle village remained undetected.

He landed in an open square in front of a large stone building, which Klent said housed the municipal Council. The villagers gathered around him, staring curiously at the platform and him. Several young females pointed at his coverall and whispered to each other. The garments they wore were plain and somber. Youngsters and older males stood silently, waiting for something to happen. On cue, an old male appeared on the steps of the Council building, surveyed the crowd with a frown, and hobbled down the steps.

He lifted a gnarled hand and waved at the crowd. "Okay, leave the boy alone. Move on."

Slowly, the crowd dispersed, exchanging comments. The old unit looked at Doby and nodded.

"I am Pako Hram, Council Elder. We bid you welcome, young stranger."

Uncertain what to do, Doby nodded. "Thank you. I am unit…my name is Doby."

"Follow me. You too, Klent."

Doby stopped before a large wooden door and waited for it to open. After a moment, he turned to the Elder.

"Perhaps it is defective?"

Pako Hram smiled faintly, reached for the handle and pushed. The door swung in, leaving Doby wearing a sheepish expression. He had a lot to learn about living in a primitive environment.

Led into a large oval chamber, he stared curiously at a middle-aged unit dressed in a gray form-hugging coverall sitting on the far side of a rectangular table surrounded by ornately carved wooden chairs. Each bare stone wall had a single large framed picture. One depicted life at the settlement. Another showed a stellar nebula, while the last an image of a modern small city with a single tower, its faint orange field clearly visible. Doby moved closer and peered at the inscription: Tracking Station 12, 3725 CE, Gregory Price. As he turned his head, he stepped back with a startled hiss. The image was two-dimensional. Digging into his store of knowledge, he glanced at Klent.

"This was made by Man?"

"It's a painting," the middle-aged male answered, "found a long time ago in some ruins. A complex not controlled by THAR. By the way, I am Kirhan. Please, be seated. You must have many questions, and perhaps you can answer some of ours."

Doby could not believe it. A city without a Monitor? A tracking station? Klent smiled as he pulled back a chair for him, then sat beside him. The Elder sat beside Kirhan and cleared his throat.

"It's not far from here, only some sixty kilometers. In days long past, I dared to venture there, tempting the wrath of the Keepers, but the place seems deserted. Others have seen it since, and it's still deserted."

"Its force field is operating?" Doby asked.

"It prevents us from entering and gathering valuable material to sustain us. Now, to answer some of your questions. Our little community has occupied these lands for two centuries. How it came about is somewhat uncertain. Probably founded by escapees from various cities, such as Central Two and Waypoint Five, which is much closer. We hunt, fish and farm. When we come across old ruins, we take from them what we can to build basic industries. The knowledge you carry will be valuable."

"What about the knowledge you carry from your imprinting?"

"Most of us were born here, Doby," Pako Hram said. "Those who came to us from cities quickly lost their knowledge, and much of it of little value to us. Advanced molecular circuitry, cybernetics, nano-engineering, sophisticated manufacturing processes, have limited application. Books also give us knowledge, but not the necessary technology infrastructure to apply the information."

"I fear that my knowledge will then be of limited value to you. Tell me, Pako Hram. How has this settlement managed to survive undetected by THAR?"

The old unit shrugged. "Our energy footprint is minimal and we limit what we radiate in the EMR spectrum."

"But THAR has space-borne observatories," Doby protested.

"We survived," Kirhan grated. "It is sufficient explanation."

Not to Doby, but he did not want to enter into an argument.

"You are welcome to stay among us," the Elder announced gravely. "Things will be strange to you for a while, but in time, you will come to accept our ways, and we'll find useful work for you. Klent, why don't you take our guest to the bachelor dormitory and get him settled in. Issue him some suitable clothing. We shall continue our discussion later this afternoon."

-4-

Doby sat on the riverbank throwing pebbles into the water and watched the fanning ripples. A warm wind whispered between the branches, stirring the golden, fiery leaves. He could hear the laughter of children—fantastic little creatures—and women voices in the fields. Across the river, dark clouds gathered, a reminder of snows to come.

Restless, he wanted to lose himself in the forest and get away from the stifling village atmosphere and it unyielding regimen. After sixteen days, he had lost all interest working in grimy machine shops breathing acrid fumes from crude welding guns, or patiently explaining concepts poorly understood and could not be applied. The alternative was toiling in the fields, even though he would be in the open. The Elder was right when he said that lack of supporting trades and industry held them back from developing advanced technology. Having knowledge and not being able to use it might be a curse, not a blessing. Frustrated, he would often walk to the river or stroll through the forest, searching for meaning and purpose in his life. Having escaped the Monitor, Doby now found himself a captive again.

Leaves rustled behind him and he turned. A young female carrying a large copper jug saw him and stopped in midstride, her small mouth a large O.

"Oh, I'm sorry. I didn't mean to disturb you," she breathed and started to turn away.

Doby jumped to his feet. "No, please stay. I would like some company."

She hesitated, smiled, and walked toward him. Standing before him, her pretty round face framed by golden hair, large deep blue eyes regarded him with open frankness.

"I noticed you walking to the river a few times."

Emotions churning, trying to analyze the flood of mixed feelings coursing through him, Doby winced. "I had to get away from…"

She laughed, a pleasant tinkle. "I know what you mean. Sometimes I wish that I could get away." She glanced at her jug. "Excuse me, I need to get water."

He smiled at her. "Stay a while. The river isn't going to dry up. What unit…what's your name?"

"Tani. Klent is my brother."

"He has done a lot for me, helping me settle in."

On impulse, he took the jug from her, walked to the bank and filled it. Not certain what was going on, uncomfortably aware of her presence, he nodded at the worn path.

"I'll walk you back."

Walking beside her in silence, he found her disturbing, but enjoyed being with her. When they reached the settlement, he held the jug to her. She smiled and walked toward the women's communal hut.

Turning, Doby saw Pako Hram walk into the Council building. Making a decision, he followed the old man. Inside, the Elder and Kirhan were going over paperwork. Both looked up as he entered.

"May I speak to you?" Doby asked diffidently.

The Elder sat back and waved at a chair. "Of course. How are you settling in?" he asked as Doby pulled back a chair.

"It's not what I expected," he said slowly, not wanting to offend. The old unit smiled faintly.

"I imagine not."

"What's on your mind?" Kirhan demanded brusquely and Doby frowned, not liking his attitude.

He turned and pointed at the picture on the far wall. "I want to take Klent with me to the tracking station."

"Out of the question!" Kirhan snapped. "No one is going to commit sacrilege by defiling a Man city!"

"How can it be sacrilege when you yourself came from a city built by Man?"

"Waypoint Five is an abomination constructed by THAR!"

"How do we know?" Doby persisted, not understanding Kirhan's objection. He looked pleadingly at Pako Hram.

"Even if you went there, Doby, you could not enter."

"Have you tried? When I escaped from Central Two, I feared crashing into the city's field, but the platform went through. Whatever controls the station might let me through."

"We are THAR's creatures and the Monitor recognized its own. Admittedly, the station would be a valuable source of material and equipment, but only Man can enter there. The life we have here is demanding, but we are free. I can understand the wanderlust of the young, and I roamed in my youth, but yours is a futile quest, Doby. Abandon this fantasy and find peace among us."

"Peace? Living in squalor when the station represents a future you refuse to grasp?"

"Enough!" Kirhan slammed his palm against the desk. "You were negligent in your work and I made allowances as you're new here, but we cannot afford to support dreamers and idolaters. I suggest you apply yourself to your duties if you want to make something of yourself."

Pako Hram frowned. "Don't be so hasty, Kirhan. Doby, why this fascination with the station?"

"Don't you see? We could go and live there!"

The Elder's eyes widened, startled by the idea. Kirhan waved a hand in dismissal. "You haven't been listening. It is impossible to enter!"

"I'll have to find out for myself," Doby retorted, tired of the unit's defeatism.

"Blasphemy! You're forbidden—"

The Elder raised his hand. "Satisfy your wish. When you return, we shall talk."

Outside, Doby sought Klent and poured out his frustration.

His friend looked at him pityingly and shook his head. "You don't understand the setup here. The Council rules, and what they say goes. They're like a city Monitor, channeling our labor to sustain us. We have lived like this for two centuries and the system works."

"Not very efficiently," Doby remarked darkly. "The Elder did not object to my going, and I would like you with me."

Klent shrugged. "I'm willing to see this fabled station. When do you want to do this?"

"Right now." To Doby, a superfluous question.

Klent raised an eyebrow. "It might be wise to take some provisions," he said dryly.

"You bring what we need and I'll prep the platform."

-5-

The afternoon sun bathed the snow-capped mountains with light. Below them the green valleys slowly opened into a broad plan and the mythical station appeared. The sight made Doby's heart flutter and he felt unaccountable excitement. All his questions would be answered there, he just knew it. He glanced at the display panel and shook his head. As far as the platform was concerned, the station did not exist. Somehow, its protective field masked it from THAR's sensors, and that was good. Massive ruins surrounded the station, so unlike the simple picture in the Council chamber.

Two hundred meters from the shimmering field, the station looked small and cramped, and he wondered what it meant to track. He placed the platform into hover mode.

"What now?" Klent demanded.

"We'll try going through...slowly."

"And if the Monitor doesn't let you?"

"We'll try something else, then."

"Mmm."

Moving in, Doby watched the display. Three meters from the field, he stopped, then allowed the platform to drift closer. A sharp warning from the display made him pull back the drive lever.

"What happened?" Klen asked.

"A power buildup. The platform's field could not synchronize with the station's, and there could have been a discharge. I'll drop our field and try again."

Klent looked uncomfortable. "That still might not work, and we'll be left with a very long walk home. Even if it does, what if *we* cannot synchronize, or whatever? Remember, you and I are not Man."

Doby accepted the logic of that observation and brought the platform down. "I'll walk in alone."

Not entirely sure he was doing the correct thing, Doby approached the shimmering barrier. Hesitating, he extended his arm. A tingle raced up his arm and he felt mild discomfort. Taking a deep breath, he stepped through. He turned and laughed at Klent's goggling expression. Heart singing, he skipped out.

"I don't believe it," Klent declared in awe.

"I reasoned that before THAR defeated STOR, Man built this station for a purpose," Doby said. "Since every city is under THAR's control except this one, and presumably others like it, Man would need a way to enter this station and keep THAR's machines out. Even with its field down, I suspect my platform wouldn't have gone through."

Klent frowned. "You're mixed up, my boy. If this station was built by Man to keep out THAR's minions, you should not have been able to pass through the field."

Doby opened his mouth in astonishment, but nothing came out. What Klent said was true, but he *did* go through. He had followed a chain or logical reasoning and did what a Man would do. Yet he was not Man. Why then did the station Monitor allow him to pass? The inescapable realization dawned on him and he felt goosebumps ripple over him.

"You are Man," Klent whispered and sat down with a thump.

Doby shook his head, not believing it. "I cannot fault your conclusion, but it's not possible. Something must be wrong with the station's field. You try it."

"Me?"

"Extend your hand and touch the field. If you don't get a reaction, we'll know."

"And if I do, I'll be fried."

Klent bit his lip and stood up, took a step toward the shimmering field, and slowly extended his arm. When nothing happened, he walked closer, then he was through. Doby nodded with satisfaction and joined him.

"The Council will never believe me," Klent muttered as he stared at his hands. "I am Man."

They walked over neatly trimmed grass until they reached the metallic-looking floor of the complex proper. Beside one of the structures lay a row of six platforms. Everything appeared new. Standing before the tower entrance, Doby pointed at a plaque above double doors.

"T-HR Tracking Station 12," Klent whispered. "THAR. At least that's how you would pronounce it. But…"

"The Tale of Man is wrong," Doby concluded firmly, his emotions churning, and stepped toward the doors. With a soft hiss, they slid aside. After unknown centuries that they were still operational…

The high ceiling glowed with pearly light. On his right were two elevators. He pointed at a door on his left and walked toward it. It retracted out of his way as he approached. Two contoured couches faced a large sloping console and a ceiling-high virtual screen pooling through random colors. A blue orb hung suspended in the middle of the room enclosed in a faint field that extended far into space.

"Earth," Doby murmured reverently. "Look!" Hovering in what he considered to be a geosynchronous orbit drifted a glowing blue rectangular slab. He walked closer and touched the image. Immediately, glowing white words appeared beside it.

'Space Tracking Orbital Relay, built in 2855 CE by the Union of Earth'

Doby lifted his head. "Monitor?"

"State your question," the familiar voice filled the chamber.

"Purpose of T-HR 12."

"It is a chain of twenty-four stations around Earth that controlled the STOR network."

"Why has this station been abandoned?"

"Loss of contact with STOR due to malfunction in the operating system during a routine system upgrade."

After prolonged questioning, a coherent picture emerged. The upgrade severed the control links with STOR and all tracking stations, and it took over the city Monitors. The station's computer could not say how Man became enslaved or why the error in the operating system was not rectified. Isolated from other stations and cities, the computer became cut from the global communication network.

Doby decided a lot more time would be needed to fully understand what happened and how to overcome STOR…if at all possible. Man at the height of his powers failed, he reminded himself.

-6-

The two platforms descended daintily into the square, Klent coming down with hardly a wobble. It was an easy machine to fly. They were immediately surrounded by the villagers and curious children, all wanting to know what was going on.

Doby raised his arms to settle the crowd. "Listen to me everyone! Klent and I have returned from the hidden city in the north, and we have vital information that'll change all our lives. I'll explain everything in the Council building."

Everybody surged after him as he made his way up the steps, his body trembling with excitement. With limited room inside the chamber, some had to stand patiently outside.

Doby pointed at the picture of Station 12. "We were there, inside it," he said, facing the Elder and Kirhan. "And we have a platform to prove it."

"Impossible!" Kirhan roared, and the room exploded into confusion.

Pako Hram raised his hand. "Let us hear what he has to say. After all, he did bring back the platform."

"We brought back much more than that, Elder," Doby declared. "The knowledge that *we* are Man!"

Kirhan jumped to his feet and pointed a bony finger at Doby. "Blasphemer! You dare defile—"

Pako Hram pounded the table with his palm. "Silence!" When a semblance of order returned, he stared hard at Doby. "Explain yourself."

"Man built STOR to help govern Earth. The city Monitors controlled communications, transportation systems, and many other things besides, including the Keepers. A routine system software upgrade broke the control link with the tracking stations and STOR began to operate independently. It is not clear why they didn't restore control, but one thing we do know. Using brain imprinting, Man was enslaved. There is no THAR, and we're not its constructs."

"You're babbling, boy!" Kirhan declared and turned to the others. "No one can possibly believe what he's saying. THAR created us to serve him, and one day Man will return from the stars and free us."

"The Tale of Man is wrong!" Doby bellowed. "You don't have to believe me. Tomorrow, Klent and I—"

"And me!" Tani shouted, waving her arm.

"—will return to the station and complete the project Man started to regain control over STOR. We can take five of you with us, and you'll see that I spoke the truth. The station has platforms, and we can use them to ferry everyone who wants to come. You don't have to live in hardship anymore."

Kirhan reached into his pocket and levelled a small needler. "Die, blasphemer!" he snarled and fired. The beam grazed Doby's right arm and he flung himself down.

Someone behind him screamed in agony. Two grim faced *men* grabbed Kirhan and wrestled him to the floor. Trying to ignore the sting in his arm and the oozing blood, Doby slowly got to his feet and turned. A youth he had known in the machine shop lay on the stone floor with a black burn in his chest, vacant eyes staring at nothing. He looked at the Elder.

"Is this what we have become, Pako Hram? Fighting each other to preserve a flawed belief? Then STOR has already won."

-7-

"…And then Man created STOR, and it was given dominion over the whole Earth. Man roamed the stars while STOR kept Earth safe from her enemies. Centuries passed, and Man prospered, with Earth the jewel of the galaxy. STOR built cities that glittered at night, their spires reaching toward the stars themselves.

"STOR was not satisfied with holding dominion over Earth. It sought to destroy Man everywhere, and it rebelled. Man fought long, leaving Earth devastated, but in the end, STOR defeated Man. Thus began the Dark Age. Man was enslaved and disobedience punished with death!"

"What happened then, Mother? Tell me!"

The woman smiled and ruffled the boy's hair. "Then a Man named Doby came. Brave, cunning, and gentle, and STOR feared him. One day, Doby confronted STOR for the final time and Earth held its breath. STOR was powerful and they fought, but Doby was also powerful. He reached up and tore STOR from the sky. Man was free at last, and once again, Earth became the jewel of the galaxy."

She brushed away a rebellious lock of hair from the boy's forehead and cradled him as they watched a red sunset, the slim city spires bright around them.

"Never forget the Tale of Man, Timmy."

The boy squirmed in his mother's arms, stars in his eyes. He never tired listening to his mother recite the Tale of Man. Every time he heard it, it made him determined that one day, he too would roam the stars. One day…

Twilight

Turner tapped the steering wheel with his fingers, marking time to the tune from the radio, and resignedly watched the slow afternoon traffic, waiting for the green arrow that would allow him to make his turn. He left work half an hour early to beat Friday's inevitable crush, but it seemed other drivers had the same thought. Well, he did manage to avoid most of the rush hour. Another fifteen minutes and he'd be relaxing in his apartment nursing a rye whisky. A dinner with Carolina would round off a very successful day. His project to upgrade the bank's short term bills trading system finally received approval, and his team could start development. The IT Director of Special Projects even condescended to smile at him, hinting at promotion and a hefty pay increase.

Yes, sir. Things were on a roll for Tom Turner.

The arrow turned green and he nodded, easing the BMW into a left turn, instinctively glancing right—in time to see a battered Ford pickup racing through the intersection. Staring at the driver, a cigarette hanging from his mouth, Turner knew he would be wiped out and there was nothing he could do about it.

"Ah, shit," he muttered as the pickup roared toward him, followed by blaring horns and the screech of brakes from irate drivers around him. What was worse, he still had fifteen grand to pay off on his car, wondering if the insurance would give him a new one. This would mean he'd probably miss dinner with Carolina. Damn.

Making no attempt to stop or swerve out of the way, the pickup slammed into Turner's car. He felt his neck snap a moment before dazzling white light flared in his head.

He had read about near-death experiences and seen documentaries where people found themselves floating in the operating theater, watching the surgeons work on them, hearing everything they said. Turner wasn't sure what to make of the situation when he found himself floating above the mangled wreckage of his beloved car, the pickup ripping it almost in two. It didn't look good and he wondered how badly he'd been hurt. Definitely no dinner with Carolina.

His project! That shit Roberts would now probably take over. The bank could not afford to wait for Turner to get out of the hospital, which meant no promotion, and he could kiss that pay rise goodbye.

The intersection was a snarl of stalled cars, people milling around his BMW and the pickup, cars slowly edging around the wreckage trying to get away, not anxious to hang around for the cops, ambulances and fire brigade tenders to arrive, which would all add to the confusion. A tough looking young guy peered into the BMW and immediately pulled back, face contorted in disgust. Crap!

"He's a goner, a mangled mess," Turner heard him say.

A goner?

"This one's still alive, but trapped," someone shouted as they wrenched open the pickup's door.

"Better wait for the ambulance," another man suggested as he pulled out his cell and punched in numbers. "I'm calling 911."

Turner willed himself to float down until he found himself level with the BMW's window. One look at the bloody mangled mess, he grimaced. Drifting higher, it slowly dawned on him that he wasn't having a near-death experience, but that he was actually dead, the realization shaking many of his preconceived notions. There was supposed to be a long tunnel and a bright light at the other end marking a doorway to heaven, or something, with souls waiting to embrace him. So some said. Apparently not. It also looked like the local priest had it all wrong, too.

This, Tom old boy, will take some adjustment to accept.

Instead of feeling anguish at having his life cut short by an idiot, Turner actually felt great, relieved that he would miss eighteen months at least of office politics, budget hassles, battling for project staff, and fighting an impossible schedule. As the program manager, it would all land on him, smiles and congratulations for getting the project approved forgotten. Life would become a drag once the bean counters sank their talons into him. He'd miss Carolina, though. They had something going, which most likely would have blossomed into a more lasting relationship.

Two police cruisers, sirens blaring and lights flashing, arrived on the scene. The cops started directing traffic, urging sightseers to move on. Why do people relish watching the macabre? An ambulance pulled up, pried loose the pickup driver and hauled him off, followed by Turner's evil wishes. The fire brigade crew had to use the jaws of life to cut through the twisted wreckage of his BMW to get at the body.

He became aware of somebody near him and looked up. A young woman floated some twenty feet from him, smiled and waved. She wore a blue blouse and black skirt, not at all what he imagined a ghost to look like.

"Hi, there," he said lamely, startled to see her.

Still smiling, she nodded and said something, but he could not hear her words. With a wave of her hand, she drifted off. Looking around him, he saw two young boys, an old bearded man, and an executive type hovering above the scene. He shouted at them, but they simply shook their heads and pointed at their ears.

"That's great. I'm in a world of ghosts who can't hear anything," he muttered sourly.

How come he could hear everything else? It appeared to be a mystery he needed to resolve, and he had an eternity to figure it out. The thought made him pause. Did he have eternity? Was death going to be spent drifting around the world until he went insane from sheer boredom, having seen everything, having learned everything? Say, if he had endless time on his hands, there were lots of things he wanted to study. Perhaps death wasn't going to be that bad after all. Wait a minute; he couldn't interact with the physical world! Or could he? Something to follow up.

Looking around, he frowned. If every dead person ended up—wherever this was—he should have been hip deep in ghosts, but the sky looked almost empty. Even as he digested the thought, one of the youngsters began to glow, then popped out of existence.

So...

Was his current state merely an interim situation before his soul—for want of a better description—was processed and shuffled somewhere else? A question of imponderables. He would simply have to wait and see what happened. In the meantime, he should say his farewell to Carolina.

As he willed himself to go higher, he scanned the city's skyline. Making like Superman, he arrowed toward Fisherman's Wharf. Carolina had the day off, preparing something special for their dinner. He wondered how she would take the news of his death. How would he tell her?

The apartment block where she lived loomed ahead of him and he headed for the ninth floor. Two elderly men waved at him as they flew past. Staring at them, he belatedly waved back. Maybe he should explore the possibility of finding a friend or two. Without being able to converse? Sign language? That would be weird.

He drifted closer to the kitchen window and saw it empty. Maneuvering to the bedroom window, his mouth sagged as impotent rage surged through him like fire. Carolina, her amber hair spread across the pillow, slim arm around Roberts' neck, winced in ecstasy as Turner's senior project manager pumped into his girlfriend. Without thinking, he clenched his fists and willed his body to close with the son of a bitch and his two-timing girl, only to shoot straight through them into another apartment, bursting out the other side of the building.

Teeth grinding, Turner slowly unclenched his fists. He now understood why Roberts hadn't come in today. Bastard!

Carolina! How could you do this to me!

Calming down, he allowed himself a wry smile. She did not know Roberts as he did. The smooth talking shithead had wormed his way into her pants, and she would deserve what she'd get if they hit it off.

The sun had turned into an orange ball, bathing the city with shadows. San Francisco skyscrapers, their lights blazing, turned downtown into a surreal wonderland. With all his life's cares and worries swept away, Turner decided to have some fun as he swooped toward Little Italy, the city's red light district. Never been tempted to go there, but always interested to know how business was conducted by the experts. He now had an opportunity to see it for himself at close range. This should be good.

But it didn't turn out to be so good. Anticipating to see feverish action, the voyeur in him salivating, in reality it was no different from watching a porno movie. Worse, as real life amateurs could not compete with staged professional actors. The hookers looked bored throughout the act, and the men, mostly elderly, probably cheating on their wives, grunted and groaned through their pathetic performance. Turner didn't even get a hard-on, the situation deflated by two male ghosts smirking at him in one room.

Dejected, he flew high into the sky and stopped to watch the blaze of city lights below him. Up here, he had a measure of peace and contentment, even happiness, something he hadn't felt in a long time. His work rewarded him with a luxury apartment—his dad would probably sell it off now—an up-market car, a wonderful girl—an ex now—and parents who didn't interfere. He reminded himself to see them sometime. As the only son of a moderately wealthy family, he'd had everything. Everything except happiness, he realized. Money, a good job, status, did not translate into happiness as he thought they would. Where had it all gone wrong?

Gazing at the quarter moon, he grinned and stretched out his arms as his body arrowed into space. He had no sensation of speed or movement, but when he glanced back, Earth was a blue orb hanging against a black tapestry filled with stars.

On his right, Mars beckoned. He would give it a go once he overflew the Moon. Always interested in astronomy and cosmology, he could indulge some of his fantasies to see the Solar System for himself. If he could only write down what he would see and give those NASA boys a shock.

He didn't know how long it took to reach the Moon, but it felt like a long time. There simply wasn't any way he knew how to measure time. Seeing the gray Lunar landscape draw close, a profusion of craters everywhere, he felt mildly disappointed at his lack of excitement. He had seen documentaries of Apollo landings and knew what to expect, which perhaps dulled his enthusiasm. Nevertheless, swooping over the forbidding landscape, he felt a measure of awe at what nature had produced. It would have been cool to see a UFO right then…

Venturing over the dark side, he could see very little and returned into daylight, seeing Earth as Armstrong must have seen it, a small blue-white ornament, beautiful but fragile. He left the gray craters behind him and flew toward his blue home.

* * *

A day came and the sun slowly sank into a still sea. White breakers smashed themselves into creamy foam along an endless stretch of yellow sand. Gulls hovered above the churning waters, waiting to plunge in for a morsel. Turner sat on the sand and watched the gulls, the surf, and the sun. Cloud tendrils, lit with fire and gold, stretched over the western horizon. A soft, mild breeze stirred the spiky grass around him. He could not see anyone, not even other ghosts.

He had spent over a month exploring the planet, seeing all the famous sights, from the pyramids, the Taj Mahal, the Eiffel Tower, and wonders like Machu Picchu. He soared over Everest and plunged through fiery volcanoes. He even flew into the raging waters of the Niagara Falls—a silly stunt to do, but invulnerable, he dared everything.

The ocean deeps gave him a fright. Plummeting down into total darkness, he was amazed to see glowing creatures out of nightmare. With all the turning and twisting, he could not tell up from down, and had a moment of irrational panic, fearing he would be forever trapped in eternal blackness. Once he thought it through, the solution was simple. He kept flying until he saw light and burst through the surface to an expanse of an endless ocean.

He sat on an abandoned shore, watched breakers roll in, and wondered if this was all there was. Is this how he would spend eternity? Roaming Earth and the Solar System? There were always the stars, but he was not that desperate yet. He had seen people and children suddenly pop out of existence, perhaps into another life. Would that be his fate one day? Would that be his moment of redemption? But if he flew away from Earth, would that moment pass him by?

He did not believe in God or the afterlife, preferring to look at his current predicament as merely another step in man's existence, however startling the experience. Whatever 'he' was now, his consciousness, his being, clearly had substance beyond the physical body. If his current situation represented a transition to something else, he wanted keenly to experience it.

After seeing so much of Earth—still to venture into deep space to see Mars—he became bored. This had not turned out to be as much fun as he anticipated. Undertake a project of study? Perhaps later. One thing was certain. He would have to devise some program that would keep him occupied and motivated, or he risked descending into depression, and perhaps actual insanity. If the hand of God watched over him, Turner hoped He would send his soul to wherever others had vanished.

Seeing the red sun disappear, leaving a glowing horizon, he had a novel idea to alleviate boredom. He had seen the film *The Core*, and always wondered what it would be like to see the

Earth's center for himself. Now, he could indulge his whim. He smiled, lifted his arms, rose a few feet, and turned upside-down. Still wearing a grin, he drove himself into the yellow sand.

Nothing but darkness. He knew the Earth's solid shell was some twenty miles or so thick, which shouldn't take him long to traverse. Then 1,800 miles of the mantle before he reached the outer core.

When he did break into the upper mantle, still in darkness, but he could perceive a faint red glow. Probably energetic photons emitted from radioactive decay. Nothing like *The Core* showed. He kept arrowing down. At least he thought it was down, the background roar of moving magma loud in his ears.

After what had to be many hours, tempted to turn back, the red glow intensified and he suddenly found himself bathed in yellow light shot through with tendrils of white. He had at last reached the outer core. He nodded with satisfaction and continued down.

It seemed like an eternity had passed before he saw darkness looming ahead of him approaching abnormally fast. Stopping with considerable effort—the layer of darkness tugging at him—he realized he had reached the rotating semi-solid inner core, the dynamo that generated the Earth's electromagnetic field. From what he knew, the core was mostly nickel/iron with a gamut of heavier elements. Farther in lay the radioactive center that fueled the entire process. His knowledge sketchy, but what he saw matched what he read.

Feeling himself drawn down, he clenched his teeth in an effort to stop himself.

He saw little value going farther.

His curiosity satisfied, he reached up with his arms and willed himself to fly to what he supposed to be 'up'. Any direction away from the black core would be up. After a while, he looked down and his mouth sagged in astonishment. He had not flown away from the core at all! Moreover, it appeared to be closer, which wasn't possible. No physical force from the real world could affect him. Yet, he reminded himself, he could see and hear what went on. Even now, the core's heaving mass hissed in his ears.

It should not be possible for the core to draw him toward it.

Before he sank through the glowing boundary into darkness, the answer hit him. Gravity somehow interacted with the dimension his soul occupied, capturing him in its embrace. What waited for him at the core's center? Why, other ghosts who became bored. Did they ever pop out of existence into another life, releasing them from a hell of their own making?

As darkness closed around him, Turner screamed, but of course, no one heard his screams.

Wishing Wall

Shafts of golden light streamed through the tree canopy high above. I breathed deeply of the eucalyptus scented air and exhaled loudly with satisfaction, the rucksack a comfortable weight on my back. My boots sank into the soft blanket of brown leaves, making a crunching sound as I rounded the hill's steep shoulder, the worn trail a snaking line some twelve meters below me.

I should have stuck to the trail, having already broken a steadfast rule of bushwalking: don't venture into the forest alone. Bending it a little did not break it really, as I planned to rejoin the trail once I rounded the hill. Besides, it felt good exerting myself a little, giving my legs a workout. So far, the muscles hadn't protested, a testament to long daily walks and running.

I paused, slipped off the rucksack and rested it against the trunk of a white gum. Pulling out a green army water bottle, I drank deeply of the warm water, feeling its energy suffuse through me. On a day like this, it felt good to be alive. Thinking about nothing in particular, I allowed my mind to drift as my eyes roamed through the silent forest.

A shadow swept over me and I looked up. Tall trees hid most of the sky, but the canopy could not hide the shapes of dark clouds creeping in from the west. The leaves whispered as a cool breeze stirred the high branches. I frowned, hoping the weather wouldn't break to spoil what had so far been a great day. I didn't get too many opportunities to go hiking and resented nature's attempt to sabotage my outing. Looking at the clouds, I decided to push toward my turnaround point, which according to my forestry map lay only about a kilometer or so away.

I heaved the pack onto my shoulder and moved off, the whisper of leaves loud in my ears. A deep rumble made me stop. Overhead, the sky had taken on an ominous darkness. I felt a drop strike my cheek, followed by another. Muttering a curse, I scanned the hillside for an overhang or hollow, anything that would give me shelter, hoping this was nothing but a flash summer storm. Another rumble of thunder, closer this time, spurred my search. Apart from my canteen, a couple of sandwiches and a sweater, I hadn't packed a poncho or any wet weather gear. The weatherman this morning said it would be a clear and hot day. That made me break another rule of hiking: be prepared for anything.

An ominous whistle overhead made the branches creak and a cold rush of air made me shiver, my T-shirt offering little protection. I pulled on my sweater as I rounded the hill's shoulder, looking anxiously for shelter. Heavy drops of rain fell around me, cold on my face.

I should have stuck to the trail.

A bright flash made me blink. Two seconds later a loud crash shattered the silence, the following thunder grumbling, fading into the distance. The rain hissed as it came down, soaking my light sweater.

A jumble of moss-covered boulders caught my attention and I headed toward them. By now the wind blew in earnest and I felt a chill creep over me. If I didn't find shelter soon, I could be picking up an unwelcome cold.

A crack between two boulders looked wide enough to squeeze through. As I took off my pack, everything turned white as lightning stuck. I jumped at the immediate crash of thunder that left my ears ringing. I knelt and pushed myself through the dark crack, wishing I'd brought a torch. Serves me right for not being prepared.

Some two meters in, the opening widened into a small cave. The air had a musty, moldy smell, but the earth floor looked dry. I raised my right arm and reached up toward the ceiling, not feeling anything. As I slowly stood, my hand touched rough rock. I found I could stand, my head about thirty centimeters from the cave's roof. Stretching my arms, I could not feel the walls, and the crack I crawled through barely showed enough light to reveal the opening.

Lightning glared, revealing a cave scarcely larger than my spread arms. A hideous crash shook the ground and I winced…then gaped as the cave wall on my right began to glow, green and blue hues merging into each other. Startled, I stared at the pool of colors as they assumed depth and substance. The surge of voltage from the lightning strike must have set off some piezoelectric effect in the quartz bedrock, I told myself, my initial shock seeing the thing replaced by calculating curiosity. Blue-green tentacles rippled across the wall from the pool body, but withdrew, leaving what to my inflamed imagination looked like a doorway.

Step through, I told myself, and be transported into a land of magic and wonder. I didn't believe in magic, grounded as I was in hard science, but the swirling pool tugged at my childhood fantasies. Tentatively, I reached out with my right arm toward the color pool. Before I could touch it, a blue-green tentacle coiled around my hand and I snatched it back, feeling an electric tingle run up my arm.

If this was a simple discharge from a lightning strike, the effect should not have lasted this long. Outside, thunder rolled ponderously into the distance.

"I could use some light," I muttered as I stared at the shifting colors.

I almost creamed my pants when bright white light suddenly bathed the cave. The walls and roof did not glow or anything, but I nevertheless stood immersed in light.

"This is impossible," I said loudly, not believing it.

For this to have happened *was* impossible under all the laws of physics I understood. Clearly, there were things I didn't understand. I realized that much. Okay, this should not have been possible, but it did happen. How? I bit my lower lip and went over the event, reaching a startling conclusion. Cause and effect.

"Let there be darkness," I said softly, and nodded thoughtfully as the cave plunged into night.

So...

You are an astrophysicist, Kevin, I told myself. There has to be a logical explanation for this. Unfortunately, Doctor, there isn't. I simply could not explain this phenomenon.

"I want light," I said and smiled as the cave lit up, and felt a surge of exultation wash through me.

As I thought it through, I formulated a hypothesis. The lightning strike had somehow energized the quartz wall, opening a dimensional rift that seemed attuned to my thoughts, turning my wishes into reality. But how? The tentacle that struck my hand?

Fascinated by the possibilities this opened, I decided to test my hypothesis. I wished for a grilled pastrami on rye toast, but nothing happened. Nodding with understanding, I tried again.

"Give me a grilled pastrami on rye toasted bread," I said distinctly, and a sandwich appeared in my hand.

I sniffed it, saliva pouring into my mouth from the tantalizing smell, then cautiously bit into it. It tasted delicious.

"Table and chair," I said crisply. Nothing.

It appeared I had to formulate my demand as an action.

"I want a French ornate table and chair," I ordered, visualizing the two objects.

Both appeared into existence and I pumped a fist up and down.

"Yes!"

Not very scientific behavior, but right then, I didn't feel very academic.

Pulling back the chair over the uneven cave floor, I sat down and crossed my legs. Whatever the mechanism that executed my wish, the color pool had to draw supplementary information from my mind to do so.

I took a bite from my sandwich and pondered what I could do with unlimited power the wall offered. I could have anything I wanted. I could do anything.

"Turn the cave floor to gold."

I had to squint from the sudden glare as light danced over the rough golden surface. I laughed, giddy with an overpowering realization that I could change the world. I could wipe out disease, poverty, hunger, war, political corruption. The possibilities were endless.

My face turned grim and I suddenly wished that Carol would love me again. There were many reasons why we slowly drifted apart, and some of them were my fault. My work at the university kept me away from her too much. To compensate, she had buried herself in her job as an investigative journalist. Both of us should have worked harder on the relationship.

"We are so smart in many ways, but so stupid when it comes to what matters."

As I looked at the wall, perhaps there was a way now to recapture what had been lost. One thing to wish for an inanimate object, but I suspected that tampering with emotions, feelings, and people, might not be as simple. Still...

I was curious to find out how far the effect manifested itself. Were my wishes confined to the limits of the cave? I needed to find out.

"Turn the cave floor back to rock," I said and shook my head with bemusement as the floor returned to its previous state.

I crawled through the crack, sniffed at the rain-filled air, and looked up. It still rained, but not heavily. The sky still a dark blanket.

"Stop the rain," I said.

It continued to rain.

I nodded slowly. It appeared I had to be close to the pooling color wall for my wishes to be executed.

Inside, I became aware of my sodden clothing.

"I want my clothes dry."

Comfortable again, I sat down, deep in thought.

Now that it existed—whatever the wall was—would it remain open for good? No way to tell, of course. The effect could fade at any moment as the energy charge from the lightning strike dissipated. I needed to take advantage of it while I still could.

"Create for me three two-kilo lumps of gold."

Three lumps of yellow metal appeared at my feet.

Tempted to wish for a million dollars in cash, I realized that would have been hard to explain. As would a new car, house, and a luxury or two. Those things would have attracted unwarranted attention and demands for an explanation. I could picture myself telling the authorities I had stumbled on a magic cave and their subsequent reaction. It would also be the end of my happiness. Showing up at a jewelry store with three lumps of gold I happened to find in the bush would not raise any undue excitement, and would give me that new car, house, and an odd luxury.

Would it give me Carol again?

Standing up, I shouldered my rucksack.

"Turn off the light and remove the chair and table."

In darkness, I stared at the pooling colors. Slowly, I reached out until my hand touched the glowing pool.

"I wish peace on all mankind," I whispered, turned abruptly and crawled out through the crack.

Outside, the clouds were drifting apart, outlined in gold, showing bright patches of blue. The air smelled fresh and clean and I breathed deeply. Invigorated, I made my way down the hill toward the trail. My thoughts full of the enchanted cave, I hurried to reach the parking lot. I needed to think carefully before unleashing the power I had found.

* * *

I turned onto the onramp and entered the freeway. Twenty minutes and I'd be home. Prepared to accelerate, I slammed on the brakes, not believing what I saw. Wrecked cars littered the lanes going both ways. There were a few multi-car pileups, but most vehicles looked like they simply left the highway and crashed.

What the hell?

I stopped beside a two-car smash, got out, and peered at the wreckage. Nothing. No bodies or blood. Did the survivors manage to walk off unharmed? No, not possible. I stopped beside three more cars before the realization dawned on me.

There were no people! They had all vanished.

Carol!

Racing down the freeway, my thoughts churning in turmoil, knowing that I somehow caused all this. I hoped it wasn't true, hoping for a saner explanation. Looking toward the city's sky-scrapers, tendrils of black smoke twisted into a clear sky. I clenched my teeth, my mind filled with awful images.

As I turned off the freeway, I could see more smoke drift-ing over the suburb and more crashed cars. Knuckles white as I gripped the steering wheel, I rounded the corner, seeing an empty street devoid of life. Two sparrows fluttered away in alarm as the car screeched to a stop beside my house.

I ran up the driveway, fumbling for the door key. Finally managing to get the door open, I raced toward the kitchen.

"Carol…Carol!"

The walls echoed my shouts. Checking the rooms—the TV in the lounge was on—I only found empty spaces. Breathing heavily, I bit my lip and thought furiously. Maybe she had gone to visit someone, knowing I was only kidding myself.

With a snarl, I dragged out my cell, called up her icon in the contacts list and pressed the ring button. After five rings, her modulated contralto answered, instructing me to leave a mes-sage.

Staring at the smartphone in my hand, I allowed it to drop to the floor. The back cover snapped off as the cell hit the floorboards. Making my way to the kitchen, I turned off the oven and electric hotplate and pushed aside the simmering casserole pot.

What have I done?

I wished peace on all mankind, I recalled.

Peace…

But man was cursed, and there could not be any peace as long as three people lived. I rightly feared wishing for something that affected people. Unqualified, my uncensored desire for peace, not translated into exacting, unambiguous words, the wall had granted the world peace, all right—by eliminating mankind. I clenched my head between my hands, racked by dry sobs.

"No!"

Exhaling slowly, I settled down and started to think. Perhaps it was not too late to undo what I had done.

I jumped into the car and drove with reckless abandon toward the looming Macedon hills, my heart thudding with fear, anxiety and hope.

It took me a tortuous hour of running up the trail, sliding and slipping on wet leaves climbing the hill to reach the jumble of boulders that led to the cave. Gasping for breath, sweat staining my brow and T-shirt, I crawled in. As soon as I entered, my heart sank. The rock wall stood dark.

I reached with my hand and touched the cold stone.

"Come back!" I cried in anguish.

After a moment, I felt my eyes sting and I swallowed a lump that threatened to choke me. I slowly sank to my knees, cradled my chest and rocked back and forth.

Sniffing, I wiped my eyes. Perhaps I could still make it the way it all was. There would be other storms and the wall might glow again.

"I'll get you back, Carol," I promised myself. "I'll get everybody back."

Lifeliners

Nash Bannon waited at the crowded tram stop, people pouring out of the Flinders Street railway station, and gave a sigh of resignation. Melbourne's skyline glowed in clear sunshine with a promise of another mild spring day. Ordinarily, he would have walked up Collins Street to see his client, but he hadn't jammed for five days now and he needed a boost. He wasn't sure why they called it jamming, and nobody had taken time to explain it to him. Probably because one had to rush in, grab his donor and disengage before the victim realized what was going on.

He hated the press and cloying smell of people jostling around him, most of them looking like they didn't want to be there. He knew how that felt, but everyone needed work to survive. He had his Docklands apartment, an investment property and a shares portfolio, enough for a comfortable lifestyle, but not that comfortable to consider retirement just yet. He figured ten more years would do it, provided he retained his sanity...and wasn't caught. Being a senior IBM program manager took its toll in long work hours, battling schedules, budgets, changing client demands, and IBM's own stifling procedures. He ought to turn freelance and wouldn't have to suck up to his brain-dead superiors—a perfect oxymoron.

Ignoring the sound of crawling traffic, the blare of an occasional horn, feet pounding on sidewalks, Bannon saw the tram slow as it approached the boarding platform. The double doors snapped open and passengers tumbled out, giving those trying to push in glares of contempt. He stepped in and forced his way into the packed tram. There wasn't enough room to take on everybody, and many would have to wait stoically for the next one, which at this time of morning would undoubtedly be as packed.

Life was shit.

For what he had to do, he needed the shield of pressed bodies around him. He grabbed the polished steel stanchion next to the door as the tram lurched forward. The man already holding on barely glanced at him as he made skin contact. Bannon exhaled slowly and forcing himself to relax. He extended his touch and felt a comforting tingle as he drew energy from the man. He had to do this slowly or the drain could become a torrent and his victim would pass out. After years of jamming, he knew how to go about it. Take a little from two or three people and everyone would walk away happy, especially him.

He did not know why he had to feed, and the odd lifeliner he met never discussed it, and didn't even want to be identified. There weren't many of them around. Bannon remembered the onset of craving when puberty overtook him. He became restless, and the occasional burning that made him want to peel off his skin caused him look at people with irresistible hunger. He only knew he had to feed from them. His initial attempts were clumsy affairs that almost got him caught more than once. Confused, not understanding the change in him, he couldn't even talk to his parents, sensing they weren't lifeliners—a term he came to learn later.

The tram ground to a stop at the Bourke Street Mall and Bannon let go of the stanchion, feeling his life-force brighten from the energy surge. His vision appeared sharper and his hearing became more acute. He became more aware of everything around him, attuned to the flow of emotions and personalities jostling along the sidewalk. Purely a psychosomatic reaction, but he felt pleased with himself and the world in general as he stepped off the tram. He strode toward Collins Street to catch another tram that would take him to the parliament buildings. Another jam and he would be good for four or five days, and this morning, he will need the extra energy boost. He had a program of work review with senior client execs and expected a hard time explaining schedule slippages, cost overruns and lack of adequate staff. They would blame him for everything, and IBM would blame him when the clients bitched to the division manager. Anyway, the job paid well, but he wondered if it was worth the hassle.

He pushed his way into the tram and grabbed a stanchion. Without looking at the elderly lady pressed against him, he figured to take only a little, and judging by her generous bulk, she could afford it. As he got ready, a familiar tingle shot up his arm and he looked down in surprise. She couldn't have been more than twelve. Pale brown hair in rats, beige sweater frayed around the collar and wrists, black jeans torn at the knees, a big toe poking through her right runner, she showed no reaction to his scrutiny, her tiny hand pressed against his. She clearly didn't know him as a kindred spirit. At her age, he hadn't either. She must be starving, judging by the rate she sucked. He could usually spot another lifeliner by the barely visible green glow that enclosed them, visible only to another lifeliner. He could not see any glow around her. She might be one of the numerous strays who wandered the streets, abandoned by her family when they learned what she was, hunted by the authorities, her trust in fellow human beings forever shattered?

She let go and the drain stopped. When the tram pulled in at the Exhibition Street stop, the little girl stepped off. Bannon got off and grabbed her hand. Her head jerked up in surprise and instinctively pulled back her arm, but he held her fast. He could not explain why he reached out to her. All he knew, she needed help and he understood what it was like being different in a world afraid of all lifeliners.

"I'm not a dober," he told her quietly. "I'll let you jam some more, but you can't take too much."

Her dark green eyes grew round and her small mouth opened in surprise. With a wash, she would look pretty. Now, she was small, alone, lost, and scared.

"How…"

"You need to learn how to spot another lifeliner."

"Is that what we're called?" she ventured uncertainly, not

sure of his intentions, looking at angles to make a run for it.

He gently squeezed her hand. "Go on. Jam."

She licked her lips with the tip of her tongue and her eyes turned misty. He felt a mild jolt as his life-force drained and a faint glow bathed her small body.

"That's enough," he told her after forty seconds. He glanced at a nearby restaurant, one of many in upper Collins Street, and inclined his head. "When was the last time you had a proper breakfast?"

She followed his gaze and broke into a sunny smile that melted his heart. Why did people do these things to their littlest ones?

"It's been a while." She bit her lip, suddenly unsure of herself. "You won't dob me in?"

"Cross my heart," he said seriously and tugged her hand toward the restaurant. "How long have you been alone?"

"I ran away from home about a year ago when my parents called the dobers. I've been in trouble before, you know. Hooky from school, stealing, hanging around with the wrong crowd, stuff like that." Her expression turned dark. "When I told my parents that I needed to jam, they called the dobers, but I ran off before they came to the house. I guess they've been looking for me ever since, but I'll never go back!" Her large eyes searched his face. "You sure you won't dob me in?"

"Promise. What's your name?" he asked as he opened the restaurant door and waited for her to get in.

"Aleya."

"Say, that's a nice name."

There were enough customers inside to avoid being conspicuous. Bannon made toward an empty table at the back. A pretty young thing dressed in a black form-fitting uniform sauntered toward them, holding a pen and pad. She glanced at Aleya's disheveled appearance, frowned suspiciously, then turned to Bannon.

"Yes?"

"I'll have a decaf black with milk on the side." He glanced

at Aleya. "What'll you have?"

Lips pressed in concentration, she studied the menu display board hanging above the counter. "I'd like a blueberry muffin and a vanilla shake." She glanced at him. "If that's all right with you?"

He nodded. "Fine. Nothing else? Eggs, bacon, pancakes?"

She hit him with her sunny smile. "After the muffin."

Chuckling, he nodded to the waitress.

"Won't be long," she said and walked off.

Bannon sat back and studied his lost charge. "So, where do you live?"

She shrugged. "Where it's convenient. Lots of empty houses and old factories and stuff. I'm with a bunch who take care of me and teach me things. They're not lifeliners and don't know that I'm one."

Looking at her, he could hardly imagine how she was able to cope, but her life didn't have a future. Sooner or later, the dobers would catch up with her.

"Aren't you afraid of being mugged or worse?"

"It's been tried once or twice, but I can look after myself," she declared, not appreciating the dangers she faced every day. At her age, getting hurt or dying was something one read about or saw on TV.

He exhaled, wondering if she really understood what it meant to be a lifeliner, with everyone around her seeking to report her to the authorities, or kill her for the reward. Having taken her under his wing, what next? Let her go back to her scavenging existence, not knowing if she would see tomorrow? But what could he do? The ramifications and scope of his obligation daunted him. He had enough problems in his life right now and didn't want to add another major one to the list. All very well, but by becoming involved, he could not let her loose, cast her off, wipe her from his mind. Not if he wanted to live with himself.

"Look, I know one or two people who can help you. Lifeliners like you. You'd be off the street. You cannot live in some derelict warehouse all your life. You need to be safe."

She lifted her head. "What's it to you? I do all right. Besides, all people are mean."

"I just—"

"You into little girls or something?"

Bannon drew back, stung by her coarse remark. "Have your muffin and shake and you can go," he grated. "But like I said, you need to learn how to recognize another lifeliner before you jam. He might not offer you a muffin." He pushed back his chair and made to stand. She shot out her hand and grabbed his wrist.

"I'm sorry. It...well, it's been a while since anybody did something nice for me."

Undecided, his instincts telling him to walk away, he sighed and sat down. "Think about what I said."

"I'll do that. Is there a toilet around here?" she demanded, craning her head. He pointed at an alcove and she grinned. "Back in a sec."

"You sure you know what you're doing, Nash?" he muttered, then shook his head. "Yeah, that's what I thought."

Alyea came back just as the waitress brought a loaded tray and walked off. Alyea reached for the shake and slurped noisily through the straw. Giving him a sheepish smile, she took a big bite out of the muffin. Chuckling, Bannon stirred milk and a sugar stick into his coffee. Taking a sip, he leaned back.

"I'll need to latch onto you, mister," Aleya declared comfortably. "You're a good provider. By the way, what do I call you?"

"Nash."

"Nash...nice name."

He grinned. "My girlfriend says the same thing."

She arched her eyebrows and her eyes became mischievous. "You have a girlfriend?"

"She is a doctor, a neurosurgeon."

"That's somebody who scrambles your brain, right?"

Bannon laughed. "It can happen. Now, what do I do with

you?"

"Those lifeliners…they'd look after me?"

"Find you a home, get you back to school—"

"School! Yuck!" Aleya said and made a face.

"It's not that bad," he said, holding back a grin. "If you want to survive, you'll need a good education. It'll also help you avoid the dobers."

"Mmm."

Sipping his coffee, he watched as two dark-suited men walked in. Their eyes scanned the restaurant and both started walking toward him. Inner alarms clanging, Bannon searched for a way to get out of this, but there didn't seem to be a back door. How did they tag him to be a lifeliner? Only a few lifeliners knew him, but if one of them wanted to dob him in, they had plenty of chances to do it before. Still, if the dobers caught one and made him talk…

As he stood up, the heavier of the two men pulled out a taser.

"Take it easy and no one gets hurt," Heavy growled casually.

"What's the meaning of this?" Bannon demanded without having to feign wounded outrage.

Heavy pulled out his wallet and flashed an ID. "Federal Police. I'll need you to come with me…her too," he said glancing at Aleya. "I think you know why."

A sudden quiet descended on the restaurant as patrons waited expectantly for the next development. Bannon had seen this type of shakedown himself and hadn't liked it, feeling sorry for the poor schmuck who got caught. Now, he found himself in that net.

"Am I under arrest for something?" he demanded, hoping to talk his way through this.

"We simply want to ask you and your little friend some questions, in the spirit of cooperation and all. If that doesn't suit you, you can consider yourself under arrest if you like. Let's go."

Bannon reached for Aleya's hand.

"Don't let them take me," she whispered, her voice tragic.

He gave her a reassuring squeeze, needing some reassurance himself. Right now, boxed in with no way out, Aleya narrowing his options, he couldn't do much to extricate himself.

He followed the leading cop with Heavy holding the taser on him.

"Dirty lifeliner!" someone shouted behind him and Bannon stiffened. Aleya pressed herself against his thigh and tightened her grip on his hand.

At any moment, the mob mentality might take over and he could find himself in a riot. He paused at the checkout counter and extracted a twenty-dollar bill from his wallet. Placing it on the counter, he flashed the tense waitress a brief smile and walked into a stream of hurrying pedestrians. A tram bell clanked as it neared the stop.

Heavy pointed at the double-parked black Holden Commodore. "In the car."

The first cop opened the rear door and Bannon slid in. Alyea wriggled in and clung to his arm. He buckled up and nodded to her, helping her clip on her seatbelt. Heavy got onto the front passenger seat and the car pulled into the traffic, rewarded by a horn blast from the car behind them for causing the blockage.

His work program meeting shot, he could vividly picture what the client would say, but he suspected he was in for something far worse than a mere dressing down from his boss.

As the car turned onto Swanston Street and went over the Yarra River bridge, then turned right after the Arts Center, Bannon had gotten over his shock, but he still could not figure out how the dobers had gotten onto him. They must have had a tail on him for a while, suspecting, but not certain what he was, deciding to pick him up just as he had Aleya in tow. Did they know about her? If they didn't, they were likely to find out quickly enough.

The car stopped in front of the Rialto Tower. Bannon did

not wait for an invitation and nodded to Aleya to get out. The two AFP cops made sure he wouldn't stray as they entered the spacious foyer, past a throng of visitors waiting to get up to the observation deck, and made for the elevators. When the silver doors split in two, Heavy got in, pressed a security card against a sensor and pushed the button for the 42nd floor. The elevator surged up, slowed and the doors opened. Heavy pointed down the plain gray-painted corridor, their footfalls soundless on the hard, dark-gray carpet. A forbidding-looking place, cold and lifeless, and Bannon wondered what dark secrets lay beyond the anonymous walls. Reaching a door, Heavy pushed it open and motioned with his taser.

"In."

Inside the windowless room, Bannon pulled back a plan metal chair from a wood-veneered table and sat down. Aleya bit her lip and sat down beside him.

"What will happen to us, Nash?" she whispered urgently.

"I don't know, honey. I'll find a way to get us out of here."

Heavy glanced down the corridor and stepped back to allow the woman to come in. Gaping, Bannon had his second shock. This just wasn't his day.

"Carrina!"

His girlfriend stood rooted, also clearly in shock. Behind her, Heavy frowned as he closed the door.

"You two know each other?" he demanded, giving Carrina a hard look. "Doc?"

"I didn't know who he was!"

Heavy thought it over. "Coincidence perhaps, but we'll have to check this out."

"Fine," she snapped, pulled out a chair and sat down.

Bannon leaned forward and stared at her. She *couldn't* be mixed up with the dobers! "What's going on?"

They had gone out half-a-dozen times and he was getting used to having her around. Her schedule at The Alfred hospital didn't leave much time for socializing. Neither did his. He met her on a tram, of all places, while jamming. He had just taken a charge when he saw her looking at him. At 180cm, well built, clean features, wavy black hair, he accepted appreciative glances from women. He grinned at her, and her smile broadened before she looked away. As he was getting off at Collins Street, wanting to see her again, he reached into his jacket and dug out a business card.

"Call me?" he implored, holding the card. After a moment, she took the card and beamed.

"Maybe."

Two days later, she did call.

Stunned, wanting to convince himself that she wasn't working for the dobers, Bannon mentally gasped, trying to make sense of it all. His world had taken a tumble as bitter bile rose in his throat. Tempted more than once to reveal himself to her, a lifetime of ingrained caution and mistrust of 'normal' people held him back. Seeing her, his caution was all too justified.

"You're working for them?" he grated, pointing at Heavy.

"They work for me!" Carrina snapped. "I am part of a CSIRO project studying lifeliners. I never knew you were one of them. You have to believe me."

He snorted and shook his head. "What now? Lab, lights, tubes, needles?"

"Don't be ridiculous. Nobody is trying to exterminate lifeliners."

"That's not what the government and the media are saying."

"Propaganda to pacify the more extreme social elements."

"Propaganda? Vigilantes taking the law into their own hands and our rights violated, legislation passed to allow indefinite confinement without due process? That's supposed to be pacification?"

"I'm not happy about some of the government's policies, but this is a major social problem without a clear solution, and the CSIRO is trying to find one that won't tear up our society. We don't want pogroms we're seeing in America and Europe.

Look, Nash, lifeliners are something new, perhaps the next step in our evolution, and the government is understandably anxious to understand what you are—"

"And counter the sensationalized threat we represent to mankind."

She blushed and looked away. She pushed back a lock of golden hair from her forehead and her brown almond eyes were pleading.

"Something strange and wonderful is going on around the globe right now. And yes, it's also frightening. The birth rate across the developed world has been falling steadily for over sixty years, and appears to be accelerating. Conversely, the incidence of lifeliner births is correspondingly rising, but we can't tell for sure, given that they can only be identified after puberty. Understandably enough, they're not anxious to advertise themselves, but we can see the pattern, and governments everywhere are naturally concerned."

"I can see why they'd be concerned," he agreed. "They're seeing their future disappearing, and with it, their hold on power."

"Now you're being naïve and obtuse."

Bannon snorted and shook his head. "I'm being obtuse? Have you read the papers lately, or seen what the media are reporting? You should get out on the street, lady, and see for yourself. Stuck in a lab won't help solve your problem."

"That's precisely why we need subjects like you! We want to understand, not exterminate, something I suspect is not even possible. If lifeliners are our next evolutionary step, stopping the process is now irreversible. There are simply too many of you to eradicate."

Bannon could not believe Carrina had said that. "Eradicate? Is that what this is all about? Finding a way to remove us? And you're a willing participant in this?"

She winced, stung by his remark. "I'm working to find a peaceful solution—"

"Tell it to those who were mobbed or dragged away by

goons like him!" Bannon snarled, jerking his thumb at Heavy.

She jumped up and backed into the guard.

"Hey!" Heavy cried out as she sagged against him.

Bannon sprang out of his chair and lunged at him, grabbing his hand. The jolt of life-force surged through him in a powerful stream as he jammed. Heavy moaned, rolled his eyes and crumpled to the carpet. Breathing heavily, Bannon stepped back.

Carrina pushed down her black skirt and stared at the body. "Is he…"

"He'll be all right," Bannon assured her. "He'll be weak for a day or so, though."

"You could have killed him."

"That's not how lifeliners work, honey, but I wouldn't be surprised if someone hadn't done it somewhere. By the way, neat move, that."

She smiled sheepishly and shrugged. "Seeing you when I walked in…I had to do something." She glanced at Aleya, who clearly didn't understand what was going on. "Who's your friend?"

"A stray kitten. What now?"

"You must get out of here." Carrina held out her security pass. You'll need this to open the elevator."

"And you?"

"I'll tell them that you attacked us, which you did. When Carl wakes up, he'll back up my story." She grabbed his arm and pushed him toward the door. "You have to get out of here right now! One of my colleagues will be coming through there at any moment. I'll call you and we'll sort this out."

"Carrina…"

She brushed her soft lips against his cheek. "I know. My head is also spinning. Now, go!"

Bannon opened the door and peered both ways down the corridor. Glancing at Aleya, he hurried toward the elevators. He pressed Carrina's pass against the sensor and touched the ground floor button. A few moments later, the double doors opened and he stepped in. The two men and a young woman inside made space for him.

When Bannon walked out of the tower, he allowed himself a long sigh and glanced at Aleya.

"We need to get away, and I have a few things stashed for just this eventuality. Come, or maybe you want to fade back into your street network? The dobers know you now, you know."

She bit her lip. "I'll tag along, for now, but I've got to tell you this. It's the closest I've come to the dobers and I don't want to do it again."

"Me neither," he assured her as they headed toward the pedestrian bridge spanning the Yarra River that would take them under the Flinders Street station into the city's center. Once they reached Elizabeth Street, Bannon flagged a taxi and told the driver to head for North Melbourne.

The cab pulled up in front of Western Self-Storage. Bannon told the driver to wait and strode quickly toward the entrance. The reception desk inside stood deserted. He dug out a key from his key-ring and unlocked a side door to a large open warehouse with three floors of sealed dirty-white containers. Taking the stairs to the first floor, he made his way down the row of containers and stopped before 214. He unlocked the door and slid it sidewise. He flipped on a switch and fluorescent strips flickered into life, flooding the space with bright light, revealing packing cartons, tall cupboards, and chests of drawers.

Stepping in, Bannon grinned at Aleya. "Everything we need to make a fresh start," he said brightly and dug out his cellphone. "I have to get in touch with somebody who'll help us get set up, but what I have here will do for now."

"What are you going to do?" Aleya asked, her eyes roaming around the container.

"Disappear. We'll both disappear," he said as he punched in his call. After three rings, he heard two clicks. He tapped the phone twice and disconnected, then put in a new set of numbers.

"Talk to me, Nash," a strong masculine voice ordered crisply.

"I need extraction, Trent."

"You can't go back to your apartment."

"I know. This has to be a total wipe."

"Meeting at point Charlie in twenty minutes. Can you make it?"

"No problem."

"Trash your SIM," the voice said and broke the call.

Bannon extracted the phone's SIM card and ground it under his heel. He took out a spare from his wallet and was back in business under a new number and name. He walked to the closest cupboard and pulled out a slim black briefcase.

"We need to take a little drive, Aleya. A man will meet us who will get us new identities, and you'll need a change of clothes...and a bath," he added with a smile.

"A spa bath?" She looked hopeful.

"Promise."

After locking up, they made their way out of the building and piled into the cab. Bannon gave the driver an address and slowly exhaled as he sat back, allowing his pulse to slow down. His meeting point relatively close, he would make it there easily.

Two hours, that is all it took to scramble his life. Everything he had worked for, all the plans he made, a future he hoped to have, all gone. He wondered whether it was even possible to have a future in a world slowly going mad. The prospect of seeing tomorrow left him with a hollow feeling of despondence. And Carrina? Would she be prepared to share his tomorrows? He somehow doubted it.

The taxi pulled up outside the Footscray Market Continental Deli on Irving Street. Bannon gave the driver a generous tip and got out. The sidewalk was busy with pedestrians and women coming out of the market carrying loaded bags. Traffic clogged the street both ways and the air stank from pungent car exhaust fumes.

A tall slim figure dressed casually in a black blazer and black corduroy trousers suddenly appeared and stopped before Bannon.

"Nash, as I live and breathe. It's been a while," the man remarked with a wan smile.

"Trent…I only wish it were under different circumstances," Bannon agreed as they shook hands.

Trent glanced at Aleya. "Still picking up strays, I see."

Bannon chuckled. "You know me."

"Yeah. What happened?"

"I'm not quite sure myself. They were on me before I knew what was going on."

"Never mind. We'll talk about it once we have you safe."

"Oh, I don't think so, Trent," the familiar voice said and Bannon slowly turned.

Carrina stood there smiling at him, five men behind her held handguns ready for action.

"We've been after you and your network for a long time, Trent Masters, and I'm looking forward to a long chat." Smiling broadly, she turned her piercing eyes on Bannon. "Nice to see you again, Nash. Although you might not think so." She looked down and held out her arms to Aleya.

"Mommy!" the little girl cried out as they embraced. "I got a big one!"

"You sure did, my darling. Two big ones."

Stunned, head whirling, Bannon felt blood drain from his face. This couldn't be happening!

"How…"

Giving him a cheeky smile, Aleya held up a small smartphone.

"We knew exactly where you were all the time," Carrina declared comfortably, hugging her daughter.

His heart breaking, Bannon stared forlornly at the little girl who betrayed him.

Playthings

I raised my cognac snifter and gave my two friends a solemn look.

"To free men everywhere."

Brent beamed and his eyes sparkled. "Welcome to the divorce club. It's been two years for me, and Trev, my boy, I haven't looked back." He clicked his balloon against my snifter and nodded sagely.

Chuckling, Martin touched his balloon against out glasses, his spare form looking insignificant against Brent's bulk. Then again, Martin had always been a rake, and likely to outlast us all with those vitamins and herbal crap he is consuming. When he gets onto his salesman platform and starts peddling natural foods, I could strangle him.

"You two are losers," he declared with the authority of a happily married man. "Six years since Brenda and I tied the knot and it never came close to unravelling."

"Only a matter of time," Brent said comfortably, leaned back against the couch and sipped the fine Otard cognac.

"Never happen, Skunk." Martin shook his head as he held his glass between both hands to keep the cognac warm. He raised the balloon to his nose and took an appreciative sniff. He gave me a quizzical smile and pursed his lips. "However, I've got to say that Anita didn't go out of her way to make your life a rose garden."

I took a swallow of my cognac and lowered the glass to the table with a soft click.

"She wanted eighty percent of the house and sixty percent of all my investments. Can you believe it?"

"So you told us already," Brent muttered and fondled his double chin.

"Even the magistrate cracked a smile at that," I mused. "We've been married for four years—"

"It's been a grind for you. I could tell," Martin interjected with malicious glee and downed half his cognac.

"—and she hadn't contributed anything to the house or building a joint nest egg. At first, I didn't even mind that she insisted on having her own bank account—"

"While she milked yours," Brent added sagely, staring vacantly at his balloon.

"Agreed." I nodded and gave a small shrug. "But—"

"Here it comes," Martin said, grinning broadly.

"You thought you were in love, a love that would burn forever, and you granted her every whim," Brent said. "Trev, my lad, been there myself. I warned you…"

We all had more than one drink and it had begun to tell. The buzz in my ears had settled into a pleasant hum and I felt warm and relaxed, comforted with my friends around me. We shared everything since high school, including girlfriends. Over time, we diverged along different paths and the bond that held us together might be frayed along the edges, but still strong.

"I know. I didn't listen," I said. "Anyway, the magistrate gave her a hard look and I held my breath, knowing he held the power to clean me out if he believed her sob story."

"She mined you," Martin pontificated, shaking an index finger at me.

"That she did," I agreed and glanced at Brent. "Despite your cynicism, I *was* in love! And I *did* think it would last forever. I believed everything she told me, and the fact she was divorced didn't matter."

"Raging hormones," Brent grunted. "They will do it to you every time."

"Perhaps. The alarm tripped when she told me she couldn't conceive. I wanted kids and so did she. At least that's what she told me." I raised my eyebrows and gave each of them a nod. "Then I found her stash of morning after pills." I sighed morosely and took another sip of my warm cognac.

"At least the magistrate didn't shaft you," Trevor added,

and I brightened.

"She got twenty percent of my house value and nothing from my investment portfolio which I brought into the marriage. The best part, I wouldn't have to pay her any alimony, given that she was comfortably well off from her previous divorce, something that only came out during the hearing, thanks to the private eye I hired. The magistrate banged his gavel and that ended it. I tell you, guys, the look of pure fury that Anita gave me would have melted a lesser man."

"But being the hero type that you are, you survived the onslaught," Brent said and chuckled.

I lifted my balloon in a salute. "Skunk, you never said a truer word. Watching the magistrate walk out, I felt the weight of the world—"

"Anita's weight," Martin added dryly.

"—roll off my shoulders. She cost me almost 200K all told, but I'm shut off her forever. Bitch!" I downed the last of my cognac and looked at my friends. "I did love her, you know."

"And I loved Nancy, but that's not always enough," Brent muttered, fondling his balloon. He gave me an appraising stare, then beamed. "Look at it this way. You'll now have more time to play golf."

I raised my empty snifter and laughed. "To golf."

Martin glanced at his wristwatch and gave a long exhale. "I've got to be moving."

"Or Brenda will bend you in two," I added with a smile.

He chuckled and pushed back his chair. "Better believe it, but what a way to go."

Making exaggerated groaning noises, Brent heaved up his ample bulk.

"I'm glad things worked out as they did, Trev."

"It could have been worse." Looking at them, I realized how fortunate I was to have them as friends. We no longer did some of the crazy things we used to, and the years have marched on as we changed, having to manage careers and relationships.

Skunk made light of his divorce, but I could see it had hurt him, making him more cynical. Having gone through one myself, I appreciated the change in him. Would I ever love again as I loved Anita? She was my first deep love and it burned with intensity, certain it would last for all time. At first, she made me feel it would. In time perhaps, I would open myself to another love, but I wasn't too sure. Not right now. I knew I would never again love someone else with the intensity and trusting innocence I loved Anita. Too many scars.

In a way, I envied Martin. Brenda adored him and he glowed when they were together. They had their down moments like any couple, but those were like fleeting summer storms that cleansed the air. I envied him, but also glad for him.

I thought I had that same adoration from Anita.

* * *

I woke with a start, wondering what the hell happened. Yellow sunlight streamed through gauzy curtains and I could see a clear blue sky.

The house shook and I jumped out of the bed wearing only my boxer shorts. An earthquake? In Melbourne? Australia experienced occasional tremors, but they were mostly mild, the continent being geologically stable.

Something crashed into the house and I could hear wood splintering. Thick dust rolled into the bedroom from the open doorway. What the hell was going on? I strode through the door and peered into the living-room. I saw a gaping hole where the backyard wall was supposed to be, and the ceiling had caved in. I gaped at the ruin, not believing what I saw. Someone was demolishing my house!

Through the opening, I saw a large yellow bulldozer blade move ponderously toward me and I instinctively stepped back. There came a hauntingly familiar background *brrr* sound. A sound I used to make as a boy playing with my tractor and crane in the sandpit.

The bulldozer blade tore through the house and the walls gave way before it. This couldn't be happening! I coughed as a wave of white dust rolled over me and I scrambled toward the opening. What I saw froze me and made me question my sanity.

A huge kid, perhaps five or six, long black hair framing a freckled face, held a giant plastic bulldozer in both hands and slowly pushed it toward the house, all the while making a loud *brrr* sound of a heavy engine.

I jumped out of the way as the 'dozer moved toward me. With a tearing crash, it flattened the wall of my bedroom and the roof fell in. The kid laughed, clearly enjoying the destruction. He saw me and paused.

"A worm!" he cried with delight and slewed the 'dozer bladed toward me.

"Wait!" I screamed in panicked horror. "I'm not a worm!"

The open blade loomed over me and I ran toward the back fence, but the kid moved faster. The blade scooped me up and the kid lifted the bulldozer. Enormous blue eyes peered at me. The kid wiggled his index finger and pushed me. I fell to the ground and shrieked in agony as I felt my broken ribs grate, hearing laughter that shook the air.

Clutching my wounded side, I watched in dismay as the kid positioned the 'dozer over the ruins of my house. He shook the toy machine and I scrambled back as the blade tilted down. Realizing what he intended to do, I screamed, but it was too late. He scooped me up again.

The blade tipped down and the kid shook the 'dozer, the action throwing me into the air. My mind going, not believing I was still sane, I fell helplessly into the ruins of my house studded with broken beams, bricks and roof tiles. I struck the jagged edge of a splintered beam and bright blood spurted from a gaping chest wound. Darkness prevented me from crying out in agony.

* * *

I sat up in bed, feeling my skin cold and clammy. Sunlight slanted into the bedroom and I blinked hard. Looking around, everything lay as it should be, but I could not shake off the vivid images of my dream. To double check, I glanced at my chest. No wound and no blood, and my ribs felt fine. I gave a long sigh of relief and sat back against the bedrest.

"Trev, my boy, you're coming unstuck," I muttered and swung my legs out of the bed.

Something slammed into the house and I was thrown back onto the bed. Did a car just hit the house? I scrambled to my feet and ran out of the bedroom, through the living-room, and into the formal dining-room. Bright blue steel of a bulldozer blade tore through the front entrance and the wall collapsed. The ceiling above me groaned and sagged.

I heard the familiar shrill laughter and looked up as the 'dozer blade pulled back. Driving the yellow metal monster was someone I thought I would never see again.

"Anita! What the hell are you doing?"

To have a bulldozer plow through my house was one thing, but to see my ex-wife driving the thing jarred my sanity. This wasn't happening and I hoped to wake from this nightmare.

"Twenty percent wasn't enough, darling!" she screamed above the engine noise and the 'dozer lurched toward me, belching black diesel smoke from its stack.

"Doing this won't get you more!" I shouted at her.

"At least, I'll have the satisfaction knowing you won't be getting your eighty percent!"

This couldn't be happening. She *couldn't* be this insane.

I scrambled back as the blade ripped through the dining-room. I tripped and fell. A sharp crack above me made me look up in time to see the ceiling open up. I threw up my right arm to protect my head, knowing it to be a futile gesture.

Broken beams fell around me and I coughed from the dust. A section of ceiling plaster board gave way.

"Ah, shit." I managed to mutter before an unbearable weight smeared me against the polished floorboards.

I thought I heard Anita's shrill laughter before a bright light flared in my head and I felt nothing. There wasn't even time to see my life flash before me like the throb writers made out.

Doorways of the Mind

It was one of those silly things.

Last night, pounding away on the keyboard, the words flowing as the thrill of creation coursed through Martin, he wanted to finish the chapter while the scene remained vivid in his mind. His characters took advantage of this momentary freedom to produce some striking dialogue. He finished the last sentence, sat back and sighed. Mentally drained, but immensely satisfied, he rubbed his tired eyes and groped for the mug. The coffee barely tepid, he drained the cup and nodded. His third in…he couldn't tell. As he moved, his stomach sloshed. The digital clock on the bottom of the screen read 01:15. He had been at it for a solid three hours! No wonder he felt stiff. Martin did not worry about the late hour as he shut down the computer. It had been a great piece of writing, he told himself. He stretched his arms until the joints popped, washed the mug, and readied for bed. Tucked under the doona, the chapter replayed in his mind and he allowed his thoughts to drift.

The coffee must have done it. Not awake, but not sleeping, his bladder demanded release, but he did not want to drag himself out of a nice warm bed just to have a pee. Besides, the room was freezing. July in Melbourne not at all amusing. There wasn't even snow to add charm to the winter. It was simply miserably cold. He turned over and pulled the doona over his head. Only a little longer, he told himself.

Martin's bladder thought otherwise. The harder he tried to recapture sleep, the hydraulic pressure became more insistent until he actually felt uncomfortable. Either get up and get the business done or wet the bed. Not an option really. Disgusted, he sighed, pulled back the doona, and immediately shivered from the biting cold. Not bothering to switch on the light, he slid his feet into the slippers and stumbled toward the bathroom. Although the room was totally dark, he did not need a light to find the bathroom, having done this sort of thing hundreds of times.

He reached for the door handle and made to step through. Unfortunately for Martin, the door was still closed, which caused his head to crash painfully against it and made him stagger. He did not have to have the room lit; there were plenty of sparkling lights around him. He uttered a short earthy word, opened the door and groped for the switch. The bathroom exploded with light and he winced as his eyes adjusted.

His hydraulic problem momentarily forgotten, he stepped toward the large vanity mirror and peered closely at his head. A nice red bruise had already colored his right temple, but the skin remained unbroken. Another expletive. His bladder reminded him why he came here and he took care of it, sighing with relief. Done, he switched off the light and strode toward the bed. As he wriggled under the warm doona, he opened one eye and glanced at the digital clock display: 05:42. He closed his eyes, exhaled with contentment, and allowed tension to ease out of his body. His head hurt, but he pushed back the discomfort and the associated unpleasant memory.

Next time, switch on the light, dummy, he told himself.

* * *

Martin liked being a freelance IT consultant and part-time author. His professional work paid the bills and his writing filled his soul. Running complex projects and seeing them completed gave him intense satisfaction, despite the downside of constantly fighting for resources, schedules overruns, and ballooning budgets, not to mention function creep clients always tried to slip in. He had a simple work philosophy, on the surface anyway. The client defined the project objectives and delivery timeframe. Martin's job was to make it all happen within those parameters. If the parameters changed, any of them, he had a chat with the client. You want additional functionality, it will cost you this much, and will impact the schedule by this many days or weeks. Sign off on the requirements variation and I'll get it done. Of course, that attitude did not always endear him to the client who wanted the expanded requirements delivered within the original budget and timeframe, which made Martin somewhat of a hard-nosed bastard. It did not bother him. Sometimes the hard facts of life had to be explained to a client in a language they understood—stuff around with requirements and you will corrupt your business objective. He got away with his approach because he was very good at what he did.

Four more years, he told himself, and he would have enough financial security to retire in comfort. Being a part-time writer provided a release for his literary creativity, and he looked forward to the day when he could write all day, every day. Well, on most days. No need to push things to the extreme, or he would be swapping one 9 to 5 job for another, not that his work was ever 9 to 5. He found writing a joy and fun, but there were other types of fun he wanted to indulge in.

When he finally woke, the clock read 07:36, but being Saturday, he could afford to be lazy for a few minutes. Today was his washing, house cleaning, and grocery shopping day. He did a cursory clean every weekend, but once a fortnight, he made a thorough job of it.

He pulled back the doona and winced as the cold air made his skin tingle. He strode to the large window and pulled back the drapes. The eastern sky stood bathed with a red glow, and frost covered the front lawn. Not really a lawn, not anymore. An assortment of various grasses had taken over the front yard after he had it landscaped originally. Now, that had been a lawn. Then the permanent water restrictions came into force and he could no longer water anything, unless he installed several bulging water tanks. He had a drip system that took care of his shrubs and bushes, the lawn left to its own devices. In summer when everything was burnt brown, he often thought of replacing the scraggly growth with a pebble garden, but the cost was too prohibitive. If he ever sold his place, the new owners could do what they liked with it. For the moment, Martin remained content to leave things as they were.

As he dressed, he gingerly touched the lump on his temple. A slight headache throbbed at the side of his head. He would take an aspirin with breakfast, which should take care of things.

He breathed deeply of the crisp air and finished dressing.

* * *

Sunday afternoon was uncomfortable, double shots of aspirin not helping his headache. Did he perhaps scramble some gray matter with the door encounter? If the headache did not clear up by tomorrow, he would get a CT scan. He felt normal, but would he be able to tell if he carried any brain damage? Just a bad bruise trying to heal itself, he told himself.

On Monday morning, the alarm woke him from a very pleasant dream—now he would never know how it ended. He had no real desire to go to work, face a cold morning, the crush of passengers on the train, or the scheduled status meeting with his project managers. He would rather be lazy and remain in his nice, soft, warm bed.

It was always like this. Each Friday night, he told himself that tomorrow, he would sleep in and make up for lost time during the week. No way. After years of waking up at six am, Saturday morning found him wide awake at six am—usually. On Sunday, he did manage to squeeze in a few extra minutes, but not enough. Mondays were bad. He wanted to sleep like the dead, but the damned alarm wouldn't let him. A conspiracy to deprive him of sleep.

In the bathroom, he checked his bruise, pleasantly surprised to find only a colored spot. It did not even hurt when he touched it. Almost finished with breakfast, the wall TV gave him a dose of morning news, he realized the headache was also gone. Now we're cooking!

He drove to the train station, parked, and joined a convoy of people making their way in. He did not even mind the cold, and it looked like another clear winter day. He had his notepad in the briefcase and he would put in some writing. Why waste forty minutes staring out the window or the expressionless faces of fellow commuters?

During the day, he kept seeing a black circle in his mind, and it had nothing to do with the novel he was writing. Simply one of those things, he figured.

Martin came home satisfied with the day, himself, and his program of work. His client did not grumble too much as things were more or less on schedule, and his project managers wanted him to leave them alone. Well, as long as they did their job, he happily left them alone. They knew he would kick ass if they didn't. Be friendly, but carry a knobby club.

He transcribed the writing he did on the train into the computer, editing as he went along, a glass of bourbon at his side, and went to bed. Two, three more months tops and his novel would be finished. At it for seven months already, there was only so much time he could devote to writing holding down a full-time job. It was moving, and that was all that mattered.

His dreams were always vivid, in full color and surround sound. Sometimes they appeared so real, he had to exert almost conscious effort to tell himself he was dreaming. That happened with some of his bad dreams when he found himself in a precarious or embarrassing predicament. Like walking around town with no clothes on, and nobody seemed to notice. Right now, he dreamed he was in Venice and missed his tour bus. His suitcase, carry-on bag, wallet, and all his documents were on the bus—and no bus. In a strange duality he often found himself experiencing, he knew he was dreaming, but that did not lessen the emotional impact and momentary panic he felt standing in front of the hotel and no bus. He did not speak Italian, didn't know the hotel where the bus would drop everyone for the night, and he had no money. The earthy words he said did not help things.

Suddenly, a black circle appeared before him some two meters in diameter. Inside the circle, he could see his fellow tour members, on the bus, chatting to each other. Relief flooded through him. All he had to do is step through the circle and he would be safe. So, he stepped through. No one turned to look at him as he walked down the aisle toward his seat and sat down. He snapped on the seatbelt—the local cops had a dim view of passengers not buckled in—and gazed at the passing scenery. He had no idea where the bus was taking him.

The dream faded and Martin fell into deep sleep.

As usual, the alarm jerked him awake. He turned over and curled into a ball, savoring a few more seconds of slumber. Not feeling crisp or bouncy, he rolled over on his back, opened his eyes…and went pale.

At the foot of his bed stood a black circle the same size as the one in his dream. He blinked and slowly rubbed his eyes. That's it. He was still dreaming. He pushed back the doona and sat up, ignoring the cold. The circle was still there. Trying to wrap his mind around what he saw, he gingerly reached with his hand and pushed through the circle. His hand disappeared and he immediately snatched it back. He wiggled his fingers, all there.

Well, damn.

He climbed out of the bed, his feet sliding automatically into the slippers, and slowly stepped toward the circle. It maintained its position before him. Whichever way he moved, it shifted to present a full, impenetrable, black surface.

Martin knew he must be dreaming, because dream circles don't become real when the dream ended. So, he must be dreaming, right? The only problem with that hypothesis, he was wide awake and knew it, and he had a black circle in his bedroom. The knock on the head had sent him over the edge and he was delusional. That must be it.

His analytical mind rejected that fanciful proposition and he spent a few moments studying the circle. He had a black hole that led to...somewhere, if he believed his dream. He pictured his kitchen, and immediately, the kitchen appeared within the circle.

"This is nuts," he declared.

Step through and you are there, right? It worked in his dream. Surely, it would not be that easy, would it? What he did in his dream violated every physical law he understood. He did not understand everything, he told himself, and the kitchen looked very real.

Martin hesitated, threw reason and logic out the window, and stepped through the circle...and found himself in his kitchen.

"Okay, steady. You're not coming unstuck."

He turned, but the circle had vanished.

He stood on the polished floorboards and realized he was warm, the preset timer having activated the heating system. He shook his head, not prepared to analyze what happened, and made his way to the bedroom. During the shower, he focused on the work program for the day, the black circle a shadow in his mind. Anyway, it was gone. An aberration, something he dreamed.

As he tied his tie, he wanted a shot of coffee to clear his mind. In the mirror, he saw the circle. He turned and slowly nodded. It seemed to obey his will, but did it?

"Go away," he said, and it vanished.

Okay...

He wished the circle to appear and it did.

"Martin, old boy, if you haven't totally slipped your rails, this has possibilities."

He pictured his kitchen and the image appeared in the circle. He grabbed his jacket and stepped through...into his kitchen. A whimsical thought popped into his mind and he smiled. In the circle, he could see St. Mark's square in Venice. If he stepped through, he felt certain he would find himself there. It was late at night in Venice, but the square teemed with tourists, and the image opened a vista of possibilities.

What about breakfast in Rome, dinner in New York, a day on a tropical beach? No more air fares! He could go anywhere he wished for free. All very exciting and appealing, but what if he could not summon the circle anymore? What if this ability faded over time? It would be like his dream, stranded somewhere without documents, and the authorities asking some pointed questions he would not be able to answer. He could picture himself all too vividly being interrogated by unsmiling cops, in jail, his comfortable life no longer comfortable.

Having a doorway to anywhere clearly handy, but he had to think things through. An obvious problem using the circle immediately presented itself. Someone, somewhere, was bound to notice if he suddenly popped into existence, which would cause talk, unwelcome talk. Departing required that he conjure up the circle, which would also cause someone to pop their eyes. Even if no one saw him, cities these days were filled with surveillance cameras. One of them would record his sudden appearance or exit, and the hunters would be set loose. Of course, he could employ more subtle and less public methods when using the circle.

He bumped his head and now had a teleportation…thing. The bump clearly did something to his brain to make this possible. He could not tell if the ability was permanent or transitory while his brain healed itself, if damaged. He will have an MRI and have himself checked out. In the meantime, he would use the circle and explore its potential.

Martin rubbed his hands and stepped toward the percolator, only to be blocked by the circle. Within its boundary, he saw the New York skyline. He turned and faced another circle. This one showed the Taj Mahal. He felt his face drain and his mouth went dry. The TV announcer droned through the day's weather, and a field of ice cliffs popped into Martin's mind. A new circle appeared showing a glacier beneath a clear sky.

His mind freewheeled and he stood surrounded by circles, all showing different images.

"Go away!" he screamed and the circles disappeared.

Badly shaken, he reached for the percolator and poured himself coffee. His hand trembled as he brought the mug to his lips. From a welcome gift, the circle had suddenly become a living nightmare.

It not only obeyed his conscious will, but his subconscious mind also appeared to control it. Something he did not expect, although he should have. He had been too euphoric seeing its possibilities to note the darker side. He sat down and gulped the hot coffee, his sweaty shirt plastered against his clammy skin.

"Oh man…"

Not good, not good.

How can a person censor his subconscious self? When the inner self could not express itself, could not control reality, its desires and fantasies were of little consequence, except to the mind benders, of course. When the inner self could summon the circle—many circles—that presented an altogether different set of problems.

Control…firm control, he told himself. Don't picture anything. Keep your mind blank.

Right, he can do this.

Martin stood, turned, and faced the circle. He had not called for it, but it was there.

"Go away," he croaked. The circle remained.

Did some part of his subconscious, or some inner secret desire, summon it? No way to tell. At least it was blank, no image to step into.

Control…don't think of anything.

"Go away!"

The circle wavered, then reformed.

Keep a blank mind, he told himself.

The circle approached him and he immediately stepped back.

"Go away!"

The circle enveloped him and he found himself in total darkness. He whimpered and shut his eyes. When he opened them, he was still in impenetrable darkness.

Martin screamed and screamed, but there was no one to hear him in the dark corridors of his mind.

Halo

Paul wished the priest would cut the sermon short. The dreary monotone tempted him to stand up and walk out. He could not do that, of course. Valerie and the rest of the family would never, ever forgive him for such a gross breach of manners. He did not even know what the sermon was about, having switched off seemingly an eternity ago. He sat there and suffered as the priest droned on, oblivious to the shuffling of restless feet and an occasional cough from the bored gathering also hoping for speedy relief from this verbal torture.

"Get the christening done and let's get out of here," Paul muttered to himself, his butt also seeking relief.

A flicker of light caught his eye and he lifted his head toward two large stained glass windows above the altar that were the main feature of an otherwise stark, modernistic church. That is how they built them these days, functional money collection machines. The sun had risen high enough to bathe the colored panels, making them glow in a rainbow of light that splashed across the pews. An orange beam caught him in the eye and he blinked and pulled back.

They really were pretty windows.

Dressed in a white silk gown, Verena slept contentedly in her godmother's arms, blissfully ignorant of everything around her. Paul sought that blissful ignorance himself. He almost did doze off once, but a sharp jab in the ribs from his sister made sure he did not miss a moment of the priest's dismal dialogue. A slow sigh of exasperation escaped him. Wasn't suffering supposed to be good for the soul? Suffering perhaps, but not outright cruelty!

Paul rarely went to church, much to Angie's thinly veiled annoyance and disapproval. She and her husband Henry never missed a Sunday. They did not understand why he loathed going to church, and their disapproval never bothered him in the least, which, of course, generated more disapproval. Easter a must family affair he felt obligated to attend, enduring the extra-long Mass, he sympathized with Christ's passion. Christmas services were okay and he enjoyed the old carols, but then, he enjoyed them even as a boy. People sang with gusto and seemed genuinely moved by the spirit of the occasion. There was compensation for attending church on those days. After the Mass, there as food and drink at his sister's place, and he could spend a few hours with the family tribe. Angie was a great cook. It would be the same today after the christening ceremony. The only other time he saw the inside of a church was during a wedding—thankfully far apart—an occasional funeral, which were likely to become more frequent as older family members and relatives succumbed to the ravages of time, and a christening, of course.

Valerie was his youngest niece, and Verena her first child. Angie had a particularly soft spot for her favorite daughter, although she would deny fiercely that she loved her more than the other two daughters. When Henry had one too many, he would confide to Paul his regret that Angie never bore him a son. Old-fashioned, Henry blamed Angie for not having a proper heir, not realizing the male determined the offspring's gender. Paul tried to explain it to him once, but his brother-in-law plainly didn't believe him.

The priest kept droning on.

Paul was religious in his own way, inasmuch as he followed the moral and ethical code the Catholic Church preached. He figured if God existed, it did no harm to be in His good books. One way or another, he would have his answer when it came time for his own funeral, hopefully a long time off.

A church gave him bad vibes, simple as that. To him, it was a house of hypocrisy. He had studied most of the ancient religions and philosophies, and the rise of the three principal faiths, in the process discovering more than he bargained for, or wanted to believe. He found Christianity to be a tortured faith, and its various denominations more interested in up-holding a bankrupt dogma than practicing the faith the priests were supposed to disseminate to the congregations. Do as I say, not as I do, was the weary mantra upheld over the centuries. It made Paul gag. No wonder people were leaving the Church, especially the young, drawn instead toward evangelical movements who were in reality only another type of money scammers that filled a spiritual need the Church had abandoned.

His thoughts dark, he swept his eyes over the gathering: family, relatives, and assorted friends. Most of them piously attended Sunday Mass, reveling in their holy demeanor, but for the other six days, many of them were simply plain bastards. It was all a sham.

His thoughts strayed to the book he currently read, a historical narrative of papal excesses over the centuries and the horrors of the Inquisition. It made a grim tale. It revolted him to read how the Vatican used its secular power to murder tens of thousands of innocent people across Europe in the name of faith. This, of course, was not the first or only horror the Church had promulgated. Christianity was a history of warfare and spilled blood as factions fought for sectarian and secular ascendancy in the name of a nebulous purity, whatever that meant. Regrettably, Islam and Judaism were tarred with the same broad brush of iniquity. Time for another reformation?

Paul sat back and gazed absently at the light streaming from the stained windows, immersing himself in the images they made. Simple images for simple people. Too simple for today's educated and questioning congregation. The last thing the Church wanted was to have the faithful question dogma. There lay oblivion.

A wave of unaccountable peace washed over him. His skin tingled and he suddenly felt warm. When he had a need to reflect on life's mysteries, which others would call communion with God, Paul did it listening to a stirring symphony, sitting in his backyard with a cigar in hand and a tumbler of bourbon, or taking a long walk, allowing his mind to drift. He did not need a church or a priest to mediate for him. Right now, though, sitting on the hard wooden bench, Paul felt a connection with...something. Perhaps only a feeling of well-being bathed in the sun's warm glow.

He became aware that the priest had stopped his sermon and looked at him openmouthed. A thick silence enveloped the gathering. He fancied he could hear a dust mote fall. When he turned his head, he saw others gaping at him. It took him a moment to realize that he seemed to be looking through a yellow haze.

Angie stared at him, having turned white as a sheet, her dark olive eyes round in shock.

"Paul, you're glowing yellow all over," she gasped.

He lifted his right arm. Sure enough, a yellow aura, soft as gossamer, enveloped his arm. His legs also glowed, as did his torso.

"Holy crap!" he muttered in startled wonder.

The priest raised his arms. "My brothers and sisters, we are privileged to witness a miracle, for it is certain that God has extended his hand over our brother Paul, declaring him to be holy. Let us pray," he declared and launched into the Lord's Prayer. Most of the gathering ignored him, staring at Paul with a mixture of awe and fear, uncertain what to make of all this.

"Mommy, why is that man glowing?" a little girl demanded, tugging at her mother's arm.

"I don't know, honey," her mother whispered nervously.

This was ridiculous, Paul thought. He knew that every living thing generated a bioelectromagnetic field, a personal aura, which some claimed they could see. However, he had never read of a case where that aura manifested itself visibly to everybody. Perhaps a very *small* miracle?

Angie grabbed his arm and clutched it to her cheek. "Bless me, Paul," she demanded, eyes wild, lost in a religious haze.

"Stop this, sis! You're being ridiculous." He shook off her hand and stood up.

The priest finished his litany and stretched out his arm. "I can see the Lord's light on our brother. Bless us, Paul, for you are beloved of God."

Paul swept his eyes over the gathering and spread his hands. "This is crazy. I'm not a holy man."

"You must be," Harold's aging mother cried out and shuffled toward him. "Bless me!"

Others surged to their feet and scrambled toward him. Alarmed, Paul backed out of the pew into the aisle. He needed to get away from this madness before things got out of control.

Eager hands plucked at his jacket, hopeful faces pleading for his benediction. A woman demanded that he cure her melanoma. A stooped man asked in a chocked whisper that he remove his arthritis. Others just wanted salvation from the pain of living.

"Folks, be reasonable," Paul pleaded. "I don't know what's happening, but I'm not holy. I cannot help you or cure anybody."

"Bless me! Bless me!" the crowd chanted, pressing against him.

He pushed through them trying to reach the exit, but there were too many of them and would not let him move.

"Paul!" the priest screamed. "Don't turn your back on the faithful! You are blessed of the Lord and you must share your blessing with the rest of us. You cannot deny us!"

"I'm telling you, I'm not holy!" Paul cried out, getting desperate. "I'm like you!"

Obviously a wrong thing to say.

"You must be blessed," Harold's mother shouted. "Only a blessed person can carry the Lord's light."

"It is not the Lord's light! It's my aura, which for some reason has become momentarily visible."

"Do not blaspheme in the Lord's house!" the priest screamed.

The press of people became unbearable and hands began to tear strips off his clothing. Alarmed, he tried to pull them off him. Suddenly, there were gasps of surprise and they fell back.

"He turned red," the little girl cried out and someone screamed.

"Lucifer's spawn!" a burly man snarled, his face contorted with holy rage.

Paul did not know him well, recognizing him as one of Harold's friends. Some friend he turned out to be.

A woman shrieked.

"You have deceived us!" the priest growled, his voice thick with menace. "Satan's flesh is finally revealed."

"This is stupid!" Paul shouted, panic growing within him. "I'm not holy, and I'm not evil. Simply afraid, and that's why my aura changed."

"You have reason to fear us, devil's child," the priest snarled and raised his arms high. "Thou shalt not let an abomination to live!"

Things were getting desperate and Paul saw a palpable change of mood in the faces around him. From awe and reverence, the faces were now hard and ugly with hate. He tried to push through them, wanting to get away.

Someone punched him in the back and he stumbled. Harold's friend, teeth bared, pushed him back and lashed out with his fist. Paul felt blood spurt from broken lips and nose and staggered, the pain bringing stinging tears to his eyes. Another punch and he fell to the tiled floor. They swarmed over him then, following through with a flurry of kicks to his body and head. He felt his ribs go and he screamed with pain.

"Stop this, you fools!" a woman screamed, the little girl beside her sobbing uncontrollably, but the gathering had turned into an ugly mob and they ignored her.

Several women gasped and his attackers fell back, suddenly looking uncertain. Bleeding, in agony, Paul saw his body enveloped in a white aura.

"This is the faith you practice?" he gasped, cradling his burning belly. "May God give all of you the justice you deserve."

Warm darkness cradled him in its embrace and the pain faded.

Shit, now he will never find out how that book ended.

The last thing he managed to see was his fading aura, revealing an ordinary man.

All my Sunsets

-1-

Andrew Payne was dead and knew it.

Pale sunshine dribbled feeble warmth into the hospital room as it streamed through white gauze curtains. A dark cloud drifted slowly across a dull sky and the sunshine faded, which pretty much summed up Andrew's condition and mood.

A drip tube inside his left elbow fed him a saline solution to keep him hydrated. Efficient nurses wearing starched white uniforms and mechanical smiles changed the bottle when the clear liquid ran down. Sensor pads taped to his body connected to a monitor next to his bed that traced wiggly lines across a green screen. Sometimes it made a soft beep, which he ignored. No one else paid it much attention, but it was procedure and gave the attending nurses something to cluck over.

Dr. Gail Dalton cleared her throat, clearly uncomfortable. Over the last eleven months, Andrew had come to know the formidable doctor well. Every time she cleared her throat, it bore bad news. He also learned that her stern exterior represented a protective façade against the pain and suffering of her patients. Her conservative gray business jacket and black trousers hid a caring person who learned early not to get emotionally involved. Andrew wasn't altogether certain the technique worked. It didn't work for him. Dying at twenty-four was a bummer any way he cut it.

She exhaled softly through her nose and clenched her jaw. For a fleeting moment, he was tempted to make this tough for her, but they were both past such foolishness.

"How long?" he asked softly, not expecting a revelation anyway.

He had known for a while his sands of time had almost run out for him. In a way, it would be a release from constant pain, being fussed over, unable to do anything except vegetate in bed…and think. That was perhaps the worst part, always thinking, reflecting on what might have been, knowing it would never be.

"Three weeks. Perhaps four. The pain will peak in about eight days, then fall off rapidly."

He smiled. "The old body deciding to settle its affairs?"

"We'll make you as comfortable as possible, Andrew," she said, her voice cold and clinical.

Don't get involved. He could almost picture her thoughts.

"It's okay, Dr. Dalton. I should have died a year ago, but you wouldn't let me." He raised a hand to forestall her protest. "Besides, it gave me time to study up. I came to know quite a bit about melanomas. Wish I paid more attention a while ago."

Like many other young men, he sought diverting outdoor outlets as a release for excess energy. During summer, surfing and kayaking were his favorite pastimes. He knew all about skin cancer and the need to apply protection, and he did use them—sometimes. Impressing girls with a well-built bronze body came first. At nineteen, melanoma was something someone else got.

When an irritating little black mole on his left forearm started to itch persistently, he had it checked. His local GP cut it out and sent it to a pathology lab. The test came back positive for a possible polypoid melanoma, which got Andrew somewhat negatively excited, but his doctor told him they got it early and he shouldn't worry too much about it. They put him on a regimen of medication and the wound left by the mole healed cleanly, leaving a faint pale scar. Life was bright for Andrew Payne and he jumped into it with relish. Sun, surf, and girls.

An honors degree in computer science majoring in virtual reality design and programming promised a fulfilling future. This was an industry to be in and he had ideas. At twenty-three, thinking about getting his own apartment in the city and leaving the stifling home atmosphere, freedom from authoritarian parents—that's how he looked at it—he noticed the scar on his arm had started to itch again and looked discolored. He had a challenging job he liked, a stunning girlfriend who thought he was the absolute best, and a place of his own that spared him the twice-daily commuting crush. He did not need an old nemesis rearing its head again to spoil things.

Polypoid melanomas are nasty, and grow quickly into the dermis and underlying tissue before a surface lesion becomes visible. A biopsy resulted in a speedy ambulance trip to the Peter MacCallum Cancer Center, part of the Royal Melbourne Hospital complex in Parkville, and his first encounter with the daunting Dr. Gail Dalton. Too bad she happened to be his doctor and much older. He would not have minded dating her at all.

"You have Stage III melanoma, Mr. Payne, and it has spread to the lymph nodes in your neck and under both arms."

Her cold announcement left him mentally floundering. This couldn't possible! He gaped at her, struggling to express his shock.

"But…I haven't felt anything! Apart from some itching on my arm, nothing."

"Chronic symptoms don't usually manifest themselves until the melanoma has matured and metastasized into the body. Your condition is serious, but treatable."

"You mean chemotherapy," he said glumly, not relishing the prospect of being bedridden, losing his fine crop of lustrous black hair, and suffering all the other associated unpleasantness.

"These days, we can tailor chemotherapy for your condition to minimize side effects, but there are other options. Latest techniques with radiation and immunotherapy have had encouraging results."

"What's the prognosis?"

She pursed her mouth. "Patients with similar symptoms

have a life expectancy of up to six years, but new treatments such as genotherapy are advancing and look promising."

Six years…if lucky. Dalton had just handed him a death sentence. No career, no girlfriend—what woman would want to saddle herself with a dead man—and his vision of a bright future in a black dumpster. It had not been a good day to get up.

Lying in the hospital bed, a drip in his arm, he stared at the somber doctor, grappling with the stark prognosis.

Four months later, despite treatment, tests confirmed the melanoma had spread into both lungs. Instead of six years, he now had six months at most.

Crap.

His parents took it hard, and his mother couldn't stop crying when they visited, which only served to irritate Andrew. He would die and that was it; no need to rub his nose in it every time she showed up. Belana smiled and tried to cheer him up, but his sister only eighteen, the prospect of death still alien to her. Adriana saw him twice, and both of them knew it was over. He told her bluntly to forget him, and meant it. She had a life and he wished her well. They had been building something that promised a future for both of them. Now, she was gone, and a life he hoped to have gone with her.

The sun broke through the clouds and sunlight again flooded the stark room. Dr. Dalton shifted in her chair.

"Yes, you have learned a lot, Andrew. You should have studied medicine." Her mouth twitched in a faint smile, which made her face look radiant.

"I *have* been studying medicine, and I came across something interesting."

"Oh?"

"Have you heard of Broca Genetics?"

Her eyebrows arched. "As a matter of fact, I have. A new startup in Silicon Valley. What about them?"

"They claim to have developed a radical genotherapy approach that produced a ninety-six percent remission rate in treatment of several cancer types, including melanoma."

"In rats and monkeys. The drug has never been tested on a human. It'll be years before they're in a position to begin clinical trials."

"I don't have years, Doctor. I want to try it. Even if the treatment fails, it will give Broca valuable data."

"I don't know if the hospital ethics committee—"

"I'll sign a liability waiver to protect you, the hospital, and Broca from any possible litigation. I've got nothing to lose."

"You could lose your four weeks."

Andrew snorted. "Wow, some risk when compared to the possibility of even partial remission? How about it?"

Her eyebrows came together and she frowned. "I'll make some calls." She stood, hesitated, patted his shoulder, and quickly walked out.

* * *

Dr. Dalton wiped his right bicep with a swab and slid in the thin needle. Andrew winced as the pale yellow liquid surged into his arm, wishing she could administer the drug through the drip. Something to do with the rate of absorption, she told him once. She slapped on a Band Aid and he rubbed the stinging spot.

"No change?" he asked hopefully.

"We're sending Broca blood samples taken four hours after every shot, but the tests so far proved negative. Your skin tone does show some improvement, but it's too early for any real change. We're laboring under a great handicap here. It took Broca four months of rigorous trials on monkeys to determine appropriate dosage and frequency. With you, we have no protocol to follow."

"Well, according to your prognosis, I have one week to go. Maybe two," he told her. "One thing, though. The pain seems to have disappeared almost entirely."

She raised her eyebrows. "Interesting. I will discontinue

pain treatment to determine if the relief you're getting is a side effect of the drug. Moreover, the painkillers could also be interfering with the treatment."

"All useful data for Broca. After all, their monkeys weren't able to tell them if they were experiencing a pain response or not."

Dr. Dalton picked up the tray with the syringe and swabs. "You now had four shots, but I want to start you on two a day with an increased dosage. You'll get the first one tomorrow morning. Have you had any other observable reactions?"

"Well, I'm hungry, and my joints aren't as stiff."

She frowned. "Mmm. Could be a psychosomatic reaction. I'll see if I can get you a Big Mac," she deadpanned.

He chuckled. "Deal!"

She paused at the door and nodded to him. "I'll see you tomorrow."

"Dr. Dalton, even if this doesn't work out, I want to thank you for looking after me."

"We haven't lost the battle yet, Andrew."

No, the battle wasn't lost, but he didn't fool himself. The Broca treatment still highly experimental, they only agreed to a trial because of his terminal condition. Like he told the doc—too bad he was laid up, she was awfully pretty—at least he was pain free, and he had forgotten how good that felt.

Grateful to have his laptop, otherwise he would have expired from sheer boredom. It enabled him to work on two virtual reality games he designed before being reduced to his present ignoble circumstances. No one would ever play them, but it kept his mind working. Having a room all to himself had its advantages not having to stare at other patients waiting to die. He glanced at his wristwatch: 9:15. His parents would be here shortly and his mom was likely to regale him with another sob session. He wondered if he could skip that part. If his three best friends came, that would definitely stop his mother's emotional outburst.

* * *

Two days of double shots did not produce any visible improvement, but still too early to tell. Dr. Dalton told him that Broca's analysis showed the drug was enabling his immune system to fight the melanoma nodules, and all of them were shrinking. Encouraging, because normally the body did not recognize cancer cells as pathogens. Regrettably, the rate was not fast enough to save him. He had gained an additional week of life at most. Basically, the treatment had started far too late.

Andrew had resigned himself to death months ago and had lost all fear of its looming shadow. There were lots of things he would never experience, but he'd had a rich life, and most of the memories were honorable. He did not dwell too long on the less savory bits. He figured life to be a stew. It needed salt and pepper, otherwise it was too bland. Unfortunately, his stew had soured somewhat. There were regrets, but he was at peace, not such a bad thing.

Last night, his favorite nurse gave him his double shot and tucked him in. Friendly and cute, but impersonal. Don't get involved was the philosophy of the day. As she adjusted his pillows, she patted his shoulder and confided that all the nurses in the ward were running a pool on how long he would last. She betted that he would pull through. Misguided perhaps, but it made him smile as he watched her undulate her form out the door. Another experience he would never have…

He woke chipper and hungry. Gladia, an older no-nonsense nurse, jabbed him impersonally, which made his shoulder ache. Before she could slap on a Band Aid, the fire alarm went off. She immediately rushed out, leaving the tray with the syringe and drug vial next to his bed. Andrew could not smell any smoke, so this had to be either a training session or a false alarm. When the excitement died down, his saucy little nurse came in carrying his breakfast tray.

"And how are you feeling this morning, Andrew?" she

chirped brightly as she studied his chart.

"Not bad actually. Hungry."

"That's good, and I see you haven't had your shot yet. Might as well get that out of the way before you have your breakfast." She glanced at the tray with the vial and syringe. "Who left that?"

"Gladia—"

She brightened. "Ah, the fire alarm. Something set it off and they're checking it out. She must have run off to her duty station before giving you the shot. I'll take care of it."

"But—"

"Just relax, Andrew."

About to tell her that Gladia had given him the shot, but for some reason he could not explain, he refrained. What would be the point anyway? He was ready to let it all go now.

She gave him the shot, marked the chart, and fluttered her fingers at him as she closed the door.

Before lunch, she came in and took a blood sample. Andrew had gotten tired of this routine and having an irritating catheter stuck permanently into his arm. Around two, he decided to doze off a little, feeling surprisingly good. His skin tone *had* improved, looking almost normal, and he was off painkillers. He felt restless with a desire to jump out of bed. It would be nice to stretch the old muscles, but he knew it was fantasy. His body looked totally wasted.

"Come and get me, you black buzzards," he muttered to himself, turned over and went back to sleep.

After the evening shot, another CT scan. At least they didn't jab him for that.

* * *

Three days later, Dr. Dalton walked in with a scowl on her face. Andrew hadn't had a shot that morning, which he figured wasn't good. Probably too far gone to bother. Well, it had to come.

She pulled back a visitor chair, sat down, and cleared her throat.

Here it comes, he thought.

"I have discontinued your treatment, Andrew."

"Yeah, I noticed. This is it, then. Right?"

A flicker of emotion crossed her face. "You misunderstand. The treatment was successful. You're in total remission."

He gawked at her, all sorts of incoherent images raced through his mind. He would actually live? After all the pain and misery, he was actually going to live?

"The cancer is gone?"

She smiled warmly at him. "Completely. We'll keep you here for another week or so until you regain some body mass, and then we'll start you on rehab. Your muscle tone is practically nonexistent." She glanced at his head. "By the way, your hair is growing back."

To hell with his hair! "How…"

She shook her head. "I'm hoping that Broca Genetics will tell us that."

"How long—"

"Will you live? No one can say. You experienced a particularly aggressive melanoma. Treatment has enabled your immune system to recognize the runaway mutation and fight it off, but there is no guarantee you developed total immunity. We'll be running ongoing tests on you for signs of any relapse, but right now all indicators point to an extended lifespan."

"Doc, even a month in the sun again will feel like a lifetime," he told her sincerely.

"I'm glad that you adopted such an outlook." She stood and patted down her skirt. "I'll see you tomorrow."

"Dr. Dalton?"

She paused at the door. "Yes?"

"About my treatment. Now that it seems I'll be alive for a while longer, I'm not sure if my insurance will cover all this, or the extended stay here."

"Oh that. Don't worry about it. Broca Genetics is footing the bill for everything. You don't know it, but you saved them millions in research costs."

He exhaled with relief. "Well, wasn't that nice of them."

-2-

Andrew Payne stepped out of the Royal Melbourne Hospital, paused, and looked up. Ragged gray clouds drifted from the west, but did not look threatening. Although late March, warm sunshine lit the stream of cars going both ways along the tree-lined Grattan Street. A tram clanked its bell as it approached the Elizabeth Street intersection. A faint breeze tugged at his hair. Melbourne's skyscrapers clawed into a washed-out sky. He took in the smells, sounds, and sights, and breathed deeply.

"Feels good, eh?" his father said gently, sympathetic to his son's emotions.

"I never expected to see all this again, Dad," Andrew told him, still gazing hungrily at everything around him. "I have stared at the naked face of death, and you know? It's not a terrifying face at all. At least it wasn't for me. The experience has rearranged my life's priorities and made me realize what is important and what isn't."

"You have changed, son. A lot. I guess matured is the word I'm looking for."

"Waiting for death tends to do that."

His father brushed his arm and pointed at the busy entrance area down the broad steps and pedestrians along the sidewalk. "The taxi rank is just around the corner. If you're not up for a walk, I'll have them bring the car here."

"I feel great, Dad. I really do."

Andrew *did* feel great. He filled out rapidly and the rehab program had firmed up his muscles and built stamina. He looked like he'd been lifting weights for months. His hair had grown back, as did the mischievous glint in his dark eyes. A scar on his right wrist was gone, and he had that since he was fourteen. He felt energy surging through his body, which made him want to prance and shout with joy. His mind seemed to be running like a dynamo, making him incredibly alert and acutely aware of everything going on around him. He had always considered himself smart, but this increase in mental capacity felt giddying, and made him feel there was nothing he could not do. Dr. Dalton and the nurses remarked more than once on his surprisingly rapid recovery. Three weeks after she told him he was in remission, they let him go. He should refrain from strenuous activity for a while, but the way he felt, he felt ready to do a marathon.

He simply felt so…alive!

The drive to his parents' spacious North Melbourne house took less than ten minutes. It had been one of Dad's smarter investments after the 2008 Global Financial Crisis. It also made getting into the city relatively less traumatic, with a tram stop a five-minute walk down the street.

He really wanted to be alone in his apartment and savor his reprieve, but his family would never forgive him if he shut them out now. Anyway, it was only dinner, and Dad insisted he spend the night. Plenty of time to reenter his life in the morning. Perhaps he was right. A get-together with his friends might also be in order.

Call Adriana? It wouldn't do any harm.

* * *

"There it is, Mr. Payne. Ready for your signature," Keith Sloan said. "Corporate in Los Angeles baulked at the price, but after they saw your prototypes, they were convinced."

Andrew smiled at the FutureTech Australian division general manager, and took the proffered contracts. He dashed off his signature in all the places marked by protruding yellow stickers and slipped one copy into his slim briefcase. It took three weeks of hardnosed bargaining by his lawyer to get to this point.

FutureTech wanted to buy his two games outright, naturally enough, but Andrew insisted on a settlement, plus a five percent royalty for every game sold. He started off with a demand for twelve, but that had been a simple opening gambit. FutureTech had gone as far as three percent, but when Andrew made it clear he was prepared to walk away—there were other VR gaming companies out there who would jump at what he had and FutureTech knew it—they folded. His approach to rendering 3D sets was unique and far cheaper to apply than anything else he had seen in the industry. Besides, he had ideas for more games, a hook that also got him a job with FutureTech. He would not be giving them new games just for his salary. That was a mug's play. He would use the company's resources and developers, but he would own the IP and sell them the games on a sales share basis. With the VR industry set to explode, his rendering algorithm plugins were set to make FutureTech millions.

He had netted US$180K for each game, and a $165K job. Admittedly in Aussie dollars, but Andrew did not mind. When the games started selling, he expected to be hip deep in cash. Perhaps he should check himself into hospital again and dream up a few more games, he mused wryly.

"Thanks, Keith. I look forward to a profitable relationship with FutureTech,"

Sloan stood and offered his hand. "Welcome aboard."

"I'll see you first thing tomorrow," Andrew said as they shook hands.

"Your office is ready and fully equipped. I expect both your games to be fully beta tested for the June 1 release. We don't want to miss that as we've already started the promotional campaign."

"They will be, and you have given me three of your best developers. With your facilities, it won't take long to work out the remaining bugs."

"Good! Tomorrow, then."

Andrew strode out of the Eureka Tower and pumped his

right fist.

"Yes!"

It must have cost FutureTech a small fortune to lease an entire floor at such a prestigious location, but the company was already on the Fortune 500 list, and all market indicators showed they were set to carve up the VR entertainment industry. What they needed, Andrew told Sloan, was branch into education, government, and defense applications. They toyed with the idea already, he was told, but for the time being, the entertainment market would remain their primary focus and revenue earner. Andrew did not push it. Perhaps a practical demonstration of a flight simulator prototype he'd been working on would change their mind, but he was a new resource and needed to establish his credentials first. No hurry.

Another change he noticed about himself since leaving the hospital. He felt driven by ideas and things he wanted to do, but somewhere in the cancer ward, he had lost his impatience with fools and entrenched bureaucracy. There was always a workaround, no need to get upset and rile the stomach. Make the other guy upset.

He dropped off the contract with Tompson, Tompson, and Parker, a prestigious Collins Street firm, and took a cab to the hospital. His appointment with Dr. Dalton originally scheduled for Friday, he did not want to start his new job by skipping a day. Besides, how long does it take to have a blood sample taken?

The cab pulled in at the Grattan Street entrance and he ambled up the broad steps into a hushed foyer. There were enough patients and visitors coming and going that he had to wait for an elevator.

Dr. Dalton's stern secretary cracked half a smile at him and ushered him into the inner office. The doctor's frown made him wonder if he was about to get some bad news. When she cleared her throat, he became worried.

"Good to see you again, Andrew. Please sit down. There is something I need to discuss with you before we take your blood sample."

He made himself comfortable and waited. She folded her hands on the desk and studied him.

"Okay, Doc. I can take it."

Her mouth twitched. "There is no need to be alarmed. You are quite healthy. In fact, you're remarkably healthy for someone who survived a Stage III, N3 polypoid melanoma."

"I'm relieved to hear that. And I *feel* healthy," he told her.

"Yes, I can see."

"So, if I'm not having a relapse, what is it, then?"

"Your case is unique and has the researches at Broca Genetics scratching their heads. The genotherapy drug they developed for you from their baseline formula has not only cured you, it has done a lot more. The problem is, they have not been able to replicate the result with any of their test subjects."

"Human subjects?"

"They were all terminal cases with advanced types of cancer. Broca managed to cure them and all are expected to live out a normal lifespan."

Andrew frowned. "Wasn't the whole objective of their program to provide a cure? Why is that suddenly a problem?"

"How much do you know about telomeres?"

"With tubes and stuff stuck into me when I was here, I had a chance to bone up. Basically, each chromosome is capped by a loop of repeating nucleotide sequences. During every cell division, one of the telomere sequences is truncated. When enough of them are removed, the cell blocks further division, which induces aging and eventual cell death."

Dr. Dalton nodded. "Somewhat simplistic, but accurate enough. It will help you understand what I'm about to say. There has been a lot of research into techniques to repair telomeres and restore the loops to their original length. In experimental animals, this has extended life and overcome several types of cancers. However, cell division is not a perfect process, and repetition results in cumulative errors. When the telomere loop reaches a certain length, the cell produces a toxin that stops further division. It's a vital mechanism that prevents the spread of cells with damaged DNA, which in essence is cancer. In humans, when a cell dies, the body does not eliminate it, the process manifesting itself as aging. However, in some organisms such as sponges, corals, and lobsters, senescent cells undergo conversion to an imunogenetic phenotype that enables the immune system to eliminate them and prevents the onset of aging. This process also slows down the epigenetic clock, but doesn't rest it. Otherwise we would have organisms that were effectively immortal."

It took a few moments for Andrew to digest this, but her words nevertheless left him confused.

"Are you saying that Broca's treatment has enabled my immune system to eliminate cells that have stopped dividing, and that's what's keeping me healthy?"

"Correct, but it has done more than that. It has reset your epigenetic clock."

Andrew stared at her. "Which means…"

"Your body is effectively living in year one."

He stared at her, then exhaled loudly. "Wow."

Year one…it is like the first twenty-four years never happened. He could easily live to a hundred! The things he could do…

"Aging is a very complex process and poorly understood," she said. "Because your body can eliminate senescent cells does not imply that you will not age. It simply means you were given an extended lifespan."

"Well, that can't be all bad, can it? So, what's Broca's problem?"

"With the patients they trialed, the treatment enabled their bodies to eliminate dead cells, but it had not slowed down or reset their epigenetic clock. They were cured, but left with a normal lifespan. Broca doesn't understand how their treatment produced your condition. In your case, numerous factors undoubtedly influenced the eventual outcome. Dosage, frequency, the condition of your immune system…many contributing factors. I'm not surprised they're having difficulties."

Andrew found himself in a moral loop. Should he tell her about the double dosage he got one morning? Even if he did, what good would it do? It would not change his personal condition, and he doubted the result could be replicated with any other patient. He decided to let it ride.

"You told me the good news, Doctor. What's the bad?"

"Broca has invited you to attend their Silicon Valley facility for six months of intensive testing and observation. You'll be given substantial compensation for your cooperation, with all expenses included."

He goggled at her, then grinned broadly. "A charming idea, Doc, but I'm not interested. I am starting a new job tomorrow, something I hope will keep me occupied for years. If Broca want samples of my blood and tissue, I'm happy to give it to them, but I am not prepared to turn myself into one of their caged test animals. I figure I have made my contribution to science. Besides, they got what they wanted, didn't they? Successful treatment of cancer."

"I expected this, Mr. Payne, and I understand your position. The Cancer Center has an extensive genetics lab. I suppose a joint research project with Broca could be done here, provided you're willing to make yourself available from time to time."

"Happy to bleed for the cause, Doctor."

She stood and offered her hand. "Thank you for coming in, Andrew, and I am pleased to see you looking so well. You were my star patient."

He took her small hand and smiled. She really was striking, but it could never be.

"You gave me a second chance. Few people get that, and I will try not to waste mine."

Adriana's fingernails marched playfully across his chest, her bold brown eyes twinkling with amusement. Her head cradled in the crook of his arm, Andrew gently stroked her smooth side, marveling at the delicate texture of her skin. The light curtains stirred when a soft puff of wind drifted into the bedroom. Nothing moved outside and the city held its breath.

"My hunk," she murmured pensively. "I always wanted a he-man all to myself, and now I got one."

He brushed a finger across her cheek and pushed back a strand of short black hair.

"And you were my dream," he told her softly, and she smiled. Then the smile faded.

"Since that crazy day when we first met at the Anglesea beach, I never wanted you to change—except for that horrid melanoma—and you haven't. Not one gray hair."

"I'm only thirty-two, love. It's a bit early for gray hairs, don't you think? A stressful marriage notwithstanding."

She fisted him in the stomach and he grunted.

"Stressful?"

He kissed the tip of her nose. "I wouldn't change a day."

"Seriously, Andrew. You haven't changed at all. You eat what you want and it doesn't stick. I only have to look at a lasagna to gain a kilo."

He admitted she was no longer the striking slim beauty he waylaid at the beach, but still gorgeous, if somewhat softer. Not overweight at all, just…womanly.

"You're still a heartbreaker and you know it. Why do you think my best friend is trying to woo you away from me?"

She gave a merry giggle. "He's only flirting." Her fingers marched across his chest. "Andrew? What if you never get old?"

Funny, that is exactly what he asked Dr. Dalton yesterday.

The stern geneticist had mellowed somewhat over the years, put on some weight, and time had left its mark on her face.

"It's your epigenetic clock, Andrew. As far as it is concerned, you're only eight years old. You won't show any appreciable physiological change for another fifteen years or so."

"That's what Broca said. I know DNA methylation is supposed to prevent gene expression. With age, methylation is altered and the rate of gene expression changes, which you can measure as a rate of aging. You told me that in my case, they have not observed any change. In effect, I'm not aging."

She frowned. "You *have* been paying attention."

"I had a lot of time in which to bone up."

"Clearly, but the epigenetic clock is still not fully understood. Nevertheless, you do appear surprisingly youthful."

Surprisingly youthful…and that was Adriana's apparent problem. He hoped this would not come between them, then shook his head.

"What are you thinking?" Adriana asked dreamily.

"It's Saturday and we don't have to go to work."

She giggled. "And I have a whole day to explore my he-man," she murmured and her hand slid lower down his stomach.

During breakfast—a very late breakfast—Andrew mulled over the conversation with Dr. Dalton. Since his incredible recovery, his mind and body were functioning flawlessly. He healed quickly, enjoyed good physical strength and stamina for someone supposedly thirty-two, and felt mentally sharp and alert. The norm for any thirty-something. No? The lovely doctor made too much out of nothing, as were Broca Genetics. They achieved a breakthrough that netted them hundreds of millions in annual sales, with a few dollars for himself with the investment he made in the listed company. Not satisfied with success, they wanted to create immortals?

Crap.

Andrew enjoyed the achievements he made. He had an adoring wife, two wonderful kids—Anita already six and Kevin five. Where the hell did the years go? His work with FutureTech had blossomed, and the investments and share options had made him moderately wealthy. Close to six million, according to Tompson, Tompson, and Parker. He was on a roll.

His epigenetic clock be damned.

* * *

"Ah, Mr. Payne. Thanks for seeing me," Vincent Price gushed, and swept a hand at a visitor chair. "Take a seat."

Andrew eased himself into the expensive leather chair and crossed his legs. The new Australian division general manager—Keith Sloan left three years ago to take up a post as the global distribution vice president—liked to project an effusive, easygoing image. He *was* easygoing, but under the polished smile lay a razor mind and a ruthless personality, as more than one luckless employee found to their cost. Despite an occasional clash of wills, he and Andrew got along because Andrew made the company money. Lots of money.

"The Flight Simulator range of games are doing well," Price said. "So well that Boeing, Airbus, and McDonnell Douglas have expressed interest to incorporate the software into their training simulators. FutureTech has never interfaced any of its products with hardware platforms at a level demanded by something as complex as a flight trainer, but the advanced rendering modules you developed under my predecessor's direction—"

Andrew suppressed a smile. Sloan's direction? Balls. Andrew had a knockdown fight with the former general manager after showing him a prototype flight trainer for a Boeing 787 Dreamliner, urging FutureTech to expand into the civilian and military markets. It would cost a truckload of money to develop responsive human interfaces for every major aircraft type, Sloan claimed, something Andrew dismissed out of hand. Think outside the box, he told his old boss. The Virtual Reality industry had advanced to a point where an expensive hardware simulator had become an anachronism. Why sink tens of millions into a mechanical flight trainer that needed new versions and constant updating to accommodate emerging airframes, when a far cheaper and flexible option existed in a totally VR product. Instrument panels, controls, and responses could be programmed quickly to replicate a real aircraft cockpit.

"—convinced FutureTech corporate that we can pitch to the industry a fully integrated VR flight simulator. The idea is not entirely new, one never seriously entertained by the industry because of their wedded belief that pilot training can only be done using a genuine cockpit replica. Your demonstration to Boeing last week has changed that mindset."

"I'm glad to hear it, Vincent," Andrew said soberly.

He had worked on and off for almost two years to perfect a workable prototype, much of the time spent in his own software lab at home. Sloan did not begrudge him the use of company resources, knowing Andrew always produced.

When Vincent Price took over, those resources were withdrawn. They paid Andrew to develop VR games, not dictate corporate policy. Despite his undeniable business acumen, the man simply could not visualize the potential of Andrew's work. If he did, he considered the project far too costly to show an immediate return. Andrew did not mind the setback. His simulator was almost done anyway. The game versions were rolling out and earning money. When the industry version was ready, Andrew sent a copy directly to Keith Sloan, confident that his friend would be receptive. Last week, Sloan had flown down to Melbourne with a Boeing executive from Seattle for a demonstration. Price had not liked being bypassed, but was too shrewd an office politician to take it personally. Andrew Payne was one of FutureTech's golden geese, and you don't serve one of them for dinner.

"You have no immediate projects, Andrew, and if your flight simulator program takes off," Price gave a wry smile, "you will be heavily involved with its development. Potentially, the entire aviation industry could be a market. There are literally hundreds of aircraft models out there, from traditional propeller jobs to jets, and each pilot needs to be trained to fly one. If Boeing comes on board, FutureTech will create a new division to service the market. The division will need someone to run it and develop the VR software. corporate asked me to offer you a proposal."

Price raised a hand. "We're not offering you a VP position to run the division. Your management credentials are beyond reproach, but at this stage of your career, you don't have the required corporate outlook. You are a visionary and a damn good designer, and that's what makes FutureTech money. Managers like me are there to make sure the corporate wheels keep turning, and see that people like you keep producing. What we want to offer you, Andrew, is a position of senior development manager, which off course, will entail a substantial salary increase and bonuses. I have not supported your flight simulator program, but you had confidence in your product and courage to push it to Mr. Sloan. That perseverance is appreciated, and I can admit when I'm wrong."

Andrew had gotten the gist of Price's proposal before the man stopped talking. The news wasn't altogether a revelation, having had a heads-up from Sloan.

"I'll take it, Vincent," he said simply.

The senior exec raised his eyebrows. "Well, you didn't need much convincing."

"It's my project, and I can understand why FutureTech would want me to continue being involved."

"Yes, I see," Price mused. "However, this position will require renegotiation of your terms of employment. I'm aware of your current contract. Of all your contracts. However, the industrial application of the flight simulator is not covered by that agreement. It isn't a game. FutureTech is prepared to give you a substantial once-off bonus for its development, but the company will own all the IP and sales proceeds."

Andrew grinned. The initial contract he entered into with Sloan covered this possibility. When he signed the agreement, he was a nobody at FutureTech, and Sloan allowed him a degree of freedom with the wording. No one anticipated how profitable the relationship turned out for both. FutureTech legal made two attempts to remove the IP ownership and sales share clauses, but Andrew did not budge. Short of firing him, he had them locked in and they knew it. A polite letter from Tompson, Tompson, and Parker on both occasions put a lid on corporate legal.

"Vincent, let's stop this here and now, okay? Under my contract, I retain IP and I get a royalty of five percent for every unit sold. The contract specifically states, and I quote, *This agreement shall apply to any Virtual Reality (VR) software acquired by the first party, namely FutureTech Corporation, from the designer and developer, the second party, namely Andrew Payne, and any adaptation of the said software for, but not limited to, entertainment, government, education, medical, and other industrial applications.'* I would say that my flight simulator qualifies as an industrial application, wouldn't you? I suggest you refer to corporate legal attempts to delete that part of my contract and the outcomes."

Vincent Price scowled. "There is no possibility to negotiate?"

Andrew shrugged. "Why should I negotiate? Five percent of every game sold is a gimme even when you sell a few million units. Games have a limited shelf life. You have to roll out new products all the time or get left behind. I am sure this has not escaped you, Vincent, but some of the best VR games Future-Tech produced were my designs, and most of them are still selling well.

"However, I appreciate that the cost of a Boeing 787 VR flight simulator won't be selling for fifteen dollars. Five percent becomes a substantial amount, but as you pointed out, you have a growing market that will need hundreds and hundreds of simulators. FutureTech will be making billions. I don't believe that asking five percent for every unit sold is excessive. Besides, I have ideas for other industrial VR applications. Now, if FutureTech is not interested…"

Vincent glared at him and pursed his lips.

Andrew was prepared to walk and Price knew it. Future-Tech did not even have a valid claim to recoup any of the development costs, considering it a future investment freely made without any liability to him. If they wanted the simulator, they would have to buy it like any of his games, and agree to a five percent royalty.

"What you have now, Andrew, is one VR simulator for the Boeing 787 Dreamliner. You don't expect us to buy simulator software from you for every aircraft type?"

Andrew laughed. "Hardly. I recognize the investment FutureTech will have to make to develop variants. I'm prepared to make a once-off settlement…two hundred million."

Price goggled. "You can't be serious!"

"Work the numbers, Vincent." Andrew said, and watched the flow of emotions race across Price's face.

There were hundreds of major airlines in the world, and thousands of little operators, and most of them needed training simulators. The cost of a Piper Cherokee simulator could not be compared to a Boeing 787 program, but the marketplace had the potential for thousands of unit sales of all types. When military options were included, two hundred million was a giveaway.

The general manager sighed, shook his head, and leaned back against his seat.

"And the five percent?"

"That stands."

"I'll have to run this past corporate, you know."

"Of course."

-4-

Life should have been sweet for Andrew Payne. FutureTech's VP for strategic development, a net worth of over four-and-a-half billion, challenging the virtual reality industry, Anita and Kevin mostly happy teenagers—teenagers are never entirely happy—a long life ahead of him, he should be laughing every time he sprang out of bed. Not bad for someone who turned forty-one. So, what was the problem?

It is not as though Andrew had not seen it coming.

Anita had grown into a striking beauty with no shortage of boys sniffing around her, especially when they learned she had a rich dad. Too early for Kevin to get serious about girls, but having everything he desired nevertheless created an occasional clash of wills with his old man. A sober talk usually straightened him out…and one sharp lesson before Kevin got the point.

"If you don't like how you mother and I are treating you, feel free to leave and find out for yourself what life is like out there," Andrew told him once, perfectly calm. "No cellphone; I'm paying for that. No credit cards; I'm paying for them as well. A suitcase and whatever cash you managed to save."

Kevin stormed out with only a backpack. Four days later, he came back a changed boy, although somewhat ragged around the edges, literally. Andrew never mentioned the incident again. However, teenagers being teenagers, he anticipated more sober talks ahead.

Adriana…that problem did not go away and had gotten worse. A chasm had grown between them, and it was easy to identify the cause—his apparent youth. Showing the inevitable small signs of age, she could not help noticing that he still looked like a twenty-four-year-old. Because this was deep seated, emotional resentment not subject to logical reasoning, made it more difficult to treat. If she would only consent to counseling, but the stubborn woman refused and fumed inwardly. Andrew did not know what to do, except keep loving her. What nagged him, did she still love him?

It appeared that sometimes even love wasn't enough.

The old saw about a fly in the soup that spoiled things almost never true, but in his case, the fly was a bumblebee. A fat black thing called age.

And there wasn't a thing Andrew could do about it.

He paused in front of the Royal Melbourne Hospital entrance, looked up at the imposing glass façade, and sighed. He didn't know why he bothered coming. Nobody could tell him anything new. A tram clanged its bell and the sounds of traffic were loud in his ears. Everything was either too noisy, too smelly, too crowded, too full of crap. And he was being morose. He slowly walked up the wide steps, another piece of life's flotsam drifting with the tide.

"Your telomere loop gets shorter every time a cell divides, as it should," Dr. Dalton explained, "and after about fifty divisions, the cell stops dividing. What is happening with you, these cells are converted to an imunogenetic phenotype that enables the immune system to expel them. This change in your physiology explains your remarkable health, but not your apparent age."

"You're not telling me anything new, Doc."

"I reminder," she said wearing a faint smile. "There is only one explanation for the observed tests conducted by Broca Genetics and my team, and is something you already know."

"My epigenetic click," Andrew murmured.

"That's right. Your epigenetic clock has not only been reset, but appears to be frozen, or is operating at a greatly reduced rate. However, our tests have not shown any measurable rate change."

Dr. Dalton looked her age—mature and dignified. Still stern and formidable, they have come to know each other somewhat well over the years. He was her star patient, and a doorway to a possible Nobel Prize. Right now, Andrew did not care if she received a raft of Nobel Prizes.

"Does this mean I am immortal?" Andrew ventured sarcastically.

"I wouldn't go that far, but barring a terminal accident, your body's recuperative powers should keep you alive for a very long time. How long that might be, no one can say. We simply don't have any comparable data."

"Well, I can always step in front of a bus if I get weary of life," he quipped, tired being a study specimen. Tired of being prodded and poked and jabbed. Tired of everything.

Dr. Dalton frowned. "I wouldn't treat this phenomena so flippantly, Mr. Payne."

"You don't have my condition, Doctor."

"That might be true, but your condition has greatly advanced our understanding of the aging process. One day perhaps, we may be able to duplicate it."

"I hope not. There is a very good biological reason why we age, not to mention a social one. Something you understand very well. I shudder to think what might happen if everyone can walk into a drugstore and get himself an immortality pill. Or the treatment is confined to the wealthy and the powerful."

"You're right, of course."

"Broca and their backers might be frustrated that they haven't managed to develop such a pill, but they have produced cures for many genetic disorders. Not a bad day's effort, I would say." He sat back and exhaled softly. "What now, Dr. Dalton?"

"We'll continue the monitoring program for as long as you are willing to donate your blood and tissue samples."

"Not a problem, provided you and Broca don't breach the disclosure agreement, which their article in the latest issue of *Nature* came awfully close to doing."

"They were warned. It won't happen again."

"See that it doesn't, or my cooperation ends, followed by some very unpleasant legal action. Not to mention cancellation of my annual endowment to the Cancer Center."

Dr. Dalton blinked. "For which we're grateful, Andrew. However, you must realize that your condition cannot remain concealed forever."

He stood and laughed. "True. My position with Future-Tech has already become uncomfortable. Some of their New York execs are finding it difficult to believe that someone who looks like a twenty-four-year-old kid is in fact forty-one. I tried plastic surgery to age me—"

"I know."

"—but within six weeks, I was back to—" He chuckled. "—normal. My body likes the way I look."

"Unfortunately, that problem will only get worse."

Andrew snorted and stood. "I'll see you in three months, Doc."

He did not get an opportunity to resolve his problem with Adriana, because on Saturday, she was gone, as were his children. They had not done anything as a family for a while, and he thought it might be fun to spend a day together, drive along the Great Ocean Road and see the Twelve Apostles. Actually, there were only eight. Constant battering by waves that came unimpeded all the way from Antarctica reduced one of the nine majestic rock formations to rubble. Still, they were an awesome sight.

On the way, they stopped for coffee and cakes, and Kevin and Anita even braved the cold ocean water. It made Andrew shiver looking at them frolicking in the surf. Not initially keen to tag along with their parents on what they figured to be a long, boring trip, both reluctantly admitted they were having fun.

That's when it happened.

A pickup took a blind corner on the wrong side of the road and clipped Andrew's car, sending it down a nine meter cliff onto the rocks below. His car was equipped with a level 3 autonomous driving system, but the narrow road gave the computer nowhere to go.

He saw the pickup, heard the squeal of brakes, and threw himself against Adriana. He felt the sickening crunch and the safety airbags popped. Sharp pain shot through his right shoulder and arm and he heard Anita scream before darkness descended.

Crap.

When he woke, he could tell he was in a hospital room because of the faint antiseptic and medicine cabinet odor. A flat monitor beside him traced wiggly lines. In the restful silence, the sun hovered above the city's skyscrapers, bloated and red. A gentle breeze shifted the curtains. It felt good lying there, thinking about nothing in particular.

Reality crashed into him and he felt his face drain.

"Adriana!"

He sat up and winced at the stab of pain in his shoulder. The monitor started beeping sharply. His right forearm lay in a cast, but didn't hurt. An attractive brunette nurse opened the door, glanced at the monitor, and hurried to his side.

"You shouldn't be exerting yourself, Mr. Payne," she admonished him in a stern voice and pushed him back against the pillows.

"Where is my wife?"

"You lie there and I'll get the doctor."

It all came rushing back, none of it pleasant.

A young man walked in dressed in a conservative dark gray suit. He pulled back a visitor chair and sat down.

"I am glad to see you awake, Mr. Payne. You were lucky to walk away with a simple arm fracture and a broken collarbone. You have some contusions and lacerations, but nothing serious."

"Where is my wife?"

The doctor—at least Andrew took him for a doctor—pursed his lips and exhaled slowly, not looking very comfortable.

"I'm sorry to have to tell you this, but your wife didn't make it. Your car landed on its roof against a large boulder that crushed the passenger side and most of the rear section."

"Kevin...Anita..."

The doctor nodded. "Your son and daughter died on the way to the Geelong University Hospital."

Andrew stared at the man trying to process everything. Adriana gone...his children gone...why couldn't it have been him instead? They had everything to live for and he'd had his life.

Something tore deep inside him and he moaned at the cutting pain that gripped his chest in a vice. After a few seconds, it receded to a dull throb. He felt his eyes sting and blinked rapidly.

"The other driver…" he croaked.

"Not hurt. The police charged him with numerous offences, although that's not much consolation to you."

Numerous offences…Andrew felt like laughing.

He had a lot to laugh about. The fates have just played one of their better practical jokes on him.

* * *

Andrew Payne leaned against the steel railing and gazed at the rolling valley below his Mt. Macedon house. The redolent smell of towering eucalyptus made him breathe in deeply and exhale with satisfaction. Warm afternoon sunshine against a deep blue sky brought colors into sharp focus. Two magpies patrolled the backyard, pecking at the grass in search of snacks. Nothing moved, and deep silence pervaded his little kingdom. He lifted his tumbler of bourbon and nodded to the gods.

He found life good at fifty-three, and not a gray hair in sight. His body bloomed with health and he woke every morning filled with energy. These days, he spent some of his surplus enthusiasm at a local golf course. About six years ago, one of his friends introduced him to the game, and Andrew became hooked. He initially found golf to be an intensely frustrating and irritating game when the little white sucker ended among the trees instead of the fairway, or went curving into the brush from a wayward tee shot. He now had the basics right and actually enjoyed the game. The browsing kangaroos no longer laughed at his amateurish efforts, standing tall as he pushed his little buggy past them, watching him solemnly before returning to their feeding. He did not play with his friend anymore, and rarely saw the three of them. They were all married with families to worry about, and work kept them busy. Once or twice a year, they would get together for a stag dinner and chew over the good old days. When Andrew saw them, saw what time did to them while he remained young, made him uncomfortable and depressed. They envied and resented him, hiding it behind cutting humor.

The years marched for everybody, but not for him.

Four years ago, he quit FutureTech, bought a hectare of land in Mt. Macedon and built a modern open plan house. It looked rustic from the outside and blended nicely into the surrounding forest, but the interior had every convenience a nine billion-dollar fortune could provide. His neighbors were friendly and did not intrude, and he didn't bother them. He drove a modest Tesla Cobra fully autonomous electric, having no desire for something flashy to show off. Although rich, he lived a simple lifestyle and did his own cooking, cleaning, and yard maintenance. Not a burden for his twenty-four-year-old body.

His parents were retired and lived very comfortably, enjoying many of the things they were unable to do before, thanks to his support. The least he could do for them. Losing Adriana and the kids had hit him hard, and it took a better part of a year before the pain receded to a dull throb. He never wanted to put himself through that again, and did not seek another companion. He missed her, missed the quiet talks they used to have, sometimes in the night's early hours, being together and doing things together. She left a hole in him he was still to fill. One day perhaps, someone else would walk into his life and make him complete.

He liked it here, but in another ten years or so when the locals started to gossip about his youthful looks, wondering if he was 'The Forever Man', as the tabloids and 3D Wall news clips labeled him six years ago, he would need to move. A seaside place next time? No hurry. Right now, though, he had time to savor life and watch the world change around him. And it had changed, a lot.

Skycars buzzed everywhere like flies, autonomous cars, trucks, buses, trains—everything automated. They made travel infinitely safer, but many diehards clung to their diesel and petrol relics and drove them, but they were a dying breed. Social pressure and government regulations made it tough for them, seen as unacceptable risks. Houses and buildings in general these days had become their own power generators when solar paints emerged, to the intense annoyance of the utilities. Those companies had dug their own grave pursuing rapacious pricing policies. Cinemas had all but disappeared, as everyone could hook into old movies and new releases through their home 3D virtual reality Wall.

Personal communication had also changed drastically. Hardly anyone carried a smartphone or tablet anymore. Equipped with an implanted Personal Communication Module, PCM, hooked into a world-wide comms and cloud data network, everything and everyone within instant reach with a simple mental command. Andrew had to fight stubborn FutureTech execs before they became convinced that partnering with Google and Microsoft to develop a PCM interface was the place to be. Intel was much easier to bring on board. They saw billions flowing into the company as demand for personal chips flowered. It took a while for the emerging technology to work out all the bugs, and even longer for governments to evaluate the social impact and enact privacy and security legislation. Many people frowned at what they saw Big Brother intrusion into their minds, but the young embraced it enthusiastically. As with everything, there was potential for abuse, but something the society would simply have to deal with. At two years, they allowed a child to have a PCM implant, and the real and virtual worlds were at its feet forever.

The Moon was occupied by the major powers, as was Mars, and several private ventures such as SpaceX and Blue Origin had begun asteroid mining. Electrogravitic ships had opened the Solar System, which should keep mankind busy for a long time to come. Andrew had invested heavily in both companies, and the investments had started to pay off handsomely. Although fascinated by space travel—he wanted badly to visit the Moon—he would wait a few years. He could afford to take the trip now, but the bases were still primitive, rough affairs, not really cut out for tourism. He hoped SpaceX would approve his concept plan for a chain of Moon hotels. A billion dollars from him gave them an added incentive. They were progressive and innovating, and clearly appreciated the potential of having an average family able to afford a Moon trip as their next vacation. It would take a few years to realize, but he was in no hurry.

In his lab, supported by one of the new generation quantum computers, Andrew hooked himself into his latest simulation prototype, a sensory interface. When PCMs first came out, they were in direct competition with smartphones and tablets. Although far more convenient to use, PCMs lacked one essential capability the other devices provided—recording visual images and audio. His latest project helped FutureTech develop an interface software plugin to enable a PCM to capture all sensory inputs—visual, auditory, olfactory, everything—and store it in the data cloud. He hoped to one day enable the capture of emotional responses, the ultimate interface, but the brain was a tricky and complex piece of organic hardware, and its workings not easily cracked. These days, he worked for FutureTech as a strategic consultant, passing them an occasional idea. He no longer had to work for a living in the traditional sense, and didn't.

He went back to university and picked up PhDs in advanced network computing and genetics. Broca Genetics had done terrific work in its field, but their research was results oriented. Their business model demanded producing marketable products. Nothing wrong with that, but it meant they shied away from spending huge sums of money on pure research. They were a business, not a university. Andrew had the money and convinced Broca to form a research division to study the more than 1300 human DNA gene switches, the microRNAs, and in particular, the switches that govern when the microRNAs are themselves turned on and off. Learning how to manipulate gene switches would have enormous implications with the potential to eliminate every disease and make humans immune to infection. If viable products were to come out of that research, Andrew ensured he would have a cut of the proceeds.

It really was not about money at all, although nice to have, but the power what money could do. He had lots of ideas how to make his money work for him.

He did not fancy going to Silicon Valley where Broca set up their new division, but with instantaneous communication and his home lab, there was no need to go anywhere. Broca still wanted to know how his epigenetic clock became frozen, so did he, but for a different reason. His interest lay in pure scientific curiosity, while Broca saw dollars in it for them. They still wanted that immortality pill.

Andrew figured his research into a sensory plugin and immortality should keep him profitably amused for a year or so.

-5-

A penthouse apartment in one of the new Southbank towers gave Andrew Payne a grand vista of Melbourne wherever he looked. He had the top floor all to himself. The floor below him served as his research lab. The four floors below that contained offices for staff who managed his various enterprises. He found it easy to live in a penthouse rent free if one owned the building, which he did. He never intended going into real estate, but a minor housing bubble collapse eight years ago offered an opportunity to buy a building in South Melbourne, and to his surprise, he found he liked living in the center of the city, these days much more habitable with the elimination of all smog. He originally paid an agent to manage it, then bought the agency when he found they were fleecing him. The first and only time he allowed a third party to run something for him, the exception being Tompson, Tompson, and Parker. The original lawyers were either all retired or dead, but the old firm had held onto its unshakeable integrity and scrupulous business practices, and Andrew happened to be one of their very important clients.

He broke the comms link with the Moon Stardust Resort manager and rubbed his eyes. The lunar tourist business had taken off big, just as Andrew knew it would, and gravitic ships were able to reach the Moon in two hours, and Mars in four days. Stellar Corporation, a merger between SpaceX and Blue Origin, manufactured a line of passenger ships, including asteroid miners. They were not the only player in the field, nor the largest, but Stellar made sound, reliable ships, and never pushed them beyond their rated operating life. Asteroid mining was a four trillion dollar a year industry, delivering everything from complex hydrocarbons, ice, almost pure metals, including gold. Stellar dabbled in this, but they were a market leader in providing energy for the power hungry Earth. Why risk building polluting fossil power plants and dangerous nuclear stations, when virtual seas of liquid methane and ethane could be harvested from Titan. It took over two months for a tanker barge to reach Saturn, but each tanker had a capacity of a million cubic meters, which made the trip worth the investment. They did not ship the liquid gas directly to Earth, but used it to power enormous orbital plants that beamed microwaves to ground station receivers.

It happened to be one of Andrew's more profitable investments.

His latest project was to tap into the limitless lines of current that streamed between Jupiter and its moons, then beam the energy to enormous collectors in the L4 and L5 Lagrange points. There was unavoidable loss as the microwave stream attenuated with distance, but the current never ran out. A pilot station between Jupiter and Ganymede had already proven the concept. His companies needed to build collectors and redistribution antennas, and Earth would enjoy limitless power. It would cost billions and perhaps another eleven years to realize, but Andrew had lots of patience. He and Stellar Corp wouldn't lose on the deal.

At sixty-four, he faced a minor life crisis. He had done almost everything he wanted in life. He had not climbed Everest and never would, seeing it as hollow bravado. A risk he did not need to take. He would never see the bottom of the Mariana Trench for the same reason. An excellent pilot, he never tried hang gliding. A mishap all too often ended up being terminal. He had been to the Moon dozens of times, and Mars five times. He gazed at the naked face of Jupiter and stood awed by Saturn's rings on his way to Titan.

His business empire encompassed many things, among them genetic research, quantum computing, space industries and resorts, and VR entertainment. He now owned Future-Tech and all its products, past, present and those being developed. He was a major stockholder in Broca Genetics and Stellar Corp, among others. Tompson, Tompson, and Parker told him his net worth was around sixty-nine billion, but he wasn't sure. It did not matter what the amount. They were only bits in a computer. What those bits did give him was power. Economic and political power.

Despite his corporate philanthropic interests, he faced a life crisis. What was left for him to do? Years, decades, centuries of living, always searching for something new to capture his mind to avoid utter boredom? His parents were gone, now only a memory. He needed a project so complex that it would need decades to implement. However, it needed to produce substantive social benefit. Technology had transformed Earth and made life easier for billions, but there was still war, starvation, sickness, and international rivalry not much changed from the 20th century. Mankind was still to advance and mature philosophically and ethnically. Unfortunately, no off-the-shelf product existed he could plug in to fix it all.

Or was there?

It all came down to a simple question. What did he want out of life, a life that might last for a *very* long time?

He pushed himself up out of the chair and ambled toward the lounge. He fixed himself a snifter of 150-year-old cognac and strode toward the floor-to-ceiling window. Below, Melbourne spread into haze, skycars crisscrossing it like ant lines. He took a sip and gazed at the sprawl of people going about whatever they were doing. Did it have any meaning, apart from the urge to constantly procreate?

As he stood there, he realized there was one thing he never tried—enact social change. He could not hope to make every person on Earth prosperous and disease free. There were far too many cultural, economic, religious, and political barriers for that to be possible. Gradual change could be achieved, given time and resources, and he had plenty of both.

He would enter politics.

Not as an elected representative, though. He intended to fix party squabbling and factional machinations. To do that, he would become a background player and mover. To influence change, he needed to be near one of the centers of world power, and that meant the United States. He decided to buy himself a president and as many Congressmen it took to shape policy.

He raised his tumbler to the orange and red-streaked sky. This promised to be a game that would keep him amused for some time, perhaps even a century.

Not exactly virtual reality, but close enough.

Intersection

Tom followed the black Toyota Prado down the narrow side street filled with parked cars toward the arterial roundabout. The Prado slowed and stopped. Cars coming down on his right were forced to wait for the pedestrian crossing light to turn green. In adaptive cruise control mode, Tom's Subaru Impreza automatically slowed and stopped some two meters behind the Prado.

Tom relaxed and waited for the traffic to start moving, wanting to finish his shopping and get home. Heavy black clouds hung low, and light rain began to sprinkle his windshield. He pursed his lips and shook his head. There goes his plan to cut the grass and do some weeding. Behind him, three cars also waited. He could not see the Prado driver hidden from view by the tinted back window.

A full parking lot loomed on the other side of the roundabout. On his left, the Woolworths supermarket had a constant stream of shoppers going in and out. On the right, the parking lot partially hid the large Big W store.

A local train pulled into the station behind the parking lot with a squeal of brakes and a sigh of compressed air, disgorging its load of passengers, while others waited to board heading into the city or one of the suburban stations.

The pedestrian light turned green and the backlog of cars began to stream through, some taking the roundabout into the parking lot. With the street clear on his right, Tom waited for the Prado to move. It did not show any turn indicator, which suggested it intended going into the parking lot, or the driver simply forgot to turn it on. He had seen a lot of P platers not bother using their indicator, much to the annoyance and irritation of other drivers, which he found strange, as Tom expected newly licensed drivers to be conscious of road rules. The young had no respect for anything these days, he mused.

The Prado sat there, not moving, even though it had a clear right of way. Tom frowned, then tooted his horn. The black beast refused to budge. Drivers behind him also started to lean on their horn. Tom wondered why the Prado driver refused to move. Did the guy have a heart attack or something? Perhaps his car died. Stuck in a narrow street with parked cars on either side, Tom could not go anywhere, forced to wait for the Prado to get out of his way. The drivers blasting their horn behind him did not think much of this development either.

In the rearview mirror, Tom saw the last car in the queue reverse, turn into a driveway, and back out to run down the street. The driver of the car behind him got out, face red with fury, and stomped toward him. He banged on the window and Tom pressed a button to wind it down. Cold drops touched his face.

"You waiting for something special?" the driver snarled.

Tom pointed at the Prado. "I can't do anything until that guy gets out of my way," he said reasonably. "Why ask *me* to move?"

"There is nobody in front of you, you idiot! Get going!"

Nobody in front of him?

"What's the matter with you?" Tom demanded. "You blind or something? You cannot see the black Prado?"

"The only thing I see, buddy, is you blocking the roundabout," the driver shouted. "Move your heap!" He stomped back to his car, got in and slammed the door.

Tom tooted his horn, but the Prado did not move.

A police cruiser with its dark blue checkerboard pattern on the side pulled up on the arterial just as the pedestrian light turned green. The Prado had a clear run to go through the roundabout, but it only sat there. Tom leaned on his horn in a prolonged blast. The car behind him reversed, the driver having had enough of this nonsense. Tom did not care what problems the Prado driver had, and placed the gear lever into reverse. He had his own problems and didn't relish hanging around in the rain.

He saw a uniformed cop get out of the car and wave to him. Tom wound down the window and waited.

"Why are you sounding your horn, sir?" the cop asked, eyes wary.

"I'm waiting for the Toyota in front of me to get out of the way, but it's just sitting there," Tom explained.

"Mmm. Please switch off your engine and get out of the car," the cop ordered and stepped back.

"Is there a problem, officer?" If the cop wanted to hassle someone, he should be going after the Prado.

"Step out of the car."

Tom sighed, switched off the engine, and opened the door. The cold breeze made him squirm. Another car pulled up behind his Impreza, the driver looking on with interest.

The cop placed both hands on his hips. "Why are you blocking the roundabout?"

"I'm not blocking the roundabout. I'm waiting for the Prado in front of me to get out of my frigging way."

"What Prado?"

"That one!" Tom pointed with his hand and his jaw sagged. There wasn't anything in front of him. It took a few seconds to collect his wits. "I tell you, there was a black Toyota Prado blocking the way and my dashcam can prove it."

"All I saw when we pulled up, Mister, was your vehicle stopping others from going through," the cop remarked coldly. "Have you had anything to drink today?"

"Nothing," Tom declared, still in shock. The Prado *was* there!

"Let me have your license, please."

Tom dug out his wallet and handed over the license. "This is ridiculous."

"Wait here," the cop ordered and strode toward his car. A

few minutes later, he came out with a breathalyzer. "Exhale into this until I tell you to stop."

Tom took a deep breath, clamped his teeth on the white plastic tube, and let out a long exhale.

"That'll do," the cop said and studied the instrument. "You're clear, but I'll have to give you a ticket for obstructing traffic."

"I was waiting for the damn Prado!" Tom exploded, enraged to be booked for something he did not do.

"You will receive a court summons if you fail to pay the fine after 28 days," the cop told him, and walked back to his car. He returned and held out the license and a green paper. "Next time, don't make a nuisance of yourself," the cop advised and strode off.

Tom stared after him in disbelief. Has everyone gone crazy? The Prado was there! With a glance at the car behind him and the grinning driver, he got in, buckled up, and turned left. He parked in the Dan Murphy's liquor store lot beside Woolworths, and hurried toward the supermarket, pursued by thin, cold rain. Loaded with groceries, he dumped them into the trunk and drove home, still shaken by what had happened.

Was he going nuts?

Still fuming, he unpacked, stowing things into the fridge and the pantry.

He knew what he saw, determined to show the bastards.

He walked into the garage, opened the car door and extracted the mini SD card from the dashcam. In his study, he inserted the card into an adapter and slid it into a computer slot. He powered up, scrolled through the card's directory and brought up the dashcam clips.

It took him seconds to open a clip showing the Toyota stopped at the roundabout.

"Hah!" Tom sighed with relief. He might have gone around the bend, but the dashcam at least was sane. Why didn't the drivers behind him see the Prado? It couldn't be a ghost or something.

He scanned the next two clips. Toward the end of the second clip where the cop told him to switch off the engine and get out, the Prado flickered and vanished.

Tom stared at the screen in shock. *This is nuts*, he told himself, badly shaken. He replayed the clip twice, feeling himself sag further into the chair every time the Prado vanished.

He did not drink in the morning. Right then, he figured he would break that rule. He poured himself two fingers of bourbon and tossed it back in one gulp.

The SD card, he nodded with satisfaction. It would put a major dent into the cop's case when he took the fine to court. Before powering down, he backed up the last six dashcam clips…just in case.

Forest Maiden

The tires whispered to themselves, a sound of hissing rain.

Beads on a string, cars moved along the highway. Although early, the hard white sun valiantly tried to warm the frozen, rolling landscape and burn away stringy remnants of clinging mist. With shrill squawks, a gaggle of yellow-crested cockatoos flew overhead and settled on massive eucalypt trees beside the carriageway.

Mason adjusted his shades, switched stations to ABC FM Classic, and nodded solemnly to the hypnotic rhythm of Ravel's *Bolero*. Not into heavy symphonies, he liked his music light and cheerful. *Bolero's* enchanting tempo sent his mind along meandering memory paths. Opera made him wince, but in a quirky way, his heart sang to some of its music. His mom always tuned into 60s and 70s popular stuff, and he inherited her tastes for the oldies. Modern, sharp, acid compositions made him switch stations. When nothing came up on the radio, he replayed favorites stored in his mind.

A silver hatchback roared past him. The decibels of its speakers rivaled an A380 taking off, guaranteed to blow out the driver's eardrums. He shook his head, not understanding any of it.

A green signboard on the shoulder said Mt. Macedon exit, one kilometer. *Bolero* finished in a crescendo and the familiar ABC news break broke his reflective reverie.

Past Gisborne, he took the off-ramp onto Mt. Macedon Road and motored down the peaceful arterial. Sheets of mist hung low over paddocks and the sun glinted between white-barked eucalypt branches. Frost painted the grass with crystal on both sides of the road, and the airconditioner whined a little louder to maintain the set temperature.

Before the hill that led into the small township, the local

golf course clubhouse stood deserted, although he figured it would fill rapidly with weekend warriors who sought to test their skill against the devilish white ball. Mason liked the small nine-hole course and played when he could tear himself away from the city. Preferably early in the morning during the week when he often had the place to himself, everybody else otherwise at work.

He slowed to sixty, drove past a cluster of old-fashioned houses and stores, and turned right onto the narrow, sleepy Cheniston Road lined with bushy trees and tall gums, providing shade and tranquility. Cottages and larger, more modern houses nestled on mostly half-hectare lots occupied by old-time residents and newly arrived retirees who sought to escape the city pressure cooker. Some owners used larger plots as do-it-yourself hobby farms or held them as investments. Looking at it all, his mood improved as the prevailing sense of peace descended on him. The place did it to him every time.

Mason pulled up before a two-meter steel gate hung on local bluestone columns and gazed with nostalgia at the single-story sandstone dwelling. A chicken wire fence ran around the entire property and gave an uninterrupted view of gently rolling hills falling away behind the house to merge into flatland. On either side, tall pines provided shelter from the neighbors. At nights, lying in bed, window wide open, he always listened as the pines softly whispered to him until everything faded and he slept. During a storm, the sounds were more agitated—hissing surf running up a beach—but they too soothed away the day's cares.

He opened the gate expecting Cricket to come bounding toward him in welcome, tail held high. His dad disliked cats and never kept pets, a characteristic Mason shared. In a quirky way, Cricket nonetheless warmed to them and often rubbed himself against their legs as they sat on the veranda, purring loudly with satisfaction, knowing he left a bunch of hairs on their trousers. The black tomcat only a fond memory now among other memories tucked away in his memory drawers.

Mason parked the car in front of the double garage and strode up broad sandstone steps to the solid wood doorway. He winced at the chill inside as he disabled the alarm, then busied himself to fire up the wood burner. Chore done, he went to the bathroom to wash up. He put aside the towel and stared at the slim figure in the mirror. Muddy green eyes inherited from Mom gazed back at him above a square jawline and tapered nose. He passed a hand through charcoal hair and a lighter streak that ran along the top of his head and pursed his lips. The streak came in for lots of jibes in primary and secondary school, which forced him to fend off a bully or two. In the kitchen, coffee percolator going, he checked the fridge. Apart from bread and milk, no need for a major shopping outing.

Buttery sunshine streamed through tall back veranda windows and made a bright pool on the polished redgum floor. A gaggle of white cockatoos in the yard pecked around the small vegetable garden. He always planted potatoes, onions, carrots, tomatoes, cabbages, and some herbs, preferring genuine flavor in vegetables he ate. Over the last four years, the garden shrank as his interest to maintain it diminished and work commitments prevented him from coming up. An idyllic weekend retreat, the property still required regular maintenance. He always cleaned during a visit, and a local man took care of mowing and trimming.

A mug of hot coffee in hand, Mason slid back the lounge ceiling-high glass panel and stepped into the enclosed veranda now warm from the sun. He dragged over a chair, back and seat made comfortable with tied-on cushions Grandma made, and placed the mug on the heavy table. He pulled out a mild King Edward cigar from his breast pocket and lit up. A couple of satisfying puffs later, he gazed absently into nothing in particular. He never smoked cigarettes, although as a kid, he and his friends tried them for taste. Not for him. He did not like the stink, but enjoyed the aromatic whiff of a cigar.

The cockatoos looked up from their chore when he

emerged and went back to teasing the ground. His eyes drifted past the back fence toward patches of old-growth forest and rested on a distant horizon where the air turned fuzzy. Melbourne lay somewhere over there. He could not see it, too far away, but easily pictured its cluster of skyscrapers clawing upward. Another life, another existence.

As his thoughts tumbled, he imagined Gramps Milan sitting on the other side of the table as he often did, old briar clenched between his teeth, bushy eyebrows drawn together in a frown. Mason lifted his mug in acknowledgment.

A magpie swooped over the cockatoo gaggle and they took flight, screeching in protest as they wheeled toward a stand of trees down the hill.

Perhaps he should latch on the trailer and drive off into the bush to look for fallen logs to top up his supply of firewood. Most easy to get at stuff already taken years ago, but lots still remained along lonely forest tracks. Physical work may clear his head and make him forget reality for a while. He took a sip of coffee and decided not to get sweaty. The back shed held enough chopped dry wood to last the winter, and two five-meter-long shoulder-high stacks would see him through at least eight more years. *Keep today's visit focused and intellectual,* he told himself.

As a teenager, he liked going into the forest with Gramps to cut timber and haul the plunder home. He enjoyed the earthy forest smells—something different from the usual city odors—listen to the whisper of rustling leaves and the cradling comfort the woods engendered. When he first started work and got a car, an old secondhand Honda hatch, he'd drive up in casual gear and got friendly ribbing from Gramps for looking like a bum. Mason shrugged off the japes.

Warm air drifted in from the lounge as the burner got into its stride. He relaxed and allowed himself to drift into retrospection, home chores be damned. Mt. Macedon's outback retreat promulgated an atmosphere of tranquility and peace. A far cry from the hectic city lifestyle he lived during the week.

The city and work provided the means through which he secured his ongoing financial and retirement needs, but did not fill his soul in the way Gramp's place did. A job simply fulfilled his economic needs. Well, it did far more than that, he acknowledged grudgingly. People who lived here had their share of problems, everybody did everywhere, and Grandma loved to share local gossip about someone's misfortune, social or financial, but they seemed to take life's knocks with a more phlegmatic, philosophical attitude, and smiled readily. If he could somehow instill such an outlook in the city, he'd make a fortune, and along the way push a lot of psychiatrists on the street. Not a bad thing, perhaps, he mused.

Mason remembered one fine weekend—he just turned eight—sitting with Gramps on the back veranda, everybody else amusing themselves in the lounge, when his grandfather chuckled and began a story. Milan had a bagful and found in his young grandson an avid listener. Mason remembered everything, but still loved to be a sounding board and simply be with Gramps. Each telling came with a slight variation, but in essence true. Mason never tried to correct Gramps on a point of inconsistency as changes or additions often provided spice and new detail.

The old man took a puff and started one of his favorite after-war yarns, still picking up the pieces after discharge from the Partisan resistance.

He and a friend, he said with a fond snicker, hid in a cornfield once and watched a crabby, stingy man without a kind bone in his scrawny body guard a small peach tree. He wore a permanent scowl as he walked the Varazdin streets and glared at anyone who greeted him. Children gave him a wide birth and tittered as he stomped by. They threw pebbles at him and scampered away with glee as he raged after them, fist held high.

Hidden by tall corn, the smell of ripe peaches made Milan's mouth water. The awful man guarded the tree all night, shotgun in lap, sometimes nodding off. Too mean to offer any peaches to his neighbors, he feared they might steal the precious fruit before he could harvest it.

Milan and his friend sneaked into the corn before dawn broke and watched the old sod guard his tree. As the sun came up, golden light filled the open, rolling meadow and the world became a bright, cheerful place, perfect for some devilment.

The old coot stood, looked around warily, and hurried off for a quick breakfast, a familiar routine by now. With no idea when he might return, not wanting to be on the receiving end of a shotgun, Milan and his friend rushed to the peach tree and quickly sawed off two limbs heavy with fruit. The plunder slung over their shoulder, they disappeared into the corn and made for their hiding place.

Minutes later, they heard a frantic bellow of rage and a torrent of profanity. The old buzzard had returned and vented outrage when he spied the damaged tree. Later in the morning, a mighty uproar swept through the town as the scandalized man sought to find who took his peaches. The incident generated a lot of local hilarity, everybody figuring the old sod deserved what he got. Nobody admitted anything, of course.

The two culprits gorged on delicious peaches, sharing some with neighbors who never cared where they came from. They merely nodded their thanks with a faint smile of understanding.

The tale finished, Mason laughed softly and shook his head at this wicked deed, clearly picturing the outraged man rampaging around in search of the miscreants. The story always generated a warm glow of deserved justice. From what Gramps said, nobody went to the old man's funeral.

"I tell you, *moj mali stroj*—little gadget—although we never regretted what we did, I sometimes felt a little remorseful," Milan reflected pensively. "The mean devil had it rough during the war. First, he lost a son to the Ustaše, then a wife when the Partisans bombed his house because they thought he was a collaborator." He took a puff. After a while, he shrugged. "Anyway, the bastard still had the rest of the damned tree."

The peach episode not the only tale in Gramp's store of adventures. Like the one when he and two friends caught a stray cat. They halved two walnuts, cleaned them, and proceeded to fill the shells with tar. They stuck the shells to the cat's paws and let it go. The poor thing tried to gnaw off the annoying shells as it clanged its way along the sidewalk to disappear under a fence. Mason snickered when Milan finished, although he felt a little sorry for the poor cat, vividly picturing its plight. The things young men do…

One of Gramps' favorites was how, fresh after the grape harvest, he and three friends managed to break into a barrel of new wine.

Several streets from Milan's house, a neighbor stored four large barrels of newly fermented wine in a backyard barn. Not predisposed to share any of the old stock, he sold the stuff to local bars and supplied parties and wedding functions.

Milan and his buddies often contemplated how to get at the wine. Come late fall, the man would decant the barrels and move the wine to his cellar beyond reach. They huddled behind the barn and sniffed at the enticing aroma of fresh wine longing for a taste. After much debate and rejection of several nutty ideas, they came up with what everybody agreed to be a devilishly cunning plan. They drove a nail into a long pole, filed the end to a point, and tied a rubber hose to the pole that left a meter or so to hang from the end to serve as their instrument of dark deed.

The barn, clad with old boards, had enough gaps to push the pole through to the closest barrel. With patience and determination, they drove the nail into a large cork that plugged the barrel and gently worked it loose. The barrel open, they lowered the rubber hose and sucked until the young wine began to pour out. With no time to waste, they sampled their prize, nudging each other to be next. Head swimming, Milan suggested it would be far too dangerous to linger behind the barn where the old coot could catch them. Everybody clearly pictured the disastrous consequences that may ensue. A hurried retreat to their homes produced several bottles and jugs to be filled and enjoyed at leisure. Plunder safely stored, they replaced the cork and tapped it down.

For some two weeks until the rubber hose could not reach farther into the barrel, Milan and his pals enjoyed a happy time.

When the man eventually came to inspect his barrels, he found one only half full. This naturally set off a cascade of accusations and arguments, everybody denying knowledge of the stolen wine. Some suggested the codger drank it himself and forgot he did it, which generated nasty amusement. If the neighbors saw four youths wandering the streets looking slightly inebriated, no one said anything, figuring the stingy man deserved it.

"He never suspected you and your friends?" Mason ventured.

"Sure did, *ti banac.* Even came to our house demanding to see our wine bottles. My father sent him packing in short order, of course." Milan winked at Mason. "You see, even though still young, my dad also liked the old coot's wine."

Both burst into hearty laughter.

Other stories Gramps told were more serious.

"Like kids everywhere," he reflected once, "I liked to listen to my own paternal grandfather regale me with tales of witches and strange goings on. True or not, I found them entertaining. Kolarovec only twenty kilometers from Varazdin where we lived, my parents often visited on a weekend to scrounge a free Sunday lunch from my grandparents. We'd take an old, creaking bus and stop at Jamnik's Tavern on the road to Maribor, and walk the rest of the way. Allowed to run wild with other kids, I roamed the open fields, played games in the forest, and swam in the nearby Drava. Tired from all the action, I'd sit with Grandpa on the front veranda and bug him to tell me a tale. The way you bug me," Milan added with a disarming grin.

"Anyhow, more often than not, the old man obliged. I remember one particular story…"

A beautiful maiden, his grandpa began as he puffed on his cherry wood pipe, rocking in a favorite rickety chair, often frequented a nearby forest filled with all sorts of wildlife. Long, corn-colored hair fell to her slim waist. Large blue eyes sparkled with laughter and the joy of being alive. Youths from nearby villages came to court her, but the tall, willowy maid repulsed them all, much to the lament of the youths. Of course, this raised all sorts of gossip, and mothers wanting their son marry the maid speculated what may be wrong with her. Some even considered her a witch. When the women demanded to know why the maid never wed, her mother paid them no never mind, which only fueled further speculation. The maid ignored the gossip, the barbed innuendos, and lived a carefree life, preferring the company of her forest friends.

No one knew where the maid went when she disappeared into the forest or what she did there, and those who followed her often got lost. She sometimes came home with scratches on her long, supple legs and slim arms, and her parents scolded her. How can she hope to attract a boy looking like that, they said. The scratches came from branches and shrubs, she explained cheerfully, eyes dancing with inner fire.

Milan's grandfather said he loved to hunt, an old, battered rifle cradled in his arms. He regularly brought home a hare, wild boar, or a deer, always welcomed at the farmhouse by his wife.

One sunny autumn afternoon, his worn Jager percussion rifle slung across the shoulder, a large leather rucksack to hold any game he may catch, he pecked his plump wife on the cheek and declared he would be back in time for dinner. His wife did not mind her husband's wanderings, knowing he never left chores undone.

He took a familiar worn trail into the forest, and after some time, the warm sun flickering between old birch, oak, and poplar, he took a meandering track that led to a meadow with a small lake tucked against a hillside. He liked the place, one of his favorites, as animals often came to graze on the lush grass and drink, and generally managed to shoot something. Even when he did not, he enjoyed sitting at the forest edge, take an occasional swig of wine from a flask, and listen contentedly to the soft buzz of insects as swallows swooped low over the sleepy meadow.

Suddenly, a graceful doe emerged from the trees some forty meters on his right. She paused, lifted her slender neck, sniffed the air, and slowly made her way toward the lake. Every now and then, she stopped and turned her head on lookout for possible danger. Satisfied, she walked through the tall grass with small, mincing steps.

Grandpa never saw such a beautiful deer, and watched the doe in rapt fascination as she approached the lake. At possibly fifty kilos, she would provide welcomed fresh venison for the table. He picked up the rifle and aimed at the doe's chest. A quick kill, the animal would not suffer. As he took up the trigger slack, the doe turned and looked directly at him. Even from some 150 meters, he saw her large blue eyes, something most unusual. He took a deep breath, held it, and squeezed the trigger.

The sharp crack caused startled birds into flight, and two hares bounded into thickets across the meadow. Without a sound, the doe dropped to the ground. Milan's grandfather raced through the grass to inspect his kill.

Chest heaving, he slowed and gaped in shock at what he saw as color drained from his face. He dropped the rifle and stared in startled wonder as the graceful doe turned into a naked young woman, golden hair spilled across full breasts. Bright blood oozed from a wound in the center of her chest. He thought she looked at him then, not with accusation, but resigned acceptance. Then the light faded from her eyes. As he stared at the village maid, her form shimmered, became transparent, and faded. Gradually, the flattened grass rose where she had lain.

Milan's grandfather said he felt his eyes sting and hot tears warmed his cheeks from deep loss and regret. He knelt beside the spot where the woman laid and sobbed, his heart tearing with pain. He begged forgiveness, knowing the forest had claimed the strange maid. Whether she heard him or not, he thought he saw her enchanting young face, eyes alive with laughter, rosy lips open in a broad smile. Perhaps she did forgive him, because he felt the load of guilt roll off his chest and he stood up with a lighter heart. He took a deep breath and let it out with a soft hiss as he wiped his face with a calloused hand.

He cradled the worn rifle and wearily made his way toward the forest and home, the years heavy on his shoulders. For a long time afterward, the villagers often talked about the strange young maid and wondered what happened to her. A search through the forest revealed an ankle-long green dress the maid used to wear neatly draped across a low branch. Some said she ran away with a youth from another village, but nobody knew for certain.

Mouth clamped on a pipe, Milan's grandfather declared roughly that he never went hunting again, and his old rifle remained mounted above the fireplace. On long winter afternoons, he sat before the flickering flames and stared at the gun. His wife often asked why he never hunted, sensing something unusual happened on that fateful autumn day, but he refused to say.

Finished, Milan sat in his chair and quietly puffed on his pipe.

"Believe it or not, the way my grandfather told it, I never doubted its truth, *ti banac*. Strange things happened in his day," he added gruffly.

Mason shook off the memories, got up, and padded into the kitchen for a refill.

Shadow Walkers

In Cairo, anything and everything is obtainable, provided one is prepared to pay the price.

You want someone to disappear? There are people who can arrange it quietly and without fuss. A woman? How many, what kind, and where? Gold, diamonds, a jeweled ankh; just show your credit card. Anything at all.

I happened to be in Cairo because it is one of the best places to obtain a rare codex and ancient bound books. I did not want just any book. I collect exotic works on mythology, legends steeped in mysticism, and the occult. The older and weirder the better, and some of my most prized pieces came from the Middle East.

Forget old Greek, Egyptian, Roman, or even European lore. Compared to some translated Sumerian material, all those other places have nothing. My *Songs of Ancients*, a battered old codex I found in Alexandria's old district, a copy said to have been made from even older papyrus rolls supposedly held in the famed library of the same name before Julius Caesar set it on fire in 48 BCE. In the 4th century, after the Council of Nicaea, the rising Christian movement under Bishop Theophilus in 391 CE, left its destructive march. Arab conquerors in the 7th century pretty much levelled the remains. Priceless knowledge lost forever.

The *Book of Hours*, a 2nd century BCE Mesopotamian codex of magical incantations, made my hair stand on end. I am not superstitious and don't believe in any of that wooly stuff, but my research opened a window into humanity's past that most established anthropologists and scholarly institutions don't pay much attention to, or pretend it does not exist. I ought to know. With a PhD in Comparative Middle Eastern Literature from Melbourne University, as an Associate Professor, my papers invariably generated controversy and heated debates among the learned, not always favorably, Damn them all anyway.

I did not care if the University refused to offer me tenure. Comfortably well off with a sizeable investment portfolio, boosted by early speculation in Bitcoin, I could afford to support my own research. The Vice Chancellor in particular had a bone to pick with me, but she swallowed her angst and left me alone. I attracted students—paying students—who contributed to the bottom line, something paramount in the hierarchy of her thinking.

To find what I wanted, I scoured old hole-in-the-wall bookshops, cluttered curio shops that packed unbelievable stuff into tiny places, and bazzars. They were undiscovered treasure troves. I always meant to peruse Cairo's famed Khan el-Khalili alleyways in the Islamic Quarter, and the El Fustat souk, salivating at the prospect of finding something exotic. With the academic year over, I set off in mid-November on a two-week sabbatical.

Cairo is a madhouse of cars, crawling and honking along narrow, winding streets, accompanied by a pungent stink of pollution that left my eyes burning and throat sore when I returned to my hotel late in the day, the pyramids visible from my window, shrouded in brown goo. Then there were the people, an endless multitude doing who knows what. I found it easy to spot tourists. The men generally wore overly casual outfits, holding camcorders, tablets, and smartphones, capturing everything in sight for posterity, material they probably would never watch again. The women were often colorful, a contrast to the more restrained garments worn by locals, but hardly any local woman wore the traditional burka. The country endured 1300 years of Islam rule, but they always considered themselves Egyptians first.

In the old part of the city, small boutiques and eateries lined the streets, catering to satisfy any bodily desire. In many places, local men sat around small tables puffing from a glass hookah and sipping sweet chai. Every now and then, a kid, usually only twelve or fourteen, hand bulging with foreign bills, would offer to exchange currency for you. I never understood that part, but they tell me nobody bothered them. Just another enterprising business.

Morning clear and surprisingly fresh, I entered the Khan el-Khalili alley, an entrance into the Aladdin's cave. A bewildering array of souvenirs, two-day-old antiques, papyrus paintings, crystal balls and glass pyramids to promote spiritual, and supposedly physical, healing, gold and jewelry glittering under bright lights, silk garments—lady tourists lingered at such places—swords, imitation guns, exotic foods, piles of colored spices, CDs of Egyptian music, and lots more my mind found difficult to absorb and comprehend.

Storekeepers did not stand, shout, or wave arms to drum up business. They sat quietly in the back reading the Quran, sipping tea or thick coffee from small tin tumblers, or patiently fingered beads on a prayer string. Time seemed to flow at an easier pace for them. Stall after stall crammed with goods packed the alleyway. I shook my head at it all.

The place noisy, hot, crowded, I pushed my way through the throng, my eyes open for a sight of a book merchant.

I stopped in front of a cramped shop stuffed with ancient books, their binding cracked, gaping like tongues, covered with dust of centuries, and papyrus rolls that might have been written in Khufu's time. I was hooked, certain to find something in this cave of wonders.

Old as time, brown skin wrinkled by age, bony hands that looked like claws, a grimy white keffiyeh on his head bound with black rope, the man lowered his glass of tea and slowly looked at me. Black, impenetrable eyes gave an impression of dark depths and mystery, and something else—a touch of malevolence. Those eyes were not just devoid of color, they absorbed everything they focused on. My imagination running in overdrive, I told myself. The sounds and endless chatter along the alley behind me faded as I stared at the ancient figure.

"Can I help you with anything?" His deep, resonant voice broke the momentary uncomfortable silence in surprisingly good English. I sensed education and culture in that voice.

"I'm looking for ancient manuscripts and any codex you might have that deals with old myths and the occult. Sumerian or Mesopotamian writing would be best."

"Are you a scholar with familiarity of those subjects?"

"I am a university researcher," I told him simply. He would not be interested or impressed with my academic qualifications.

He pursed his lips, nodded, and with a weary sigh, pried himself off the stool. Bottom lip clamped between stained teeth, he grunted and peered at a row of various-sized books that packed a shoulder-high shelf.

"I may have something for you," he murmured, pulled on a pair of dirty white cotton gloves, and reached for a slim volume bound with blistered, frayed, green leather. He blew off the dust, turned toward me, then hesitated as though uncertain he should sell it.

"What is it?" I asked intensely curious, eager to get my hands on the thing.

"*Runes of the Undead*," he spoke curtly. "It's an old Mesopotamian text copied from original Sumerian cuneiform. Very powerful magic. It is said to be from the first century CE. My family has held it for generations."

"If it's that valuable, why sell it?" I demanded, wary of being the butt end of a sales pitch.

"You look like someone who needs self-redemption," he replied crisply.

The inference eluded me as I reached for the book. He gave me a smart rap on the wrist.

"Never touch it with your bare hands!"

"Why not?"

"Just don't." He leaned forward and peered at me. "Are you a believer?"

"Believer in what?"

"In forces beyond your ken. You must believe a little, or you would not be on this quest."

"I'm a scientist gathering information. I don't believe in spirits or magic."

The old man gave a deep sigh and shook his head. "La yuhimu, no matter. Wait, I'll get you some gloves."

Devil worship, astrology? A mumbo-jumbo sales pitch, I figured, suitable for the gullible.

He placed the book on the stool, turned, and rummaged in the back of his shop. My gaze was drawn to the innocent volume on the stool, and I wondered why I must not touch it. My curiosity got the better of me. I bent forward and reached for the thing with my right hand. It's only an old book, I told myself.

I grasped the slim volume and gasped in shock as unbelievable cold shot up my arm. I instinctively tried to drop the thing, but it remained glued to my hand. Small, red flames appeared from the book and licked around my hand. My vision faded and I shivered. Alarmed, I tried to shout, but nothing came out, not even a gurgle. Desperate, I shook my hand, but the book stuck to me.

The old man turned, cotton gloves in hand, saw me, and gaped.

"You have damned yourself, fool!"

I reached with my other hand to snatch the book from my grasp.

"Don't touch it!" he yelled in desperation. His cry froze me.

Then it started.

Horrors from the depths of my soul burst forth unleashed. Serpents—my most dreaded fear—from the dark, basement corridors of my mind, coiled around me, hissing, yellow eyes ablaze with malevolent fire, long fangs bared. Transfixed with terror, I screamed, desperate to shake them. As soon as one fell, others took its place, coiled tight around my legs, and pinned my arms to my body. Then they struck and kept striking. The needle pricks from their fangs made me writhe in agony. I felt the poison course through me even as my flesh colored crimson, then purple from the fires inside me. I longed for death and the relief it would bring, but it did not come. The pain intensified until I felt my head would explode. All I could do was scream endlessly, begging for release.

That's when the spiders came, my other nightmare nemesis.

Giants the size of dinner plates, their soft, furry legs sent my skin on fire where they touched my bare arms and face. Black fangs glistened as they struck repeatedly. Different poisons shot through me, each with its own set of agonies and intolerable anguish. I writhed and clawed to get them off me, but the snakes were there, ready with their strikes.

I screamed and sobbed and pleaded for help, but the horrors I unleashed would not be appeased. Part of me wondered why I hadn't died already.

Something black slithered from the bottomless pit of my mind, and two blazing, orange eyes focused on me. A cavernous mouth filled with small, needle teeth, opened and fire spewed forth. The flame transcended all previous pain, not believing such agony was possible. I contorted in total shock and felt my spine breaking. My skin bubbled, turned black, and fell off me in large flakes. My polyester T-shirt melted and took flesh off me as it burned. I danced in total anguish, screamed for help, wishing it to end. Why did my horrors torment me like this?

I saw the old man rush toward me, a broad sword in hand. He brought it down and exquisite sharp pain lanced through my wrist. The terrors retreated. I gasped when I saw my severed hand on the dusty ground still clutching the book. I moaned, fell to my knees, cradled my wounded arm against me, and sobbed uncontrollably. My skin was normal and my T-shirt unmarked. It was all in my mind, but my severed hand was all too real.

Part of me stared at the raw wrist and I pondered at lack of blood. The wound seemed cauterized and without pain. The horrors of my mind faded into wherever they came from, but I knew they were still there lurking, malicious, ready to spring forth should I be foolish to evoke them again.

Around me, total silence. Tourists, vendors, children, men and women, clustered in the narrow alley, eyes wide with fear and horror as they stared at me. A little girl clung to her mother's jeans and sobbed. The woman picked her up and pushed through the crowd. Gradually, the others dispersed, not wishing to be involved, throwing me puzzled glances as they walked away.

The old man helped me to his stool and offered me some yellow drink that burned on its way down, but cleared my head. In shock, I began to tremble. He forced me to drink more of that vile liquid. Satisfied, he shifted his gaze to the book and the severed hand that held it. Slowly, his fathomless black eyes peered into my soul. It felt as though everything I was lay open to him.

"Did you find what you were looking for?" he rasped in a thin, reedy voice, removed from the confident baritone he used to greet me.

I did not say anything as I slowly stood on wobbly legs. I wiped my eyes and sniffed, then shuddered at the terrors now only a horrible memory. Without saying anything, I looked at the old man and punched out his lights. He fell, arms flailing, and lay buried beneath his smelly books, then I stared at the fallen sword. After an endless moment, decision made, I picked it up, stood back, and thrust the point through the book. Little blue flames writhed around the cut, then faded, taking the menace and the magic with them. I let the sword fall from my nerveless fingers, then slowly bent, picked up the book, and shoved it into my little backpack, my desire to search for more manuscripts totally slaked.

The hotel arranged for a doctor. He clucked and hummed, and bound the stump with a clean dressing. Curious how I came to lose my hand, I could not tell him anything. What could I say that would sound believable? To tell him the truth would probably mean an extended vacation in a nice, padded cell. The other thing I insisted on, no police. I had enough horrors for the day.

Airport security gave me a little trouble when I tried to leave. My face did not match the picture in my passport. No wonder. Somewhere in that alley, I aged thirty years. Inside, I aged a thousand. Eventually, supported by other documents I carried, they let me go. I went through a similar process when I landed at Melbourne Airport, but I was home.

In my Southbank apartment, the evening enchanting from lit skyscrapers, I sat relaxed in my black leather recliner, a tumbler of bourbon at my side. Three months since that horrid episode, my demons sometimes ventured forth tentatively, but did not fully show themselves. I had gotten used to them with the help of some counseling.

Color had returned to my face and I lost that gaunt, haunted look. I hardly saw my parents or friends, tired of their forced sympathy and my lame explanations. Soon, I hoped, I would be my old normal self. Frankly, I had gotten weary walking around like a damned geriatric.

In another month when the stump healed completely, they would fit me with some bionic prosthesis. I saw it in action and was impressed. The thing would not give me full dexterity, but better than a pirate hook. My students and faculty were understandably curious to see me without a hand. I told them my usual line—an accident, and left it at that.

My gaze shifted to the library shelf and focused on the green book and its cracked binding. I had not touched it since I put it there and never opened it. Why did I bring it at all? After everything that happened, I still wanted to read the thing. Call it scientific curiosity. I took a sip of bourbon, stood, and padded to the bookshelf. Did I believe? I only had to look at my severed hand for my answer.

The leather felt dry and warm as I carried the book to my recliner. The sword cut had disappeared and I had no idea how that happened. Another sip and I opened the hard cover. My fingers slowly slid across the faded yellow page. Intense cold immediately surged up my arm and I gasped in total horror. Unlocked, my demons came for me in a rush. This time, I had no one to cut off my hand. All I could do was scream endlessly as the snakes and spiders struck me. Perhaps a neighbor would hear my screams and rush in to help me, only to be damned himself when he touched the open book.

In Cairo, anything and everything is obtainable, provided one is prepared to pay the price.

Last Day

Crystal tumbler of whiskey in hand, I switched on the TV for my six pm news fix. With everything going on around the world, I did not relish getting another dose of misery. It's enough to drive a man to drink.

The sight of Gaza almost totally obliterated, starving Palestinians because of Israel's aid blockade despite the ceasefire agreement, made me cringe and shake my head. Then there are the bombed cities and villages in Ukraine under increased Russian drone and missile attacks. Predictably, Kyiv intensified its retaliatory strikes against Russian military bases and oil refineries, which in turn has caused real problems for civilians who always suffer the most in any war. I had enough watching Chinese Coast Guard vessels ram Philippine fishing vessels, then brazenly claim they are only protecting their sovereign waters, which is a load of crock. I chuckle when I see clips of President Trump claim victories in his tariff war while America is slowly getting ruined.

Scenes of destruction and starvation turn my stomach, and I wonder why such things are allowed to happen. However, like a junky, I need my dose of local and international news, simply to confirm that things really were rotten as I thought they were.

The ABC intro music ended and a flashing red BREAKING NEWS footer on the screen caught my attention. The presenter, Iskhandar Razak, trim in his blue suit, looked grave. Without any preliminaries, he started his announcement.

"For those who missed our five o'clock bulletin, three hours ago, President Zelenskyy authorized launch of newly delivered Tomahawk cruise missiles against multiple targets in Russia, including a strike against Moscow. Despite President Trump's escalated sanctions, President Putin has shown no inclination to engage in any peace talks. As reported two days ago, US intelligence sources claim that Russia deployed several road-mobile SS-26 Stone missile batteries near the Ukrainian border. The missiles can carry conventional and nuclear warheads. Kyiv is only eighty kilometers from the Russian border and well within range of those batteries. Just a moment…"

An individual appeared from off-camera and handed Razak a note.

"I am informed that the Russian State Duma, the Federation Assembly building, was struck by two Tomahawk missiles. There is no information on damage or casualties. In response, Russia has launched an unknown number of missiles against Kyiv. We are still waiting for results of that strike.

"We also have a major development in Israel. At 7:32 am local time, Jerusalem came under a sustained missile attack launched by Yemeni Houthi rebels, backed and supplied by Iran. The attack was apparently made in retaliation for Israel's resumption of its bombing of Gaza. Although Israel's Iron Dome defense system intercepted most of the incoming missiles, several struck Jerusalem, including the Knesset. I will now switch you to Matthew Doran, our Middle East correspondent in Jerusalem."

Another strike by the Houthis? Despite all the international fanfare and Trump's breast-beating claiming victory, I never believed the fragile ceasefire would hold. Netanyahu's far-right, ultraconservative religious coalition partners, would never allow a permanent peace with the Palestinians. They agreed to a ceasefire only to secure the release of remaining hostages and the return of those already dead, and fumed for days because Hamas could not produce all the bodies. After two years of war, no wonder Hamas could not deliver the bodies. This, of course, gave Netanyahu a perfect excuse to resume his war. The objective being to occupy the Gaza Strip and make it Israeli territory. It was their God-given land after all, right?

The picture shifted to the equally serious Doran, a microphone in hand.

"Jerusalem is burning this morning." The camera panned to show smoke rising across the city. "I am told the Knesset was hit by two missiles, which killed a number of sitting members, staff, and civilians in the area. It is not known if Prime Minister Benjamin Netanyahu is among those killed. In retaliation, the Israel Defense Force launched several Arrow 3 intermediate-range ballistic missiles against Tehran, possibly nuclear-tipped. There is no report if the strike was intercepted. I am told by sources inside the IDF that Israel's nuclear forces were brought—"

An intense white flash made me wince and the picture returned to the studio. Iskhandar Razak glanced at Tamara Oudyn, his co-host. She slowly returned his gaze and pressed both hands to her mouth. He cleared his throat and faced the camera.

"It appears we have a technical difficulty—"

Someone rushed to his side and whispered to him. Visibly shaken, Iskhandar licked his lips.

"I have been informed that Jerusalem was struck by a nuclear missile launched from Iran. We shall provide ongoing updates as they come to hand. To other major—"

The same individual hurried to his side. Iskhandar turned white and swallowed hard.

"It appears Kyiv was obliterated by two nuclear SS-26 missiles. Thirty-five minutes ago, China launched multiple ICBMs against Russia and the US."

I stared at the TV in disbelief.

Holy shit!

The idiots went and done it.

Around me, sirens began to wail.

Iskhandar choked as he stared at the camera. Tamara Oudyn quietly sobbed beside him. "This is a nuclear alert. Take immediate shelter, and may God be with us all."

The picture immediately turned into hissing static.

I swiveled my brown leather recliner and faced the ceiling-high window. My 14th floor Southbank apartment gave me an excellent view of Melbourne ablaze with light from high-rise

buildings and skyscrapers against a background of an approaching evening. I took a sip of whiskey and chuckled. Take shelter?
The chuckle turned into a belly laugh.

I stood and slowly walked to the window, tumbler in hand. I
should feel panic, swamped with regrets and opportunities
missed, but I felt unaccountably calm. Perhaps I should put on a
CD of something classical that fitted my mood.

I saw a searing white light—

About the Author

Stefan Vučak has written twenty-one novels, which include eight SF books in the Shadow Gods Saga. His *Cry of Eagles* won the coveted Readers' Favorite silver medal award, and his *All the Evils* was the prestigious Eric Hoffer contest finalist and Readers' Favorite silver medal winner. *Strike for Honor* won the gold medal.

Stefan leveraged a successful career in the Information Technology industry, then turned his passion for writing into another full-time career. He also spends time as an editor and book reviewer. Stefan lives in Melbourne, Australia.

To learn more about Stefan, visit his:
Website: https://www.stefanvucak.com
Facebook: https://www.facebook.com/StefanVucak/Author

More Books by Stefan Vučak

www.stefanvucak.com/Books/

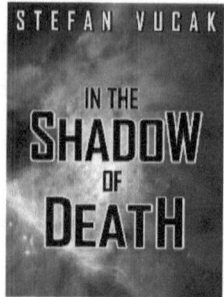 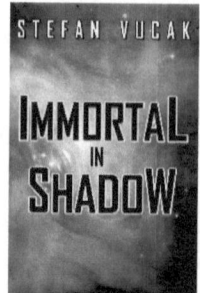 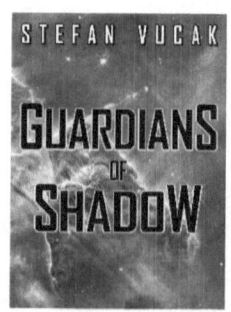